LOVE IN 3D

MARIE HARTE

This book is a work of fiction. The names, characters, places, and plot points stem from the writer's imagination. They are fictitious and not to be interpreted as real. Any resemblance to persons, living or dead, actual events, locations or organizations is entirely coincidental.

LOVE IN 3D
ISBN-13: 978-1642920772
Copyright © August 2022 by Marie Harte
No Box Books
Cover design by Black Bird Book Covers

All Rights Are Reserved. None of this book may be reproduced or used in any manner without express written permission from the author, except in the case of brief quotations used for reviews or promotion. http://marieharte.com

For exclusive excerpts, news, and contests, sign up for **Marie's newsletter** at https://www.subscribepage.com/marieharte

PRAISE FOR MARIE HARTE

"She really loves telling stories. A little too much, maybe."
    Mom

"…the novel is an infuriatingly puerile slog."
    Publisher's Weekly for *The Troublemaker Next Door*

"Why do all these books have so much sex in them?"
    Random Amazon Reviewer

"I'm not sure if you're trying to be funny or not. I don't think this is going to work."
    John S., an unsuccessful Tinder date

"She never missed a day of recess or lunch."
    Ms. Zeewy, 5th grade

LOVE IN 3D

DEAR AUNT TRUTH

Dear Aunt Truth: We've been together for six months, but now he's icing me out. What should I do? I love him more than life itself, but my brothers want to beat the snot out of him.

Dear Iced Out: Have a little dignity and find a new man who is mature enough to talk to you about your relationship. And don't send your brothers after him. What are you, five?

CHAPTER 1

"You can take your inner needs and codependency crap and shove it, you jackass!"

"Calm down, Dan. I didn't mean it like—"

"I heard what I heard. You're a real piece of work, you know that?"

Justine Ferrera peeked out from the stairwell and watched 2C, her tall, buff, too handsome-for-his-own-good downstairs neighbor, confront "Dan," a tattoo-laden giant wearing a tank top and shorts, showcasing a lot of unforgiving muscle.

More swearing. A lot of intense glaring between the men that took on new meaning as they talked about an injured third party and feelings. Was this some kind of love triangle gone bad? Was she watching two men involved in a polyamorous relationship? Her eyes widened at the thought, which then bode the question: why could *she* never be the meat in a hot-guy sandwich?

"Oh man, love gone wrong in the best way," her best friend murmured beside her. "All that hunky muscle, those sexy, testosterone-filled glares." Katie sighed. "Yum."

Justine shifted to see better. "What are they saying? It got quieter."

"Now I can't see. Move over," Katie whispered. "I am *so* jealous you live here. Yesterday at my place, seventy-nine year old Mrs. Purcell was duking it out with the Super over her dying Christmas wreath. It's the same thing every year. She tries to hold onto the brittle thing, needles everywhere, as long as she can. But by May, we've all had enough. My building is filled with old people battling over door decorations, laundry carts, and freight elevator access." Katie paused. "Of course, I constantly struggle for the elevator and always end up carting my laundry around by the basket. Hmm. Maybe I should get in on those fights, might make my life a little easier."

"Shh." Justine clapped a hand over her friend's mouth and stared in shock as angry Dan *took a swing* at the hottie from 2C.

But 2C somehow dodged and maneuvered around the brute, putting Dan in a headlock he couldn't break out of.

She eyed the straining forearms and bulging biceps from 2C and indulged in a few rushed, heated fantasies.

"Super sexy," her best friend said, muffled against Justine's hand. Then the weirdo licked her.

"Ew." She wiped her hand on Katie's jeans. "You're disgusting."

2C glanced over and saw them staring. He grimaced. "Enough, Dan. My neighbors are going to call the police if this keeps up, and I don't think you or I want any more drama. It's over." He relaxed his hold and pushed Dan away.

Dan gave him a courtesy one-fingered salute, turned, and breezed past Justine and Katie down the stairs, swearing all the while.

They exchanged a look. *What now?*

Katie shoved her into the hallway. After shooting daggers at her friend, Justine approached 2C with a bland smile.

He dragged a weary hand through hair colored a deep brown that bordered on auburn in the right light. Rocking the facial hair —a full goatee and beard lining a square jaw—he seemed a mix of tough guy and sensitive soul, judging from the apology in his expressive brown eyes.

"Bad breakup?" Katie asked, following behind Justine.

He sighed. "You could say that. Women suck."

Well then, maybe not so much an apology as stupidity shining in those eyes.

"Men aren't much better," Justine muttered.

He frowned at her.

She frowned back.

"Should you be in this building?" His deep voice held more than a thread of disapproval.

Justine had no idea her neighbors lived such turbulent lives. Aunt Rosie owned the unit but hadn't lived in it full-time until this past year. Though close to her aunt, Justine hadn't ever visited due to a grueling work schedule and her aunt's chaotic lifestyle, though they talked often. But hadn't Aunt Rosie told her the place was quiet and full of nice, fairly boring people?

Having just settled into her aunt's unit two weeks ago, she hadn't yet met everyone in the cozy TCA—which sounded much cooler than Tuscan Cosmo Apartments. But this guy seemed anything but quiet or boring.

Time to introduce herself, apparently. "Hi. I'm Justine Ferrera. I think I'm above you in 3D. I'm subletting from my aunt."

"*You're* Rosie Gallo's niece?" Instead of smiling, he looked her over with suspicion.

"You're—" *being a bit of a dick. No. I can't say that. One, Aunt Rosie will be coming back to live here at some point. I can't make enemies with her neighbors. And two, I could never say something so rude.*

"I'm what?" He raised a brow in challenge.

"Being a bit of a dick," Katie said with a wide smile, reading Justine's mind.

2C's expression darkened.

"You're just as nice as my aunt said you were," Justine blurted, lying to keep the peace. "I mean, we heard you trying to deescalate the situation. Sorry we intruded." She yanked Katie with her and fled for the stairwell. "Bye."

Once on the ground floor and headed to their ride share, she let Katie yammer on and on about getting a backbone and facing bullies. Several minutes into their ride, Katie had yet to shut up about it.

"Okay, already. And ironic," Justine cut in, "since you've been bullying me since we got in the car!"

"You really have," their driver agreed, grinning at them in the rearview. "But honey, it sounds like that guy upstairs was a jerk."

Katie nodded. "Vindication. He totally was." She turned back to Justine. "You need to stand up for yourself more."

Justine groaned. "I'm trying. It's not easy." Not having been raised in her family with so many demands and expectations. No wonder she had issues. Her oldest sister acted like a tyrant, the second oldest like a doormat, and she fell somewhere in between, doing her best to avoid domineering parents.

"I know." Katie punched her in the arm. "I'm sorry. I just hate when guys push people around. Especially when it seems like all the good-looking ones are assholes."

"Preach," the driver said.

Justine would have been more annoyed, but the girl power solidarity felt good. Then their driver mentioned a few hidden gems nearby, restaurants and shops Justine would have to check out later. She'd previously lived in Seattle's Beacon Hill neighborhood, so Fremont was a change for her. *A good one, though,* she kept telling herself, trying to believe it.

When they arrived at the club, Justine noticed a small group of guys waiting by the side, one of whom she recognized as Katie's *other* best friend. She swallowed a groan. "You promised tonight would just be for us to hang out and commiserate over how much we hate our jobs."

"And how much we hate our bosses—although mine just left

and I love the new gal. But hey, we're going to bitch and complain, sure. And maybe you hit it off with a few friends I invited. The male kind." Katie exaggerated her wink.

"You know, my head is starting to hurt. I might have a cough too." Justine gave a few fake coughs, but Katie wasn't buying it.

"Nice try." The car stopped, and they left with a goodbye and hefty tip to their driver. "Get the lead out, Ferrera. Your ovaries aren't going to wake up if there's no one to greet them in the morning."

"What the hell does that even mean?" Justine pasted on a smile as they approached Katie's friends.

"It means you're going to thank me tomorrow."

"Or I'll be cursing your name while battling a hangover and regretting a terrible Friday night where the men have no game."

"Or that. Either way, you're going. So move."

CHAPTER 2

Xavier groaned as he let himself back into his apartment. Great impression to make on the new tenant. With a splitting headache and overdue project, dealing with his ex-girlfriend's brother had been last on his To-Do list. And of course, just his luck, Justine in 3D looked beautiful and all put-together while he looked his worst. Brawling in public. Jesus. He hadn't gotten into a physical fight since college, back when Auggie had been all about doing terrible things on campus then blaming Xavier for it.

Twins. He loved his sister, but Auggie could be over-the-top on a good day.

His phone buzzed. Speaking of over-the-top... "Yo, Auggie. What's up? We doing dinner tonight or what?" He wondered what Justine and her friend had planned for the evening. If Justine had a boyfriend or significant other. Odd that her aunt had never mentioned her, considering he and Rosie had been good friends for months.

And of course, they kind of worked together.

"Bro, I need help."

Xavier swallowed a sigh. "Of course you do."

"Don't be pretentious. Buzz me up."

"Do you even know what pretentious means?"

He winced at the vitriol that accompanied his sister's answer and buzzed Auggie in, which reminded him he only had himself to blame about Dan—the guy he never should have allowed in the building. Apparently, Christine still didn't like the word "no." They'd broken up a month ago, and she continued to harass him, now using her brother to send messages.

Last time Xavier would make that mistake.

He'd known he and Christine were over a while ago, but he'd tried his best to make it work. As a therapist, Xavier knew all about dysfunction and lying to oneself. Christine had been pleasant...at first. A nice woman, attractive, self-sufficient. The perfect companion.

Until she'd revealed certain truths, become clingy and codependent, and had made his life a living hell with petty jealousies and insecurity. Auggie hadn't liked her either, and that was typically a telling sign that things wouldn't work out.

Xavier could count on one hand the number of times they'd approved of each other's relationships. A real pair, the both of them.

"We're so pathetic," he muttered as Augusta Hanover pushed through the door.

Though obviously not identical twins, they might as well have been. They shared the same features, voice inflections, and had that twin-brain, where they had a tendency to pick up on what the other might be feeling or thinking. Auggie was incredibly pretty, more redhead than brunette, tall, and had a trim and toned physique. She'd never taken crap from anyone in her life—a clear balance to Xavier's people-pleaser mentality.

He had a few inches on his sister in addition to muscle but wasn't nearly as defined. Auggie, a personal trainer and gym-worshipper, had an aggressive drive and a tendency to go after what she wanted. Unlike Auggie, he got the twin share of charm, had a smile that could kill from twenty paces—according to Mom—and the patience his sister lacked.

They were two halves of the same whole. Unfortunately, most significant others wanted the entire piece, not just a half, and neither he nor Auggie had yet to find that perfect partner for more than a few months here or there.

"Xavier, my dearest brother, you still pale beside the glory that is me." Auggie flexed, showing off some impressive biceps, looking cute and fit in a pair of workout shorts and a tee-shirt, her hair pulled back into a long ponytail. "If only you had my brain, my sense of style... breasts."

Xavier rolled his eyes. "If I wanted a 'boob' I'd look no further than you. Idiot."

Auggie grinned and flipped him off.

"Thanks. But I already had one of those earlier."

"This?" She pointed that middle finger at his face "What happened?"

"I went against my better judgement and let Christine's brother in to talk to me. The only good thing about the visit was I got to return her grandmother's necklace without meeting up with her."

"The same necklace she deliberately left here last time so you'd have to talk to her again?" Auggie asked.

Xavier sighed. "Please don't say it."

Auggie shrugged.

A few seconds passed.

"*Itoldyouso*," Auggie blurted. "Ah, that feels better."

After a second of glaring at each other, they eased into smiles and laughed.

Xavier looked his sister over. "You working out more?"

"Yeah. There's a new event I'm entering in August. It's a fitness competition with major sponsorship. Winner gets backing from the sponsors, a fifty thousand dollar prize, and emcee rights for the winter competition, which includes major branding and marketing. It's huge, Xav."

"Where's it being held?"

"Our great city of Seattle. Duh."

"Hey, for all I know you're going to Hawaii on another 'work' trip."

"I wish. And that Hawaii trip was legit. I worked out, trained two guys at the hotel gym, and had a hell of a time with Barry. You know, before we broke up." Auggie plopped herself on the couch and eased her forearm over her eyes. "My life is a mess."

"When isn't it?" Xavier muttered but didn't react when Auggie moved her forearm to glare before covering up again. Taking one for the team, he asked, "Okay, Ms. Messy, what's wrong?"

"It's Rafe."

"Wait. The guy who thinks he's a pirate?"

"Oh my God. He wore that shirt because he was modeling. It wasn't his everyday wear."

"And he looked like a pirate. Am I wrong?"

Auggie gave a loud sigh. "It's just... He's not the man I thought he was."

"Auggie, he's *exactly* the man you thought he was. Handsome, a stud in bed—your words, not mine—and not much between his ears."

"But they were such cute ears." Auggie paused. "I feel bad that I don't miss him. I'm thirty-two. Shouldn't I be thinking about a steady relationship at this age? Babies? A family? Shouldn't *we*?" She moved her arm and stared at Xavier.

"You've been talking to Mom recently. A mistake."

"I know." Auggie groaned. "I though it was you calling so I picked up the phone. Anyway, she made some valid points."

"Auggie, you know you can't force love. Mom got lucky."

They paused a moment, still missing their father though it had been over ten years since his passing.

Auggie nodded. "Ever since breaking up with Noel last year, she hasn't been happy." Though it didn't need to be said they'd both loathed Noel for a multitude of reasons. "She's too focused on us and needs to concentrate on her own life. She's got a few good years left."

Xavier snorted. "Ya think?" Their mother had just turned fifty-two and had no plan to die anytime soon. Or so she'd said just a few weeks ago when nagging him to find a wife and have a few kids while she was still young enough to appreciate running around with them. "You do have a point. It's not healthy for her to be so alone all the time."

"She'd say the same thing about you."

"Hey, I was dating Christine until recently."

Auggie gave him a knowing look. "We all knew that was going nowhere. She was your Rafe, only a little smarter."

Xavier bit back a laugh. "Okay, okay. So we need to hook Mom up, is that what you're saying?" He felt a little ill just thinking about his mother out there, dating. Noel had been bad enough.

"Do I need to use smaller words?"

This time Xavier shot Auggie the finger. "Look, I have to finish my article before tomorrow morning. But I have time to join my baby sister in a pizza and some beer."

"Baby sister? I'm barely four minutes younger than you."

"Five minutes, but who's counting?"

She made a face.

"I also have soda if you don't want beer. But nothing diet. Real sugar for us real people."

Auggie gagged. "That you're not dead yet, after all the crap you eat and drink, is a miracle. Must be all those good vibes you're passing along to your readers."

Xavier cleared his throat. "Not *my* readers. Aunt Truth's readers. Remember, I'm just filling in while she's on sabbatical."

Auggie sat up and rolled her eyes. "Whatever. I'm not gonna

tell anyone you're pretending to be the popular Aunt Truth. Sheesh. I'm just messing with you."

"Good. Because I need this break, and I'm actually enjoying the work."

"It's still therapy, Xavier, no matter how hard you pretend you're taking a break from your day job." Auggie shook her head. "Denial. The first step to accepting your faults."

"That's one of the first stages of grief, actually, so—"

"Like I care. We already have one shrink in the family. We don't need *me* telling people how to think too."

"That's not what I do. I—"

"Don't care." She grinned. "I always thought you drew better than you spoke. Stick to cartoons, Bro, and we'll all be better for it."

"Stop or my head will explode from all the compliments." He ignored his sister's laughter. "Order us an extra-large pie. One half extra cheese and—"

"—the other all the toppings. I got it."

Xavier grabbed them some beer while Auggie called in their order. In the other room, on a drawing desk, sat his current project. A cartoon to go with the advice column he'd been working on. It was silly, he knew, but he got a kick out of drawing out snippets of relationship dramas and problems.

Ever since Aunt Truth had decided to take him on as a silent partner, he'd been answering the advice column for *Searching the Needle Weekly*, a free weekly paper and streaming channel that had just sold Aunt Truth to an affiliate for some serious money. Now he had more work with better pay. Nothing close to his previous salary as an LMFT—Licensed Marriage and Family Therapist—but he didn't need the money. His father's life insurance and investments had helped the entire family avoid deep debt for the rest of their lives.

He brought the beers to the table and watched Auggie surf through channels. They settled on a reality medical program.

She grimaced. "Ew. How the hell do you get a bike chain stuck in your thigh?'

They both cringed as the doctors proceeded to remove said chain, but they didn't look away. Fascinated by other people's messes, Xavier thought with humor.

An hour later, as they nibbled on pizza while watching a true crime show, Auggie said, "I know a guy I can set Mom up with. He's nice and built like a brick."

"Uh, I don't know that she's into beefy guys."

Auggie frowned. "What's wrong with working out?"

"Nothing. But Mom's a little more cerebral."

"Stereotype much?" Auggie huffed. "You know, we're not all meatheads."

"I know that. But I've also met a lot of your friends. Exactly which one do you think's good enough for Mom?"

She opened her mouth and closed it. "Okay, so not Josh. Or Abe. But a few other names come to mind. I'll feel them out first though."

"Fine. I'll do the same. I have a few guys from work that might fit. Problem is, few of them know how to leave their therapist hats at the office."

Auggie arched a brow. "Isn't that what Christine said about you?"

"Yeah." He sighed. "But she was just annoying." He chuckled at Auggie's exaggerated nod. "Hold on. I'll get some paper and a pen so we can make a list."

So he spent the majority of his Friday night with his twin drafting a dating list for their mother. Though he didn't think any of the guys would work, at least it was a start.

And while he wrote down names, he tried not to think about how sad his circumstances had become that even his mother was gearing up to have a social life more exciting than his own.

CHAPTER 3

Justine woke up with the hangover from hell. "I hate you, Katie," she mumbled into her pillow then swore as banging at her front door stopped her from going back to sleep. She mumbled a slew of curses and stomped her way to the front door, only pausing to see the time.

Eight-thirty in the morning. An ungodly hour by anyone's account.

"What?" she snapped as she opened the door wide, expecting to see Katie.

Not the hottie from 2C.

He stood in shorts and a tee-shirt holding two coffees and a bag that smelled delicious. He also looked as if he'd stepped out of Katie's *Sexy Men with Coffee* calendar.

She looked down at her oversized *Friends Don't Let Friends Beer Goggle* tee-shirt that had seen better days. The neck had been stretched so that the shirt hung off a bare shoulder. It also barely hid her short-short pajama bottoms from view. Her hair stood on end, though she'd at least wiped off her makeup from the night prior, so she shouldn't look like a goth racoon staring at male perfection.

He tried to bite back a smile, but she saw it and scowled.

He wiped the smile from his face and cleared his throat. "I'm sorry for yesterday. I came over with a peace offering. Too early?"

A waft of coffee and sugar hit her, and she tugged the drink holder from his hands. "Come on in."

He closed the door behind him and followed her into the tiny kitchen. Aunt Rosie had an eclectic sense of design, the open kitchen and living room small but furnished tastefully with smaller teak pieces accompanied by light fabrics. It felt like one of those tiny IKEA rooms but was expensively appointed with high quality pieces. Minimalist with everything in its place. As opposed to the opulent bedroom, full of different shades of reds and pinks and clutter.

And mirrors. *So* many mirrors. It was like living in a bordello.

She nursed her coffee, letting the caffeine do its work as 2C settled in at the small kitchen table across from her. *Not 2C —Xavier.*

"I like Rosie's style. Everything's so neat and organized."

She snorted and said, "You should see the bedroom."

He paused with his cup to his mouth and raised a brow.

She flushed. "Not that that was an invitation. I'm not asking you to sleep with me."

He stared.

"Well, not that we'd be sleeping. I'm talking about sex." It was like her mouth hadn't yet connected to her brain, which kept screaming at her to shut up.

He took a sip of his coffee and kept staring.

She rambled. "I'm not saying I don't want to have sex with you. I mean, I don't. But it's not because you're not handsome enough."

He had yet to blink.

"Even with the facial hair. Not that facial hair is bad." It could be quite nice, especially trailing between her thighs. "It's fine. You're fine," she blurted, cheeks blazing.

His lips quirked.

"I just... What's in the bag?"

His grin managed to take him from sexy-hot to blazingly handsome. "Not a morning person. Noted."

She groaned and dropped her head to the table. "It's not even nine o'clock yet."

"I've been up since six-thirty."

She raised her head to glare at him, annoyed at the smirk that instead of making him annoying, turned him into a charmer.

"How about some donuts to make you smile?"

She perked up at that.

They ate donuts and drank coffee in a surprisingly comfortable silence while she woke up and tried to speak without sounding like a moron.

Before she could say anything, Xavier spoke first. "I'm really sorry for coming over too early. I felt bad about leaving a terrible first impression yesterday and wanted to make it right. I swear, I don't normally pick fights in the halls or intrude on my neighbors' privacy."

"It's fine, really." She paused. "Can I ask what that fight was about?"

He blew out a breath. "My ex-girlfriend sent her brother around to—hell, I don't know. Convince me I was making a mistake?" He ran a hand through his hair. "We broke up over a month ago, and honestly, it should have happened a while before that. She's a nice person, but we didn't fit."

"Sorry to hear that." She finished her coffee and needed more. "I need more coffee. You?"

"Sure, if you're offering."

"You did bring the first cup." She left the table to fix a pot of the good stuff, grinding beans from a local brewery. She glanced over her shoulder to say something and saw him staring at her ass. She flipped her gaze front and felt another blush heating her cheeks. "Do you think your ex's brother got the message?" A tentative glance back at him showed him fixated on one of her aunt's funny dish towels that hung over the handle of the oven door, so maybe she'd been mistaken about him staring at her butt. She rejoined him at the table.

"Huh? Oh, Dan. Right. I hope so. I'm not into fistfights over women." He snorted. "I'm not into fights, period. Now my sister, she's the one you need to worry about."

"Yeah?"

"Auggie—short for Augusta, and she hates that name—lives for drama. She breaks up with her fifth boyfriend in two months? Drama. Loses a quarter? Drama. Thinks I'm not answering her calls fast enough? Drama."

Justine snickered. "That's funny. My sisters are so the opposite. My oldest sister is the son my father never had. She's smart, pretty, and vicious. Basically, his mini-me. She married his protégée, a financial guru with the personality of burnt toast." She paused. "I can't believe I'm telling you this. I sound like a horrible person."

The coffee machine beeped, and Xavier got up to refill their cups, then helped himself to creamer from the fridge. "Sorry, Rosie used to make me serve her when I visited. I haven't yet broken the habit." He brought her creamer and a bowl of sweetener packets from the counter.

"Thanks. No worries."

As Justine fixed her coffee, Xavier continued, "Please don't apologize for being honest. I love my sister and love being with her, but she's a drama queen and knows it. So your older sister is a carbon copy of the old man. What about the other sister?"

"She's the middle child; I'm the youngest. Mallory is the family pleaser. That sounds really mean, but it's sadly true. She'll do anything to earn my parents' approval. It drives me nuts, but there's not much I can do about it. I don't like her fiancé much, but he's approved by my parents so it's a done deal." Justine sighed. Just thinking about Ted made her ill.

"And you? The youngest, you said?"

"Yeah. I'm the only one who didn't go into business. I'm a PR stooge with a graphic design background. I work at a marketing firm in town." She didn't like thinking about work on her off time. "But it's the weekend, so let's not go there. In any case, my dad still nags me to come work for him. He's also constantly trying to fix me up with his employees, which is just embarrassing. My mom helps him by springing these poor guys on me, when I think I'm going over for some mother-daughter bonding and end up doing coffee with a stranger. I've stopped visiting." And was *more* than overdue for a family dinner.

"Whoa. That's rough. But I think it's a parent thing. You look..." He paused. "How old are you?"

"How old do I look?" She laughed, which was odd. Normally around a handsome guy, Justine felt like a bundle of nerves and typically said the wrong thing at the wrong time. But since she'd already put her foot in her mouth earlier, she felt surprisingly comfortable around Xavier. He hadn't been eyeing her breasts or making moves. Just talking about family, making eye contact, and *listening*.

It was...nice.

"What's that look?" he asked.

"Oh, just thinking that this conversation is a lot better than the ones I had last night." She grimaced. "And for the record, I'm twenty-nine."

"Ah. Well, I was going to say that when you near thirty, a lot of parents seem hit some kind of switch that has them nagging about marriage and grandkids. I'm thirty-two, and my mom has been all over me about finding the right girl and having children."

"It's not just me, then."

"Nope." He grimaced. "Last night, while you were having terrible conversations with people, I was watching bad reality TV and making my mom a boyfriend list with my sister. Because when Mom has a boyfriend, she leaves us alone. What can I say? I live a sad life."

She laughed. "Wow. And I thought my night was bad."

"What was so bad about it?"

"Katie, my best friend you met last night, keeps trying to set me up with her friends. And I'm just... I'm done dating for a while. My last breakup sucked. And frankly, I don't have time to date just dealing with the day-to-day in a lousy job and dealing with my stressful family. Did I mention my middle sister is getting married next month, and I'm one of her bridesmaids? It's a nightmare."

Justine paused, suddenly embarrassed about confessing things to a stranger. And in her pajamas, no less! "I'm sorry. I've been sitting here in my PJs talking your ear off."

"What? Oh." He gave her shirt a brief glance and looked quickly back up at her face. "I hadn't noticed, to be honest. It's been so long since I've been able to talk to someone and not feel pressured to perform or impress." He paused. "That sounds horrible. I just meant you're easy to talk to."

She gave him a shy smile. "You are too. I hope you don't take this the wrong way, but this is nice. Like, I feel like I've made a new friend. One who understands difficult family and the need for quality coffee and donuts."

He held up his cup. "To new friends."

"To new friends." She focused on how good it felt to share coffee with someone without pressure to be anyone but herself.

"And to no more fights on the second floor."

She laughed. "We'll keep them to the first and third floors only."

"Exactly."

"Now what can you tell me about the other tenants in this building? Because the super stares at me like he hates me, and I've been warned not to screw around or the cop in 1A will write me up in a heartbeat."

"Oh boy. We might need something heavier than caffeine and sugar for that. But I'll give you the abbreviated version."

And that's how Justine spent her Saturday morning, with coffee, donuts, and a smile on her face as she learned the best way to navigate life in the TCA with a new friend.

CHAPTER 4

Saturday passed in a blur of errands and time spent with Katie at aerobics, which Justine had dearly needed. Out of breath and out of shape, she added a walk around the neighborhood as the sun set, enjoying the wonder of Fremont in the pre-summer warmth. Seattle could promise a cold breeze at any time of the year, even in late May, but the weather had held, and she made use of it as she passed by the thinning crowd as storefronts on Fremont Way readied for the night life.

She made a note to try Dreamland Bar & Diner and remembered last night's driver mention Stampede, a cocktail club. Then she recalled exactly who she was and why she hated bars, the nightlife, and dating in general. Yeah, that would be a *no* on the nightlife and dating scene for a while.

She hadn't been lying to Xavier earlier. Though she secretly found him *more* than attractive, she didn't want to sex him up. At present, she wasn't looking for more than a friend. She'd been burned not long ago by a boyfriend she could never satisfy. And dealing with an ultra demanding boss at work and her father at any given moment, she just didn't have it in her to have to please one more man.

Justine enjoyed her walk home, the trees and bushes now a vibrant green, bulbs springing to life into rich color, and the sweet smell of life breezing past, carrying the scent of barbecue and beer from a nearby restaurant.

She let herself into the TCA complex and headed for the inner courtyard—the outdoor area enclosed by a security door and walls, yet open above and through a few windows to qualify as a true outdoor space.

The building from the outside looked like a long, boxy rectangle. But inside, on the first floor, there was a cute brick courtyard with a water fountain, picnic tables and chairs, and a bevy of plants making it a wonderful relaxation spot.

She headed for the fountain and spotted a young boy sitting on a nearby bench, playing on his phone. She'd only met two tenants, not counting Xavier, upon first moving in. Kai, her third floor neighbor, and this boy, who lived on the first floor.

He saw her and stared.

After an awkward pause, she waved and said, "Hi. Hope I'm not intruding."

His bright grin was infectious, his warm brown eyes sparkling. "Nope. I'm just messing around on my phone." He tucked it away and patted the bench next to him. "There's plenty of room right here."

She decided to take him up on his offer and sat, a little surprised he didn't seem to mind her being so close.

"Are you the new girl?"

She nodded. "I'm Justine Ferrera. I'm living in my aunt's apartment for a little while."

"Oh, you're related to Rosie. She's nice. Always gives me cookies when I visit." He flashed her a charming grin. "I'm in high school."

"That's nice." Huh. She'd have pegged him as much younger.

"Yeah, school gets out in a few more weeks." He nodded,

staring at her so hard she wondered if she had a smudge on her face. "How old are you?"

A blunt question, but she answered, "Me? I'm twenty-nine."

"Cool. I like older women."

Huh?

"There's a free concert at Seattle Center next weekend. Wanna go?"

She didn't know what to say.

Fortunately, a frazzled man who looked around her own age approached, taking the boy's attention. "Sam, give it a rest."

"What?" Sam scowled. "I'm being nice and neighborly, like you said."

The man sighed as he turned to her. "Hi there. I'm Adam, Sam's uncle. I hope he's not bothering you."

She stood and shook his hand. "Not at all. We were just talking."

"I asked her out, Uncle Adam. She hasn't said yes yet, though."

Justine felt her cheeks heat.

Adam blinked. "Were you going to say *yes?*"

She turned to Sam and shook her head. "Sorry, but I'm busy with family stuff for the next few weekends. And I have a feeling I'd get into trouble if I tried dating a high schooler."

Adam pinched the bridge of his nose. "He's in eighth grade."

"I'm almost in high school. That counts." Sam winked at her.

She found herself laughing as he scampered out of his uncle's way and headed for the door to his unit. Once there, he stopped to blow her a kiss.

"Sam," his uncle barked.

The boy quickly let himself into the apartment.

"I'm sorry for Sam," Adam said.

"No worries. He's cute." She hurriedly added, "Not in a dating kind of way. Honestly, I had no idea what to say when he asked about going to a concert tomorrow. I didn't want to hurt his feelings. Good timing on your part."

Adam groaned. "Between him and Rylan, I'm about to crack. Sam's twelve going on thirty. Rylan's the sixteen year old who thinks he's the boss of his brother *and* me. I take it you haven't met him yet."

"No. Technically, I haven't met you either." She held out a hand. "Justine Ferrera. Rosie Gallo's niece."

Adam's expression brightened as he took her hand. "Hey, it's nice to meet you. I'm Adam Baker. When Rosie told us she was leaving for a few months, the boys were bummed. She's been super great to us all."

"That's Aunt Rosie. Always willing to help out." Like subletting her place so her pathetic niece didn't have to move back in with her family. Justine still wasn't sure if Rosie had truly planned her vacation ahead of time or had just made up the excuse to give Justine a place to stay.

"I'll say." Adam studied her. "You look familiar. Have I seen you before?"

"Not on a wanted poster," she blurted, which made him laugh.

His smile eased the tension on his face and turned him from mildly attractive to handsome.

Yet another man she wanted nothing from but friendship. Justine wondered if something was wrong with her, because for so many years she'd been what her sisters had long ago termed "boy-crazy." Wanting a boyfriend, wanting to get married, have babies, live in the dream house. But after breaking up with her ex and moving out, fantasies of happily ever-after paled next to the reality of headaches and heartbreak.

"Well, I'd better get back inside. Dinner isn't going to cook itself. I'll see you around." Adam gave her a pleasant smile. "And please let me know if my nephews start making a nuisance of themselves. Sam especially."

"I'm sure they'll be fine." She smiled back. "If only dinner would make itself, right? I'm having a PB&J and cutting off the crusts. Fancy, huh?"

He laughed, waved, and left.

Alone, contemplating the soothing sounds of the water spilling from a stone floral centerpiece in the center of the fountain, she wondered about the neighbors.

On the first floor, according to Xavier, lived Top, the crabby super who stared at everyone as if contemplating murder. Then Adam, a police officer and his two nephews. Xavier thought something had happened to the children's mother, so Adam had stepped in to care for them. Sam was a cute if a little precocious. Rylan sounded like a handful, but Adam had been decent to talk to.

Then on the second floor, she had Xavier in 2C and quiet, introverted Benji in 2B. According to Xavier, Benji rarely left his apartment except to go to his job at a tech company twice a week. A pleasant yet shy man who liked to keep to himself. She could respect that. And Xavier was...well, Xavier.

On the third floor, the irrepressible Rosie Gallo was subletting to Justine. And across the hall, in 3E, lived Kai Strand—internationally acclaimed children's book author and her aunt's best friend. Kai had recently left to vacation in Tuscany with Rosie but would be returning sometime in July.

For now, Justine had the third floor all to herself. Instead of being creeped out at living by herself up there, she felt cozy. Tucked in with TCA's quirky residents, from the gruff caretaker to the intelligent and friendly Xavier to the intense yet caring Adam, she felt safe nestled among people with their own problems. Everyone too busy to focus on Justine.

As she left the fountain and cooling evening air, she walked up the steps to her unit and entered, still in shock at how much her life had changed since she'd broken up with her ex.

After a shower and dressing in shorts and a simple tee, she made herself a sandwich, cut off all the crusts, and added an unnecessary hot cocoa with marshmallows, just because she could.

She watched a gimmicky sitcom and laughed with the canned audience, feeling like part of the crowd, which then made her feel that much more alone, taking pleasure in fake belonging.

But then, that was kind of her pattern. Her go-to, her aunt liked to say, to seek acceptance and validation from those who would never give it back.

Her father.

Her boss.

Her ex.

All of them determined to refuse her the affection and approval she craved.

Which had her making what would probably be a huge mistake, calling her mother, the woman who would always love Justine more than anyone in the world, or so she said.

"Hey, sweetheart, how are you?" Jeanine Ferrera asked, her voice light, the sound of people in the background hinting at a crowd.

"Oh, sorry. Sounds like you're busy." Justine already regretted the urge for motherly comfort.

"Not at all." Her mother must have moved, because the sound behind her muted. "What are you up to?"

"Just relaxing. It feels great to not have anything to do for once." *I'm bored, Mom. So bored I'm calling you.* "What are you up to?"

"A small party for your father's new business partner. You should see my dress, it's *so* cute. I picked it up on Thursday at that boutique downtown I was telling you about."

"Nice. You should take pictures and send them to me."

"I will. But before I forget, you are coming tomorrow night, aren't you?"

"Tomorrow night?"

"Sunday family dinner. Justine, you have to. We're going to be talking about Mallory's wedding."

"So Angela will be there?"

"Yes. Angela, Scott, Mallory, and of course, Ted. But we won't talk wedding details in front of him. It never helps for the fiancé to know too much about the bride's secrets." Her mother tittered.

Justine didn't find anything funny about the thought of her sister's flirty husband-to-be. But she wanted to be supportive. She loved her sisters, even if she sometimes didn't like them all that much. Then again, who was she to judge? Nearly thirty, no husband, no children, and a dead-end job working for a dickhead. Oh, and no home either, since she'd moved out of her place with Mitch.

Great. Now she'd depressed herself. Time for more marshmallows.

"Justine?"

"Of course I wouldn't miss a chance to talk about Mallory's wedding." Justine paused. "But this had better not be an attempt to set me up again, Mom. I mean it. If I see one guy at dinner I don't know, I'm leaving."

"Now, Justine. I've learned my lesson. It's just family and wedding chatter. I promise. Six o'clock sharp, honey. Don't be late."

Justine imagined her mother crossing her fingers behind her back but ignored her better sense. Despite their nonsense, she missed her family. "I'll see you then."

"Perfect. Now let me tell you about the people at this party. I've got dirt on all of them."

Not caring but kind of—maybe a little bit—interested in someone's life that seemed to be on track, she encouraged her mother by asking, "Who's the worst of the worst?"

"Oh, that would be Kathy with a K, who's sleeping with Cathy with a C's husband."

"Well, at least he can keep his women straight. Same name."

"That's what I said!" Her mom laughed, and something inside Justine eased.

She might not have the perfect life, but she did have people who cared about her. Life could be a lot worse.

CHAPTER 5

A lot worse. Worse than a dinner spent talking to one's sister about a wedding one loathed the idea of attending. Worse than agreeing to dress in a clingy bridesmaid gown on the big day that would show way too much boobage. Worse even than having to sit across from Ted during dinner while he leered when no one was looking, still acting like an attentive and loving fiancé while one's sister simpered over him.

Ugh.

Justine glared at her mother, who pretended not to see her glaring, and stewed because she knew better yet had still accepted her mother's invitation.

Sitting between bachelor number one and bachelor number two, two of her father's up and comers at Ferrera-Hind Wealth Management, she tried to relax, telling herself her mother had promised not to try to set her up. Was she reading too much into this dinner?

She really had planned to walk right back out the door when they'd arrived ten minutes after her. But her mother had implored her not to make a scene. "It's not always about you, dear," Jeanine had quietly pointed out.

Plus, her father had been behaving so well tonight. A kiss on the cheek without all the unwelcome advice about her career. Angela and their mother had refrained from asking after Justine's dreaded ex, whom they'd all liked. And even Scott—Angela's husband—had been pleasant at first greeting instead of treating her like a wad of gum stuck to the bottom of his shoe.

Then the proverbial sound of trumpets heralded the coming apocalypse—the dinner bell and forced conversation.

"That's the timer," her mother cheerfully announced, as if she'd cooked their meal. The catering staff came out moments later with their salads and wine.

Used to fancy dinners where the caterers came and went, Justine didn't think much of her parents' wealth. They hadn't been born rich. They'd had to work for it. But somehow, raising their three children, they'd forgotten how the average person lived. Something she knew quite well, living independently, and appreciated.

Justine made her own choices about life, living like a pauper, yes, but on her own two feet. Unlike her sisters, who didn't hurt financially but also had to obey their parents in regards to their professional and personal lives or be threatened to be cut off.

"Thanks for coming Cal, Nick," her father said in a booming voice before shooting her an expectant look.

"So glad for the invite, Mr. Ferrera." Cal—Bachelor Number One—said.

"Yes, thank you," came from Nick—Bachelor Number Two.

The pair had dark hair, similar builds, and politeness swimming in their DNA.

"We always love having Dad's people for a visit," Justine agreed and gave the perfunctory fake smile, which eased the grim expression on her father's face. He turned to Scott and started on the finance talk, including Cal and Nick. Not to be ignored,

Angela put her two cents in whenever a lull fell, and the dinner passed pleasantly enough.

A Seattle Surf and Turf platter—King Salmon and Kobe filet—sat in the middle of the table filled with mashed potatoes, rice pilaf, asparagus, roasted beets with goat cheese drizzled with a dark vinaigrette, honey glazed carrots, and a few more delectable dishes that made Justine drool. Heck, she hadn't been eating this well in...well, since the last time she'd been to the house.

She concentrated on her meal, doing her best not to fall on it like a starving woman, and gave occasional murmurs of interest when Mallory gushed over wedding plans.

Fortunately, Ted seemed more interested in her father's conversation than his fiancée's, so she was able to ignore him.

Midway through the meal, Cal and Nick began talking to her more, asking more personal questions.

"Oh, she's single," her mother sang, having apparently paid more attention to Justine than she'd thought. "She broke up with her ex-boyfriend a while ago."

Officially, two weeks ago. But technically, they'd been over long before that.

"Mom," Justine growled.

"Oh, honey, you know you're over him."

"I am, but this isn't something we need to be talking about over dinner."

Ted snorted. "You're too good for him. You'll find someone else."

Mallory beamed up at her fiancé. "She is, Ted. You're so right."

"I'm not looking for anyone else." Justine fought to keep her voice pleasant while refusing to look at the men on either side of her. "I'm happy living on my own and being single."

"Good for you," Cal said, surprising her. "So many people jump from one relationship to the next. My brother did that. Married too quickly and is getting divorced next month."

"Bummer." Nick shook his head. "But I don't think being with someone is a bad thing. You get all the feels and meet needs. Take the financial aspect, for instance."

Her father leaned in, his eyes sparkling. "Yes, let's talk about financial stability, Nick. Go on."

Justine swallowed a sigh and took a long sip of her wine while Nick and her father traded common investment strategies overlooked by most of the workforce. Then Angela explained how she and Scott had been saving, which had Ted asking more questions and Mallory trying to keep up while their mother glowed with approval.

Keeping quiet felt safe, so Justine finished her meal then excused herself for a side trip upstairs, needing a break. She dialed Katie but had to leave a voice message. In a low voice, she said, "The next time I even think about going to my parents for Sunday dinner, tie me up and shove me in my closet. Ring me later. Gotta go."

She heard Mallory calling for her and quickly pocketed her phone. "I'm coming. Just had to respond to a message."

"What message?" Mallory entered the hallway where Justine had been hiding. Like her sisters, Mallory had dark hair and dark eyes. Pretty, she and Angela took after their mother, their looks softer, whereas Justine had the eagle eyes and features of her father. Which was a joke, because clearly Angela was more bird of prey and Justine more chicken.

"Oh, nothing important. Just something Katie sent."

"How's she doing?" Mallory looped her arm around Justine's and tugged her back toward the stairs.

"She's good. Still likes working for the company. But she got a new boss, so she's not dealing with a jerk like I am."

Mallory gave her a sympathetic squeeze. "That's tough. I'm lucky Dad put me with a good team." She leaned closer. "I think I'd lose it if I had to work under Angela."

Justine chuckled. "Hard-ass Hanover's oldest is a real chip off the block. I've heard that *so* many times before."

"No kidding." Mallory walked down with her. "I know you weren't expecting Cal or Nick tonight. But honestly, I don't think Mom's trying to set you up. Dad had something come up today he was working on with the new guys, and then Angela mentioned inviting them to dinner."

"Really?"

They stopped at the base of the steps. Mallory looked around, then admitted, "Well, that's what Angela said, but I think Mom hinted to her at how nice it would be to have a big get-together tonight since you were coming. Um, you know, with more men at the table to round out us girls."

Justine groaned.

Mallory quickly added, "Look, I get that you want to be alone. But I know you were bummed out when Mitch dumped you."

Justine counted to ten in her head before repeating, "He didn't dump me. I got tired of his crap and broke up with him."

"Sure, sure."

Obviously, no one believed the truth. But how could they when Mitch had been the *perfect* boyfriend? Successful, independent, handsome, smart. A *doctor*. He never showed them the clingy side of his personality, the side that constantly demanded Justine be more and do more to make *him* happy, no matter what *she* wanted. Life with Mitch was all about Mitch. Ugh. Talk about exhausting.

Mallory drew Justine toward the living area, where the ladies gathered after the meal. "Anyway, I really appreciate you helping out with the wedding." There wasn't that much for Justine to do since Mallory's wedding planners, including their mother, had everything well in hand. Justine basically had to show up for a few pre and post nuptial events. "I'm so excited! Just one more month and I'll be Mrs. Mallory Cochran."

She hated to rain on her sister's parade, but Justine had no idea what her sister saw in Ted other than a paycheck and dimples. He wasn't bad looking, but he'd have to look like a virtual Adonis to make up for his wandering eye. She hadn't been the only one he'd subtly come on to; she'd seen him flirt with several of the administration assistants at Ferrara-Hind, and even Katie once when they'd run into him in Queen Anne.

"You're sure you're ready to get married?" Justine asked. "You're only a few years older than me. Still so young. And you could have any guy you wanted. You know that. Are you sure you're ready to settle down with just one man?"

Mallory blushed. Odd that Justine had always felt protective of her older, more vulnerable sister. Such a sweetheart, yet so easy to manipulate. So very unlike their mother or Angela.

And me? Am I that easy to control? I did come to Sunday night dinner, and I know better.

Her Aunt Rosie popped in her mind with familiar advice. *Relax, girl. Sometimes you just need to smile and mean it.*

In her place, Aunt Rosie would have flirted with both Cal and Nick, made plans to take one if not both of them home, and enjoyed the dinner her parents had shared without missing a beat. Hmm. Maybe Aunt Rosie and Katie were right. Maybe Justine was a little too tense all the time, making problems where there didn't need to be any. Dinner had been delicious and *free.* And if the conversation and company hadn't been all to her liking, no one had done anything inappropriate or rude.

She joined her mom and sisters in the living room, a lovely area decorated in pale creams with gold accents. The subtle flair of wealth, sophistication, and majesty didn't so much calm her as she sat down but forced her to acknowledge a grand effort had been made to soothe and entertain, so she should stop resisting.

"I love the redesign, Mom." Justine sipped at the cup of tea Angela handed her, though secretly she preferred the room's previous blue tones.

Angela glanced around, her lips pursed. Justine's oldest sister wore her hair up in a stylish updo and looked both elegant and professional, her black business suit and white blouse pristine, her black pumps gorgeous—and expensive. To go along with her pricey attire, her icy gaze looked more black than brown, Angela never less than 99% intense about life.

She raised a perfectly sculpted brow. "The redesign is gorgeous. Would Mom have it any other way?"

The girls laughed, their mother blushing with pleasure.

The family bonding, even though it felt a little stilted, was nice.

Then Angela ruined it by opening her big, fat mouth. "Before we get involved in the wedding plans, Justine, what do you think of Cal and Nick? They couldn't take their eyes off you all through dinner. And I happen to know they're both single and loaded."

Their mother perked up. "I saw that too! Oh, Justine, honey. What do you think? You do need a date to the wedding, after all."

Freakin' Angela.

CHAPTER 6

Xavier sat across from his sister in the dining room while their mother kept flitting back and forth from the kitchen to the table.

"Mom, sit down already." Auggie rolled her eyes. "I told you I'd help set everything out. Come on. Take a load off."

"You, hush. I'm nearly done."

Xavier would have been helping, but he'd been banned from messing up her kitchen the last time he'd been over.

Their mother lived in a lovely home in Queen Anne, a two story colonial full of family memories and comfort. The house they'd grown up in, with the same large tree swing and creaky wooden floors covered by patterned runners, always felt like home, but only because their mother had made it that way.

With short, stylish, auburn hair, a trim build thanks to daily yoga and her morning walks, and a fun-loving attitude, Cynthia Hanover could always make him smile. Though she hadn't lived like a monk since his father had passed, she seemed to take more comfort in friends, work, and hobbies than dating.

Noel not included.

He frowned, saw his sister frown, and knew they were

thinking the same thing. Noel had always insisted on sitting right next to their mother at the table. But tonight, Xavier and Auggie sat across from each other, right next to their mother. Just the three of them.

He swallowed a sigh, not wanting to see his mom dating some douche again. Heck, he never seemed to like her boyfriends, though Noel had been more irritating and lasted longer than most. But he also acknowledged she might be lonely, especially because she kept spending so much time meddling with her twins' social lives.

Thus he and Auggie had come up with a semi-decent list of good men to distract their mother. Time to make good use of it.

His sister kicked him under the table.

"Wait," he whispered and glared when she nodded to their mother, who'd left her seat again, having forgotten the rolls.

After she sat and they started to eat, he decided to ease into the conversation. "Mom, this salad is delicious. And the tenderloin is fantastic. So much better than leftover pizza." Not that he'd had that much left over after Auggie had polished off more than half of it.

"Leftover pizza? Xavier. You know how to cook. I taught you better than that."

"Yeah, Xavier." Auggie shook her head. "He's just lazy, Ma."

"And you." Cynthia tried to frown but ended up grinning at her daughter. "Do you want me to believe you're at home, cooking up a storm? The last time I visited, you had so many frozen dinners you could barely close your freezer door."

"It's a meal plan, and they're all nutritious."

Xavier frowned. "You're still getting your food from that food delivery service? Gross. Everything's all natural and frozen."

"*Natural* is not a four-letter word, Xav. Neither is *frozen*. I also shop daily for fresh fruits and veggies, you know."

"It's no wonder you have no life. All your time is spent bulking up at the gym or buying supplies to bulk you up at the grocery store." He grinned at the flush stealing up her cheeks. Auggie was so easy to rile.

"*I* have no life?" Auggie shot him a superior look. A warning.

Damn. Shouldn't have teased her.

"I'm not the one who nearly had a fight with my ex's brother. And please. Even Mom hated Christine. Why did it take you so long to break up with her?"

"Auggie," Cynthia snapped. "I didn't hate Christine." Cynthia turned to Xavier. "A *fight?*"

He sighed and quickly explained what had happened.

"Oh, Xavier. Why *did* you take so long to break up with her? We all know you were miserable the past few months. What have I told you about being too nice?"

He glared at his sister, who easily ignored him, enthralled with the tomatoes she'd isolated on her plate.

"It's not that I don't want you to be nice," his mom continued. "I just get scared you'll end up with the wrong girl because you're afraid to tell her the truth when you don't want to commit."

"Like Noel?" he ventured, thinking it the perfect time to change the subject. "Because we all know you cared for him. A lot. I know it hurt you to break things off with him. But Mom, you were too nice dealing with his drama and narcissism when you should have ended things a while ago."

She sighed. "Pot calling kettle, I know."

"Exactly," Auggie muttered but didn't meet their mom's gaze.

Xavier said, "I'm not trying to be mean, Mom. But Auggie and I are worried about you."

"Don't be worried." Cynthia snorted. "I've got more going on than both of you. And don't think I'm unaware of your many 'man friends,' Augusta Hanover."

Auggie winced.

"I know you two think I meddle. I don't mean to. I respect both of you, and I realize how difficult it is to find someone special. Heck, maybe you'll never get married."

Xavier met his sister's gaze and did his best not to laugh. Because when their mother turned all understanding, The Lecture was sure to follow.

"It's fine if you never marry. Being independent and happy is just fine."

Auggie subtly showed him two fingers near her plate. Yep. Two *fines.* There would be many more before The Lecture ended.

"Auggie, honey, the only reason I harp on starting a family with you so much is that the older you get, the more chances you have for a difficult pregnancy or problems with the baby. It's simple biology. But I do want you to know it's fine with me if you choose not to have children. I mean, it would be a shame, all your smarts and skills ending with you, not passed along to future generations. But it's fine."

She turned to Xavier. "And you. All that brain, that handsome smile and compassion, all of your fine qualities ending with you. You're thirty-two, Xavier. I just don't understand why..."

He let her words run over him while he continued to enjoy her delectable cooking, nodding or vocalizing his agreement at the appropriate times.

The Lecture ended with a whopping twenty-two fines. More than the last time.

After she'd wound down, Auggie cleared her throat. Before his sister could cut in and ruin the perfect setup for his lead-in, he kicked her under the table.

"Ow."

Cynthia frowned. "What's wrong, Auggie?"

Xavier answered instead. "Mom, I really do understand everything you're saying." His thoughts turned to Justine. Hadn't they just had this conversation about interfering though well-meaning parents? "Both Auggie and I were just talking about relationships the other day. We're trying to center ourselves, to make sure when we commit, we can give our hundred percent, because we're happy and healthy first."

"Makes sense." Cynthia started eating, and he knew the worst has passed.

Auggie gave a quiet sigh, relieved as well.

"Right. But there's something I think you're missing." He paused for effect. "You."

"What? Me?"

"Yes, you. You've spent a lot of years making everyone else happy. It's time you looked out for you. We talk a lot about being healthy and positive. You've got so much to give, why not try dating again? Noel's gone." *And good riddance.* "Don't you think it's time you gave the dating world another try?"

She blinked. "Really?"

"Yes. You're only fifty-one. That's young," Auggie said.

"Fifty-two," Cynthia murmured. "But, well, I don't know. Breaking up with Noel was hard."

"Yet that relationship showed you that you enjoy being with a partner. Noel might not have been the right one, but he wasn't a mistake." He said that more for his sister's benefit than their mother's. He hadn't liked Noel at all, but Auggie had loathed the selfish, condescending jackass.

"That's true," their mom said.

"You're always telling us to share ourselves with others, that having friends enriches our lives. Well, that applies to you too." He paused then added what would surely fire her up, "Or are you too old to date?"

Their mother glared at him. "Too old? Boy, I'm barely fifty-two. I could have more babies if I wanted."

"Oh, please don't." Auggie looked horrified.

"Shut it, you." Cynthia pointed a finger at Auggie. But her lips quirked. "I'm done having children, you little bonehead. But I take your point, Xavier. I do miss having a companion to do things with. Book club and my Bunco buddies aren't the same. I tell you what. I'll get out there and try if you two will."

"Done." Auggie shook their mom's hand before Xavier could

caution her not to agree too readily. It was one thing to say they'd date, but another to prove they were. Because their mom liked to see—with her own eyes—proof in the doing. She'd been burned by Auggie too many times in the past to trust blindly.

"Excellent." Cynthia smiled a little too widely at them, and Xavier wondered who had actually been manipulating who, exactly.

Auggie gave a tiny shrug. "Mom, a friend of mine wants to meet you. I was talking about you, and he asked if you were as good-looking as me, so I said, hell no. My mom's a straight-up honey." She laughed at Cynthia's blush. "I'm happy to give him your number if it's okay with you."

Their mother looked happier. "Sure. If it'll make you two stop nagging, then I'm all for it."

Xavier gave her a stern look. "Nagging? Really? Because we care?"

"Don't use that hurt look on me, boy. I perfected that pout with your father years ago."

He grinned. "And just like Dad, you still fall for it."

"Oh. For that, you're doing the dishes."

Auggie stuck out her tongue at him.

"And Auggie, you're drying."

"Crap."

Xavier laughed and spent the remainder of the meal telling his mother about the latest advice cartoon he'd drawn and the bevy of *Dear Aunt Truth* emails they continued to receive.

But he made no mention of Justine, though she continued to remain in his thoughts throughout the meal.

And he didn't understand why he couldn't get the sight of her fine ass and *amazing* body, loosely covered in that old, overlarge tee-shirt, out of his mind's eye.

CHAPTER 7

Monday evening, Xavier sat in the courtyard by the fountain in their apartment building, sketching in his notepad, and inhaled the fragrant scent of sweet peas, honeysuckle, and lilacs. To add to the variety in color, the red rhododendrons added another burst of vibrance to the verdant garden.

The fountain trickled, and a cool breeze eased the warmth of the encroaching summer, a surprising heat wave hitting them early.

He sat at a picnic table, enjoying the darkening blue sky with the umbrella closed, and watched Top kneeling, getting in a last bit of weeding and pruning around the bushes in one corner of the courtyard.

"Can feel you watching me," the older guy grumbled. In his mid-fifties, Max Dixon wore his salt and pepper hair military short. That gray hair and the wise eyes in his brown, craggy face the only things showing his age. He still maintained an incredibly fit body and had the spring in his step of a man in his prime.

He'd retired as a Master Sergeant from the United States Marine Corps a few years ago and had moved into the Tuscan

Cosmo Apartments to serve as the building's caretaker. He didn't say much, but he wasn't as stern and uncompromising as he outwardly appeared.

"I like watching you work, Top. Makes me feel relaxed."

The older man grunted in amusement. Xavier had gotten pretty good at reading the guy and knew Top actually liked him. Not just because Xavier was an ideal tenant, but because Xavier had served in the USMC as well, back when he'd been young and stupid.

Top glanced over his shoulder, saw Xavier grinning, and snorted. "Pain in my ass."

"So it's been said. Tell me, if you had to ask advice about something, what would it be?"

Top turned back to his work. "Hmm. I think I'd ask how to get my shower to stop leaking. Because I replaced what I thought was a damaged O-ring but nothing changed."

"No, I meant a relationship question. Are you dating anyone?" He hadn't seen a ring on the man's finger.

"Son, I'm not interested. No offense."

Xavier snorted. "That's not why I'm asking."

"Maybe I'm married."

"Are you?"

Top sighed. "No. And you're still talking to me."

"Come on. Give me a relationship question. Like, something you'd read on *Dear Abby* or *Dear Aunt Truth*."

"Huh?"

"It's almost like you're afraid that once you answer me, I'll leave and go back up to my apartment and leave you all alone."

"Well then, I guess I'd say, how do you keep a woman's interest? There. You leaving now?"

Xavier had no intention of going anywhere soon. "Good question." He flipped the page in his sketchbook to draw something for *How to Keep a Woman's Interest* and roughed out a picture of Top looking quizzical next to a beautiful woman, a large question mark hanging in the air between them. Then Xavier did another panel of what most considered men's interests versus women's interests and had fun with stereotypes.

Some time later, Top plopped on the bench across from Xavier. "You're still here." He had a drink bottle with him and guzzled it before wiping the sweat from his brow with the bottom of his tee-shirt.

"Well, I do live here."

"I thought you'd ask then leave."

"Nah. I'm still enjoying your refreshing company."

Top snorted. "What are you doing?"

Xavier showed him the cartoon.

Top frowned. "That looks like me."

"I know. I'm just doodling. But you asked a decent question. Something all men want to know."

"You're the marriage expert, Dr. Advice. What's the answer then?" Top drank more water.

"First off, I'm not a doctor. I'm a licensed therapist. Second, it depends on the woman. You find out what her interests are and see if they mesh with yours. Successful relationships are founded on shared ideas and shared interests. Most men can't see beyond what they want."

Top smirked. "Tits and ass?"

"Did you get *any* sensitivity training in the Corps that stuck?"

"I'm kidding. Keep your tighty whiteys on."

Xavier laughed.

"If you're so smart, how come you're not married?"

"Haven't found the right woman yet. What about you?"

"Tough to find a gal around here who's not into 'feelings' and 'communicating,'" Top ended in air quotes.

Xavier sighed. "You do realize *I'm* into feelings and communicating."

"But that's your job. All I know is when you're with the right person, you feel it in here." Top thumped his chest. "I was married for a time. I know what love feels like."

That was more sharing than Top had ever expressed. But before Xavier could ask what had happened to that marriage, Benji, Xavier's neighbor in 2B, waltzed into the courtyard carrying a paper sack and a fountain drink, his backpack slung over one shoulder.

He stopped in his tracks upon spotting Top.

Top grunted, gave Benji the stink eye, and left without a word.

"Join me," Xavier invited, knowing if he didn't, his neighbor would likely hot-foot it up to his room and not venture out again until he had to go into work. Benji was a mega-introvert with social anxiety. Xavier couldn't relate, as he liked people, but he knew just how to handle anxiety.

"I don't want to intrude." Benji edged toward the doorway.

"Nah. I'm lonely. Come sit by me."

Benji held up his food and drink. "I was going to eat dinner..."

"Perfect. I already ate. Now I get company." Xavier smiled and waited.

Benji ambled closer before finally lowering his backpack and taking a seat. A good couple of inches taller than Xavier but leaner, the guy had to be close to his own age and did well enough working in the tech field. Xavier had a feeling Benji made a pretty decent salary but didn't want more than a small apartment close to downtown Fremont.

The guy seemed to be trying to hide behind bad grooming. His unkempt full beard and mustache made him look a bit slovenly. His shaggy hair in desperate need of a cut didn't help any. A lumbering giant who dressed in pop culture tee-shirts and shorts, no matter the weather, Benji had a surprising sense of humor under all the facial fur.

"So Top wasn't good enough company?" Benji took a sip from his drink and pulled out a few mouthwatering burgers.

Xavier had lied. He hadn't yet eaten, but he hadn't seen or

talked to Benji in a few days. He kept doodling and promised himself a meal after hanging with his shy friend.

"Top was just fine. And don't say that too loudly or he might gut you when you're not looking." He glanced at Benji, saw him pale, and laughed. "Kidding, man."

"Ha ha. You don't see the way he looks at everyone. Like we're future victims."

"Nah, he's just cautious. He's been in some hard places."

"Yeah, I could see that." Benji bit enthusiastically into his food and groaned.

Xavier tried to look as if he wasn't salivating. "How's work? I haven't seen you in a while."

"Been busy. New roll-out has a ton of bugs. I told my bosses to wait, but do they listen to me? No." Benji continued to talk between bites about the lack of intelligent managers at his place of business.

"Why not apply to manage at the company yourself?"

A look of horror crossed Benji's face. "Are you kidding me? And have to talk to *people?*"

"Sorry. What was I thinking?"

"No kidding. You been drinking, bro?" Benji's eyes crinkled, and Xavier swore he saw his lips quirk in a grin. "See? I can make jokes. I can talk to people. Certain people."

Of the male variety, Xavier noticed. Benji could barely make eye contact with women, and when he did, he typically stammered and blushed a lot. Xavier had seen the guy stare pretty hard at Auggie, but when she'd tried to talk to him, he'd fled.

"What else is going on beside work? Anything?" Xavier asked.

"Still killing it at *Arrow Sins & Siege*. My brother keeps telling me I should livestream, but no way. I mean, I love working where I do because I only have to go in twice a week and talk to all of three people. I don't want them invading my home through my computer. My team leaders are fine with me doing all the work and leaving me alone to do it."

"You do have a pretty nice setup."

"You too. Must be nice to have a month off of work. But you still give advice to your neighbors." Benji grinned. "You're almost as good as Aunt Truth. I love reading her column. Plus, knowing it's Rosie gives Aunt Truth even more credibility."

Xavier snorted. "You know, I'm pretty sure Rosie has a confidentiality clause. But it feels like half this apartment knows all about it."

"Well, we probably do. Rosie treats us all like family. When's she coming back?"

Rosie Gallo had a way about her. Benji could talk to her without issue, at ease around the older woman. She'd taken to Adam's nephews with ease, always welcoming them at any time. She and Kai, in 3E, were best friends. Top liked her. And hell, Xavier loved the woman. She'd cajoled him into helping her write her advice column, then insisted he take over when she went on her holiday, knowing how much he loved working on it.

He wondered if Justine knew her aunt's secret identity and decided not to say anything unless Justine brought it up.

And why am I thinking about Justine again?

"Say, Benji, have you met Rosie's niece, Justine? She's really nice."

He flushed. "Um, no. Not yet. Why?"

"Just asking. I met her the other day. She's going to fit right in around here."

"Until Rosie comes back."

"Yeah, until then."

As if he'd conjured her, Justine walked into the courtyard, looking tired. Dressed in denim capris and a cute, light-blue top, her long hair down and a messenger bag over her shoulder, she looked both professional and beautiful. And friendly, he reminded himself. *Not looking for a man, and you're not looking for a woman. Quit focusing on how attractive she is.*

"Hey, Justine." He had to act fast before Benji bolted. "Come on over and meet Benji."

She smiled and drew closer. "Hi. Nice to meet you, Benji. I'm Justine Ferrera, living in 3D for the time being."

Benji turned red and stood. He glanced at Xavier, saw his subtle encouragement, and wiped his hand on his shorts before offering it to Justine. "Hi. I'm Benji."

They shook before he hastily pulled his hand back and sat, then shoved some fries in his mouth.

"Please, sit," Xavier said to her, motioning to the spot next to him on the bench. He didn't think Benji would be able to handle it if Justine sat too close to him. Benji, he noted, focused on his food and not Justine.

"Oh, I don't want to interrupt you two."

"You're not. We were just talking about Benji's rise to fame and fortune with *Arrow Sins & Siege*."

"Oh man. That game is everywhere, and I suck at it." Justine made a face.

Benji blinked up at her. "You play?"

"Please. Everyone plays. Although I don't know if you can call what I do playing. More like dying repeatedly."

Xavier chuckled. "Benji tried to get me to play. I'm not bad."

Benji snorted. "You're horrible."

Justine laughed. His friend studied her out of the corner of his eye but hadn't run yet. A good sign.

Justine toyed with her bag and set it on the table. "I have to confess that I used the game as a diversion last night at family dinner."

"Oh?" Xavier wanted to hear all about it.

"Things were going well, um, kind of. Not really, but I was hanging in there. Then my annoying sister threw me under the bus with my mom about dating. I tried to escape and overheard my dad and his friends mentioning how much money the gaming industry makes, as an investment potential. So I jumped into talk about *Arrow Sins & Siege*." She grinned. "I went through my efforts as a barbarian queen and had them so lost it was funny. You'd think they'd have played a little. Gaming isn't just for kids."

Benji nodded. "It's a billion dollar industry for a reason. The majority of those playing the games, which cost upward of $70 a pop, are men over the age of thirty-five. I would know. My company hires out for work on a lot of those projects."

"No kidding?" Justine goggled before Xavier could respond. "That's so cool. Is that what you do? Game design? Coding?"

Benji gave a shy nod.

Justine asked him more questions about his job, and Benji answered without pause, enthusiastic about computers and games and most anything that plugged in.

Then a small lull in conversation occurred, and Benji must have realized he'd been talking at length to *a woman.* He stammered something unintelligible, hurried to his feet, and lit out with a hasty good-bye.

Justine turned to Xavier with a question. "Did I say something to upset him?"

"No. I think he realized he was talking to a beautiful woman and got scared. Benji's a great guy, but he's pretty introverted. The fact that he sat here so long talking to you is amazing in itself."

Justine blushed. "He was really sweet and very into gaming. Wow. I feel stupid after talking to him. The guy's smart on top of smart."

"No kidding." He watched her for a moment, realized how much he'd missed talking to her, and leaned back. "Okay, hit me."

"With?"

"With your Sunday dinner. I caught undercurrents of fear and dismay." They both laughed. "The folks were on you about dating, huh? Tell you what. You tell me about your dinner and I'll fill you in on mine."

"Oh, the man-list for your mom." Justine's eyes sparkled. "You're on."

CHAPTER 8

Justine followed Xavier to his apartment, curious about what it looked like. In her opinion, you could tell a lot about a man by the way he lived. Was he neat or messy? Into color or black and white? Organized? Chaotic? Did he have matching furniture or an eclectic mix of pieces? Function over fashion or both?

Not surprisingly, his apartment fit what she knew of his personality. The furniture looked comfortable yet attractive and well-cared for. The unit had a light, airy feel, nothing heavy or too large for the space. Xavier knew how to decorate, or he had someone who'd helped him. She felt immediately at ease and liked the fact he had a bevy of green plants around, adding to the natural colors all around.

The few pictures on the walls were of cities and landscapes. She noticed a group of photographs on one wall, some of him and his sister, a few of his family when he was younger, and a bunch of men in fatigues. He walked into the kitchen, so she followed him after toeing off her shoes and setting her bag on a hook by the door.

"I'm starving. I'm going to make a stir fry. Have you eaten?"

"Oh, no. I just got back from work."

"Perfect. Are you allergic to anything?"

She sat at counter, where two stools hid under the overhang. "Not that I know of. And thank you. Stir fry sounds amazing."

"Good. How about something to drink? I have wine, beer, and a few sodas."

"Water would be good." The kitchen was a spacious area shaped like a U, which gave him counters for food prep and enough room to cook with a friend and not be all over him. Or her.

A surge of curiosity struck that she hastily ignored. It wasn't her business how many *friends* Xavier had. For all she knew, he was already dating someone else despite his recent breakup. A guy with his looks and easygoing personality had to have a line of potential lovers waiting around the block.

"Here you go." He set a glass with ice along with a pitcher of water in front of her. "Hope filtered water is okay. Auggie gets all over me when I drink straight from the tap." He sighed. "Girl's a health nut."

She smiled as she poured a glass and drank to sate her thirst. "Oh man. That hit the spot."

"Good." He smiled at her, and she felt herself drowning in the richness of his warm brown eyes.

An awkward pause settled, and she flushed, hoping she didn't look like she'd been mooning over the man. She hurriedly dropped her gaze and focused on her water glass. "Sorry if I'm spacey. It's been a long day."

"Oh?"

Thankfully, he turned to the stove and moved pots and pans around as he started cooking.

"Well, my boss is a huge jerk. But that's just one more thing I'm working through."

"Right. We were supposed to talk about your Sunday night

dinner." He cracked some eggs and boiled water for rice. Then he took out some veggies and started chopping.

"Do you need any help? I feel guilty for sitting and watching while you work."

He laughed and glanced at her. "I was just doing the same to Top in the courtyard. So I guess it's only fair I be the one working while someone watches me." He winked at her, and her face felt hot. "Just relax. Talk to me about your family night."

"Oh man. I don't know if I want to ruin your appetite."

"Trust me. Unless your dinner involves vomit, I'll be okay." He paused. "It doesn't involve throw-up, does it?" He looked a little green.

"What? Oh, no. Not at all. My dinner was a meal in frustration, actually. But the food was incredible."

He turned back to the stove with a relieved sigh. "Good. I mean, not good. Talk to me."

So Justine gave him her recollection of events, including her perceptions of intent, including Angela's bitchiness. "I mean, I had thought that maybe I was overthinking things. It's my parents' house, not mine. They can invite any guests they want. The guys, Cal and Nick, were actually pretty nice. No one hit on me or anything." She still felt foolish. "It's pretty presumptive to think my parents invited my dad's colleagues over just to set me up on a date."

"Which they did, though, right?" He was working magic on the stove, and she hoped he didn't hear her stomach grumbling.

"Well, it felt like it to me. I'd made it all through dinner before stupid Angela brought up that both guys are single and rich." She grimaced. "Who cares what they make? I don't want a guy for his money. I want to be independent. I mean, I lived with Mitch, my ex, and look what happened. We broke up and I had to move out. Well, technically it was his apartment. But you know what I mean."

"Ouch, that hurts." Xavier shot her a sympathetic glance.

Justine warmed to the topic, not feeling at all self-conscious about pouring her heart out. "Man, you're good. I just keep talking."

He grinned. "If I didn't want to listen, I'd say so."

"Well, you asked for it. It was Mitch's apartment, so it's not like I could ask him to move. But I gave up my place to move in with him. We dated for two years, lived together for one. And by the end, I couldn't leave fast enough. But— God, sorry. I'm off track. My breakup with Mitch was just two weeks ago. Well, really more like two months ago, but I kept trying to make it work. I just got too tired of always trying to please him." She snorted. "It's like, that's my pattern. Trying to make everyone else happy at the expense of my own happiness. Something Aunt Rosie used to lecture me about."

"You're aunt's a smart woman." He moved some plates down and continued jostling things at the stove. "And that's pretty insightful. Just what I told my mother last night. Women do that a lot. Bend over backwards for everyone else, putting themselves last. But you never did say, what happened at the end of dinner?"

"Oh, well, when we finished, the guys went in one room while the rest of us went to hang in Mom's sitting room. It's kind of tradition. We sit and talk with an after-dinner drink." She liked the togetherness with family. She just wished they'd get off her back about the way she lived her life. "It was going well until bitchy Angela opened her mouth. Then my mom was on my case about dating and who I planned on bringing to Mallory's wedding." She paused. "And I don't like Ted, her fiancé. He's a huge jackass, but my parents like him, so of course Mallory will marry him. And be miserable." She sighed.

"What's wrong with Ted?"

"He flirts with anything with breasts."

"Oh."

"Yeah, oh." She still hated the thought of her sister anywhere near the guy. "But I can't say anything, because in my family I'm the outsider, the one who didn't go into finance and has no intention of doing anything my parents like. I want to make them happy, but a big part of me likes that they disapprove." She looked at him, saw him nodding. "Should I be paying you for this therapy?"

"Nah. I'm on a break from work."

She blinked. "Wait. You're an actual therapist?"

He turned to watch her. "I am. An LMFT—Licensed Marriage and Family Therapist with a Masters, so technically I'm also an MA." He shrugged. "I'm a good listener."

"Now it all makes sense."

"What?"

"That you're so easy to talk to."

He gave a small grin that made her belly do flipflops. "My gift of gab is on account of Auggie. We're twins. She got all the headstrong, aggressive tendencies. I'm the good guy who's charming. Just ask my mom."

Justine laughed. "Okay."

"Good. Now relax and finish your story."

"Right. So where we left off... I was arguing with my sisters and mom about having to bring a plus-one to the wedding. Why can't I go by myself? Then I had to explain, yet again, that I was the one who broke it off with my ex—they all think he dumped *me*. Fortunately, my dad and the guys joined us, talking about investing in tech companies, one of which was a gaming company. And I went off about how much I love *Arrow Sins & Siege* to throw off any attempt at matchmaking. Gamer girls aren't cool, you know."

"They aren't? Who says?"

"Something I read in a magazine. Utter crap, but I figured the type of people who work with my dad likely aren't into video games. Too sophisticated for that kind of nonsense." She frowned.

"What?"

"Cal didn't seem to mind. I could just feel him getting ready to make a move. It was cowardly, but I took off." She sighed. "Mom's been leaving me texts I'm pretending I haven't seen."

"You can't avoid her forever."

"I know." She sipped her water, feeling glum. "But that was my dinner. Now what about yours?"

He laughed as he plated their food, and Justine helped him bring it to the small kitchen table, where they fell upon the meal like starving dogs.

"I'm sorry. But this is so good, and I was so hungry," she said between mouthfuls.

"Me too. Benji's burgers were killing me, they smelled so good." After a few more bites, he said, "Dinner with Mom and Auggie was fun. Great food, and I love my family. We're a lot more easygoing than your folks, it sounds like."

"Congressional debates are a lot more easygoing than my parents," she grumbled.

He laughed. "Yeah, well, even though we had a great meal, that didn't stop my mom from giving me and Auggie 'The Lecture.' It's basically her talk about how it's just fine if we never want to get married... except it's not really fine, and she finds all these soft, kind ways to tell us we're disappointing her if we don't get married and give her grandkids."

"Ouch."

"Yeah, but it's also fun, because my mom uses the word 'fine' every five seconds to try to reassure us that our lifestyles are our own business. Last night, we counted twenty-two."

She chuckled. "That's terrible. Hmm. I wonder which word my mom uses that I could start counting. 'Disappointed' might work."

They snickered over disapproving parents and teased each other about being single forever.

"But not my mom," Xavier said. "She's going to be dating if I have to drag her into a singles bar myself." He frowned.

"Do you want your mom to date and get out and have a life? Or to be so busy so that she's not bugging you?"

He pushed his plate away and sat back. "That's a good question. The part of me that's a good son just wants her happy. I love my mom. I want her to find someone special, to treat her the way she deserves to be treated. But the little boy in me wants her all to myself."

Justine softened. "I think that's sweet." Hadn't she often wanted to be Daddy's little girl? To feel loved and protected, cherished by the man she still saw as larger than life? Instead, she was the outcast who didn't care enough about his feelings that she had to do everything her own way.

"Sweet but silly." He rubbed his jaw, and she thought again how handsome he appeared despite not seeming to realize it. "I'm a grown man. And now she expects me to date because she's putting herself out there." He groaned. "After Christine, I'm just not ready."

"I get you. After Mitch, I just want a chance to breathe without anyone telling me what to do or how to live."

They sighed together, looked at each other's pitiful faces, and burst out laughing.

"You are so pathetic," he said.

"Almost as bad as you are, loser."

That sent him into more gales of laugher. And as they cleaned up together, still teasing, Justine realized she'd never felt more at ease with a man she'd just met than she did with Xavier.

So it was only natural before she left to give him a friendly hug. "Thanks so much, Xavier. This was just what I needed."

His arms tightened around her, a wall of solid muscle and warm man.

Suddenly, her platonic, *friendly* hug had her lusting after Xavier with every breath in her body.

He tensed for a moment. But when he pulled back, he wore

nothing but an affable smile. "This was exactly what I needed too."

"Next time, my place," she managed to respond, relieved she sounded normal.

He walked her out into the hall and waited until she entered the stairwell and waved goodbye before turning to close himself back inside the apartment.

She staggered up the stairs, beyond confused. What the heck was that all about?

He was just a friend.

So quit imagining him with his clothes off while you give him mouth to mouth!

Poor Xavier. Trying to be a nice guy only to have his needy upstairs neighbor fantasizing about him.

Swearing at herself all the way, she made it back into her apartment and treated herself to a nice warm bath and a book about female empowerment.

Because no. She did not want or need a man in her life. Not even one who felt like the answer to all her sexual prayers *and* cooked like a dream.

She'd learned the hard way that dreams often turned into nightmares, and she couldn't afford to screw up living in this place. If she had to leave the TCA, she had nowhere else to go but home to her parents.

And that was enough to scare her straight.

Until she slept. Because her subconscious had a mind of its own.

CHAPTER 9

Tuesday afternoon, while working out at Jameson's Gym, Xavier kept replaying his evening with Justine over his mind.

He had no idea what had gone wrong.

The dinner had been both relaxing and fun. Justine didn't seem to mind him being a therapist, which could sometimes be off-putting for people. They became self-conscious when talking to him, thinking he was analyzing every word they said. Not Justine. She'd been laughing and open, sincere about processing her evening.

He felt for her. Her family sounded worlds apart from his. Though he and Auggie teased about their mother's lecturing, it all came from a place of love. And she'd never hold their choices against them. From a young age, he'd been taught to be accepting of everyone. Race, gender, sexual orientation—none of it meant anything compared to the soul inside the body.

Yet Justine didn't seem to have that. From what he'd heard and what she *hadn't* said, she wanted her parents to accept her because she loved them, even if she didn't always like them. Why else go to a dinner party knowing she'd likely get run over by her overbearing family?

He ran faster on the treadmill as he thought about that Cal guy, the one she hadn't exactly disliked. Why did her parents need her to date the perfect man? At least she'd been smart enough to ditch her ex. She hadn't mentioned much of him, but the guy sounded like a jackass.

He couldn't imagine Justine needing that much more from a man than empathy and affection. So where exactly had Mitch gone wrong?

His curiosity was itching at him, wanting to know more about the woman he had a tough time not thinking about. And God, hugging her had been *excruciating.*

She'd felt like warm sin, all curves and strength, yet fragile. It had been all he could do not to rub up against her like some big perv. So even though he'd been aroused, he'd been careful not to show it.

Five minutes after she'd left, he'd talked himself out of being aroused. Then ended his night by jacking off to thoughts of her, unable to get her unbound breasts and tight ass out of his mind—those pajamas he'd caught her in on Saturday.

He ran harder, feeling that arousal build once more. Not about to be caught chubbing up at the gym, he ran himself into exhaustion before turning to the free weights.

He finished his workout and nodded at a few gym-goers he hadn't seen in a while.

"Well, well, Rapunzel finally left her tower." A trainer with a steel-hard frame and square jaw smirked at him.

"I'm not sure if that's a reference that I need a haircut or you're calling me a girl."

"Neither," Gavin Donnigan said, crossing his arms over a broad chest. "First, I'm not into your hair, though I've heard more than a few of our members talking about the hot redhead with guns."

"My hair's brown, not red," Xavier growled.

Gavin talked over him. "And since your sister isn't here, and they were looking in your direction, I'm thinking the guns they were talking about belong to you." He looked over Xavier's arms and added, "Puny though they are."

Xavier flushed, which had no doubt been Gavin's intent. "Dick."

"Second," Gavin said with a grin, "your sister's a girl, and she scares me. No way I'd ever insult women by lumping your sorry ass into the pool. I was knocking the fact that it's been a while since your royal highness has graced the gym with your majestic presence." Gavin sighed. "It's like, now that you're a civilian, you've lost all sense of discipline."

"Oh, please. It's been ten years." Xavier huffed. Gavin had served time in the Marine Corps, as had his brothers. If Xavier wasn't mistaken, the youngest Donnigan was still on active duty. "Speaking of discipline, how's Theo doing?"

Gavin's smile widened. "Little shit is just fine. Sergeant Donnigan has been kicking ass and taking names."

"Hell, man. That's terrific. How long does he have left on his contract?"

"I don't know. I'm not sure if he's gonna re-up or not, but he's doing well so far. He's got some leave built up. I think he's coming for a visit in the fall. We'll have a big party. You're invited."

"Well, you kind of *have* to invite me, don't you?" Xavier smirked. "Because if you don't, Auggie will throw a fit. She's all about us jarheads sticking together."

Gavin shuddered. "I know. I already admitted she scares me. You trying to give me nightmares? I've had enough of those to last a lifetime."

Xavier saw Gavin's teasing for what it was, innocent jesting. Not the call for help he'd once had. Xavier worked with Gavin's therapist at MYM Counseling, the practice from which Xavier was currently on a break. Though the therapists didn't share patient information, Xavier had spoken with Gavin at a group session a few years ago, sharing stories and embracing the service they'd all given to Corps and country. Auggie and Gavin's older brother had been there too, all of them bonding and becoming friends. That networking had in fact landed Auggie a job at the gym where Gavin managed the other trainers.

"Hey, don't tell loudmouth I asked, but how's my sister doing? She seems pumped about some exercise competition coming up."

"Your sister's a kick." Gavin laughed. "She's been talking a lot of trash to the other trainers entering the competition. I wouldn't be surprised if she wins it. Talk about driven." Gavin shrugged. "I'm an old married guy with another kid on the way. I can't keep up with you youngsters."

Xavier refrained from rolling his eyes. Gavin looked like he ate weights for breakfast and had no lack of attention at the gym from anyone and everyone needing advice on how to get huge. "You're like, forty, right? That's not too old."

"I'm thirty-eight," Gavin snapped back.

"Oh, my bad. The gray in your hair threw me."

Gavin immediately put a hand to his hair, which caused Xavier to laugh.

After slugging him and calling him something Xavier would never repeat in front of his mother, Gavin stalked away with threats about setting Auggie on Xavier's tail.

Taking that to heart, Xavier grabbed his things and left. He already had plans with Auggie the following day, when they would discuss their mom's date. Cynthia and Big Henry had plans later in the evening. Apparently, Big Henry was taking their mom to dinner and a movie.

Personally, Xavier would forgo a movie on a first date. When trying to get to know someone, having to be quiet while in a theater didn't seem productive. Then again, Auggie had set their mom up with Big Henry—a nice enough man who put more stock in bulking up than in conversation. But again, he seemed pleasant and was more than interested in their mom.

Once back at the apartment complex and rid of thoughts about his mother dating again—*God help me*—the rest of Xavier's night went smoothly. He filtered through emails, answered a few *Aunt Truth* advice questions, and went over some older notes from his practice, using his time off to update patient files and get better organized.

Despite this minor break, Xavier felt good about his job. He'd come back from his time in the Marine Corps both wiser and happier. A people person, Xavier put stock in emotions and attitudes, and wanting to serve continued in his daily life. He liked helping people, communicating. Top's sneering about *feelings* and *communication* only made him laugh; they were Xavier's lifeblood. Drawn more to relationship dynamics than individual concerns, he'd focused his career on interpersonal relationships.

Going to school to get his LMFT license, then his masters in the subject, had been enough for him. He didn't have the patience to go for a doctorate. After a good six years of college and two years to intern and license, he'd spent the past three years helping people heal. But giving his all took its toll, so his current hiatus allowed him to recover.

It hadn't helped that he'd been mired in Christine's bullshit for way too long. He needed a healthy homelife to balance work.

And hell, a healthy sex life would have been ideal too.

But after time, his relationship, both emotionally and sexually, had fizzled.

He wondered if it had been the same for Justine. She'd said she tired of trying to please her ex. Just one more thing they had in common.

As he settled into bed, he continued to tell himself to stop making more out of his friendship with the woman. He finally had a great friend—not his sister, a work associate, or gym rat—that he could easily talk to. One who had expressly said she wasn't looking for a relationship. He didn't want to ruin that by being just another swinging dick pestering her for what she didn't want to give.

No. He respected Justine. He liked the heck out of her. Every time they spoke, he looked forward to the next time they'd meet. And that was...nice. Normal. Something men and women should be able to be without complicating everything with sex.

He kept telling himself that as he fell asleep.

And woke up having dreamt of her, once again.

His dreams put his temper out of whack and, annoyed with himself, he spent the day frazzled and off-kilter. Which didn't help his meeting with Auggie later that evening.

Xavier stared at her. "He did *what?*"

Auggie shushed him. "Would you stop? Mom told me this in confidence. You know she seems to know everyone in this freaking city. Keep it down, moron."

"You just said Big Henry kissed her. On the first date?" Xavier was incensed.

"Oh my God. She's not a virgin, Xav." Auggie rolled her eyes. "Besides, she said it was like kissing a plunger, all wet, rubbery, and slobbery. But I never told you that, because she confided in me on the pain of death."

He twisted an invisible key across his lips then ruined it by talking again. "Sealed. But Auggie, you suggested they go out. Did he make moves on her as soon as he showed up or what?" As much as he didn't want details, he needed them. His poor mother.

"They did go out. And they had fun at dinner. She said she wished they could have ignored the movie and talked more, but you know, 'Big Henry ain't about talkin.'" She mimicked the man perfectly. "Don't look at me that way. He's a respectful guy and good looking. You should see what he benches."

"I don't care what he benches, so long as he's not benching Mom," he muttered.

She laughed like a loon. "Oh, relax. Mom had a nice time. If Big Henry hadn't shown what a bad kisser and talker he was, they'd probably go out again. But she told me one date was enough."

"Oh, so it's my turn, then, eh?"

"I guess." Auggie looked glum.

"My friend Lee's been divorced for five years. No kids. A really nice guy and I think he's close to Mom's age, maybe a few years younger."

She winced. "A shrink?"

"A damn good one. He helped Gavin out."

Auggie brightened. "Oh, okay then." She slugged him in the arm before he could dodge her.

"Ow. What was that for?" His sister hit like a heavyweight champ.

"For talking about me. Gavin told me you were checking up on me. Quit it."

"Hey, I'm allowed to look out for my little sister."

"Would you stop that?" She sounded exasperated. "We're twins."

"Five—"

"—minute's difference means nothing."

"I..." He trailed off, surprised to see Justine walking into the coffee shop, her clothes business casual. As usual, she looked gorgeous. Lively, pretty, yet tired. Today she wore her hair up in a ponytail and looked a few years younger because of it.

Auggie followed his gaze. "Well, well. Who's that?"

Xavier whipped his head back around, saw his sister's calculating stare, and knew it would be better to get it over with. "My new neighbor." He waved to Justine. "Hey, come join us if you're not busy."

She nodded and waved then stepped to the counter to order something.

He turned back to Auggie. "That's Rosie's niece, Justine. She's subletting her aunt's place for a awhile." He realized he had no idea how long Justine might be there. And that bothered him.

"You sure took your time looking at her."

"We're *friends*," he emphasized, glaring into his sister's crafty eyes. "Don't even think of making her uncomfortable."

"Friends, huh?" Auggie stared at Justine. "We'll see about that, won't we?"

CHAPTER 10

Justine had finished another crapfest of a day. Once again covering for Frank because he hadn't gotten his work done on time and had something "important" to do tonight with his wife and kids. So sure, Justine would stick around and cover his ass, finishing up that spreadsheet for the PowerPoint presentation tomorrow. She was mightily sick of doing work she wasn't paid for, but Frank kept saying how great her team player attitude would look at her next yearly evaluation—in two weeks.

That was if she could make it that long.

For the past year, she'd been unhappy in her job. She wanted the freedom to express her artistic background, serving the company's client more than her frustrating, lackluster boss. And what really bothered her—his condescending attitude. She kept catching echoes of her father and ex in Frank's approach.

After grabbing a chai latte, she joined Xavier and the pretty woman sitting with him. Ignoring her odd peevishness at the woman's presence, Justine concentrated on being pleasant and not irked at the woman's challenging gaze. Was this Xavier's new girlfriend? Because the woman seemed threatened by Justine's presence.

Yet... As Justine looked from Xavier to the pretty redhead, she noticed a lot of similarities.

"Justine, meet my sister, Auggie. Auggie, this is my new neighbor, Justine."

She ignored her sense of relief and smiled wider. "Auggie. It's so nice to meet you."

Xavier's sister nodded. "So you're Rosie's niece?"

"Yep."

"How long are you staying at the apartment complex?"

Justine shrugged. "At least the next three months. My aunt is taking a vacation in Italy and doing some sightseeing in Europe. I'm using the time to regroup."

"From what?"

Xavier cut in. "Don't be so nosy, Auggie."

"Why not?"

Justine did her best not to laugh. The twins frowning at each other made them look that much more alike.

"I can ask her questions." Auggie turned to Justine. "I can ask you questions, can't I?"

"Sure, I guess." She could now see that Xavier had been right about his sister being a little more aggressive, whereas he came across as charming. "I'm pretty much an open book."

"Do you like living at the building? I think it's a little claustrophobic."

"I don't," Xavier said. "I like knowing my neighbors."

Justine relaxed into her seat, pleased to be done with her work day. "Everyone seems really nice. Well, except for the Super. He's a little intimidating."

Auggie grinned. "Nothing like a former Marine to keep the starch in his shorts. Top's not a bad guy. Say something nice about the Corps and you're in."

Xavier frowned. "Um, not necessarily. I was in the Marines, same as you, and he still gives me a hassle."

Justine blinked. "You were in the service?"

Before Xavier could answer, Auggie did. "Not just any service, but the best of them all. We're prior Marine Corps."

"You were too?" Justine asked Auggie, not surprised. Auggie looked fit and trim. Her take-charge attitude only bolstered the notion that the woman had lived a regimented lifestyle. "How long did you guys serve?"

"Xav served for four years. I did five. We got out, then we went to school. Xav for mind games and me for exercise science." Auggie looked her over. "You ever think about getting into fitness? Maybe a bootcamp?"

Xavier sighed. "Leave her alone. And they weren't mind games. I majored in psychology."

"Yeah, like I said, mind games. And what's your problem with a mini-bootcamp? I'm just saying. She could use a little more definition." Auggie turned to Justine. "Guys always think they have the corner on getting buff. But women can too. Strengthening your core helps everything."

"Oh, uh, good point." Justine wondered if she looked as scrawny as she felt next to Xavier and his sister. "I like jogging when I get free time." Actually, she didn't, but she ran because she liked sweets a little too much. "And I was thinking about trying a new yoga class that opened near the coffee shop down the street from us."

"Yoga's good." Auggie nodded. "But so are cardio, lifting, and strength training."

"So wonderful to have your thoughts on Justine's fitness routine," Xavier said with no small amount of sarcasm. He shook his head. "Ignore her, Justine. When you get home after a long day, the fountain in the complex is terrific for destressing. And you don't even have to sweat if you don't want to."

"Hey, sweat is good for the skin," Auggie argued. "Opens your pores."

"I like the indoor courtyard, actually," Justine cut in before their identical frowns turned into an argument. "The flowers, the sound of the water falling. I was surprised at how peaceful it is...even though there's an occasional teenager hanging around." Justine chuckled. "I like Sam though."

Xavier grinned. "You should see him with his brother, who's a few years older. They're really nice kids, though they run rings around Adam."

"The poor guy. But good for him for helping his nephews."

"Yeah. His sister is in and out of rehab, so he finally stepped in to give them a more stable homelife. Rosie filled me in a while ago when I was new. Gave me the lowdown on everyone in the building."

"Really? What else should I know?"

"Well, I gave you the basics already. What Auggie said about Top is pretty smart. Honestly, though, he's not that bad. No one at the complex is. Frankly, I'm surprised at how long Benji talked to you yesterday. He's not a people person."

"Benji talked to her?" Auggie looked as if she didn't know what to make of that.

Xavier nodded. "They were connecting over a video game."

"Oh." Auggie tilted her head and studied Justine. "You're into video games?"

Justine felt like a speck of dirt under that intense, probing look. "No. Well, yes, I like them, but I don't have that much time to play. And I'm not very good."

"Huh."

She didn't know what to make of Auggie's answer.

Xavier asked, "So Justine, did you talk to your mom yet?"

"I finally caved and answered her texts. I told her I was really busy at work lately and that I'd call her later in the week." She groaned. "But I have no idea what to say." She needed a solid plan of defense in case her mom nagged her into committing to bringing a date to the wedding. Or worse, about going out with Cal or Nick.

Xavier looked sympathetic. "It's tough to make family happy. Auggie and I were just talking about Mom's date last night."

"Oh, how did it go?" She'd wondered about that a few times during her day. Thinking about Xavier and his family troubles took her mind off her own. How would a laid-back therapist handle family drama?

He sighed. "I think Mom's a one-and-done with this guy." He explained about Big Henry's bad kissing, which had her laughing.

"Oh my gosh. A bad kisser is terrible." She looked to Auggie. "Am I right? If they can't kiss well, that's a bad sign that a relationship probably won't amount to much."

Auggie nodded, reluctantly, so it seemed to Justine. "Yeah. That's the truth. I typically try my guys out before dating them. No kiss, not even a little tease with second base, and I'm out."

Xavier slapped a hand over his face. "Stop. Talking."

"Oh, you're okay with second base? I need a little more time than one date for that," Justine confessed, trying to ignore the fact Xavier was a sexy guy, doing her best to factor him in as a friend with whom she could tease and laugh.

"Both of you. Stop." He sounded in pain.

She caught Auggie grinning, looking from her to her brother. "No, tell us, Bro. From the dude's point of view, what's in a kiss? Or a first date?"

Xavier peeked through his fingers before putting his hand down. "This is torture, you know that?"

"Come on, Xavier. Don't be such a baby," Justine added.

He glared at her.

She grinned back.

Auggie laughed. "He always was the weakest in the family."

"Fine. Yes, a kiss means a lot when you're first dating. Trust me, women can be just as bad. Too much lip or tongue. Then all the groaning and rubbing all over a guy. It's not always sexy, let me tell you."

Auggie chuckled. "From the horse's mouth, Justine. You should take notes."

"Oh, I am." She leaned forward and cupped her chin in her palm, her elbow on the table. Manners be damned. "Do continue."

Xavier blushed, and she found the sight of his embarrassment too cute. "Look, I'm not saying a woman who goes for it isn't sexy. But she has to be a little subtle." He gave his sister the side-eye. "Not like a 5-Ton ramming at full speed."

Justine noted Auggie's glare and smothered a laugh.

"Subtle is sexy," Xavier continued. "But a good kiss shares feelings and intent."

"Oh my God, Xav. Sometimes sex is just sex. You can get down with a body and not care one fuck about feelings."

"Nice mouth."

"Yeah? Well, I know how to get what I want without all the babble that goes constantly through your mind."

"Please. You'd need to have a few thoughts to share before macking it with any beef-bod in sight."

Justine worried the two might get into a serious argument, their tones more aggressive. But Auggie burst into laughter.

"'Beef-bod?' What the hell is that?"

He gave a sheepish grin. "I don't know. It just popped out." He said to Justine, "See, this is how we communicate. Auggie drives me nuts, then I spout nonsense. It's sad."

"It's actually pretty funny." Justine snickered. "My sisters aren't that great at arguing. Angela steamrolls over you while Mallory cajoles like a whipped puppy. I end up sitting there until one of them shuts up. Then I act like I missed everything and ask them to repeat it. Never fails to annoy the heck out of them."

"Hmm. Not a bad strategy," Auggie said. "You're not as dumb as you look."

"Thanks so much for that," Justine deadpanned, which had Auggie laughing.

Then Xavier cut in with his idea of a good date, information he planned on imparting to his candidate for his mother's next outing.

Justine liked his take and added her two cents, not realizing how interesting she'd become to his sister.

AUGGIE WATCHED her brother and Justine interact, sensing a lot more bubbling under the surface than just friendly banter.

Xavier's gaze seemed glued to the pretty brunette. And though Justine tried to include Auggie in on the conversation, which was a decent thing to do, the woman had a tendency to study Xavier with more interest than she was probably aware of.

Just a neighbor? Please. Xavier had *I Want This One* plastered all over his face. That he acted super casual and not at all interested said volumes to Auggie. She'd have to keep an eye on Justine.

"I know, right? Who goes to a movie on a first date?" Xavier was saying.

"You can't talk during a movie. I think it's a lot more fun to do something together. Like going to a museum or the arboretum. Maybe on date three or four you see a movie or a play. A concert even. But you need time and space to talk."

"Exactly." Xavier nodded, a sparkle in his eyes. *"Communication,"* he emphasized with a sharp look at Auggie, "improves the more you use it. Plus, you and your date are new, so you need to feel each other out."

"What I was saying," Auggie muttered.

"Verbally," he stressed, "to see what you both like, what you have in common."

"So when do you get to the favorite color, favorite number conversations?" Justine asked, nursing her coffee.

Auggie swore she heard the girl's stomach rumble and felt for her. It had nearly reached eight in the evening, and if Justine had come from work without eating any dinner, she had to be hungry.

Xavier must have heard, because he paused. "Hey, you want something to eat?"

Justine flushed. "I'll get something later."

"No, really. I could eat too. They have great panini sandwiches. It's on me."

"I couldn't."

"I insist." He shot Justine his killer smile, that one that always knocked them dead from ten paces.

"Well, okay. But I'll buy the dessert."

"Something sweet. Sweet." Xavier chuckled. They both stood, and he waited for Justine to precede him, ever the gentleman.

The pretty blush on Justine's cheeks, the way they kept smiling at each other, then glancing away, keeping it casual, was telling.

Auggie said nothing, however, and made a mental note to discuss this with her mom. Because though she had a twin bond with Xav, would always remain loyal to him, there was such a thing as looking out for her brother. And their mother had mad instincts when it came to her boy.

No one could ever be good enough.

Yet Auggie kind of liked Justine, what she knew of her, anyway.

Might be interesting to see where this went with the new girl and her too-chill brother.

She sent a text to her mom and smiled when the pair came back with something for her as well.

"We didn't know what you wanted, so we brought back three of each," Justine said with a smile, spreading the food around.

Xavier shot Auggie a warning glance to be nice, so she nodded her thanks. "Appreciate it. I guess I'm hungrier than I thought."

Though the amount of bad carbs in this dinner didn't bode well for Justine's food and nutrition awareness.

"Don't even," Xavier warned in a low voice, reading her mind.

"What?" Justine watched them.

"Never mind," they said at the same time.

Justine stared in astonishment. "Do you guys do that a lot?"

"Not really," they both said again.

Auggie chuckled.

Xavier frowned at her and said, "Well, hardly ever. Now, let me tell you about my guy choice for my mom. Auggie, no comments from the peanut gallery."

She rolled her eyes but said little, swapping sandwiches with her brother. As twins, she and her brother were very much in tune. People always seemed to have something to say about it. But Justine seemed to absorb that detail and accept it, hanging on Xavier's every word.

Auggie made another mental note and decided a visit to Mom's was in order. She smiled widely at her brother when he frowned at her all of the sudden.

"Problem?" Justine asked.

"Nope," she said for him. "I'm just glad to see my brother's got a new friend." *Oh yeah, you know we're going to talk about Justine later.*

She laughed to herself when he kicked her under the table. She kicked him back and thought about how she couldn't wait to tell her mom all the good parts.

CHAPTER 11

Thursday afternoon, Xavier groaned as he did his best to get off the phone with his mother. Damn it. Would it have killed Auggie to stick to the twin-code and remain mute on the subject of Justine?

"Ma, I'm serious. She's a lovely woman, but we're just friends. Both of us are getting off bad breakups, and it wouldn't be healthy to jump into a new relationship for either of us."

"But honey, Auggie said—"

"Auggie's a pain. She's just stirring up trouble because..." *She's treating your dating life like a competition. Whose candidate wins Mom's heart?* He couldn't say that. "Because she's Auggie."

"If you say so, Xavier. I'm not nagging."

"You're totally nagging."

"It's only because I love you." She paused. "And I never thought Christine was a good fit for you, honey."

"I know, which is also part of the reason we broke up. I didn't feel she was a good fit for me either. Again, Justine is a *friend*. It's nice to not have any weirdness with her."

"Fine." Yet Cynthia didn't sound as if she believed him.

He had no idea why. They chatted for a few more minutes before his mother had to go to play pickleball with a few friends.

"I'll talk to you later this week. Love you."

"Love you too, Ma," he said and disconnected.

He wondered when Justine would talk to her mother, and what she'd say. He had enough pressure from his mom and Auggie, and he liked being with them. It couldn't be easy dealing with problematic family all the time.

He left the apartment and hit the gym, coming back home a few hours later. He'd managed to avoid Auggie after yesterday's coffee and late dinner. Poor Justine. She must have been starving. She really should confront her boss and say—

Nope. Not my business. Not going there.

Though it was a chore to put away good advice, he knew it best to stick to his own business and no one else's unless they asked for it. Justine would handle her family and boss the way she saw fit.

After fixing himself a quick meal, he grabbed his laundry and hauled it downstairs. Fortunately, of the two washers, only one was running, so he had plenty of room in which to work. He put in a load and left, returning an hour later to find both machines off and nothing in the dryers.

He put his load in the dryer and turned to leave when Justine entered wearing a battered sweatshirt and shorts that showed off her amazing legs.

Doing his best to keep his gaze on her face, he saw a lack of makeup and thought she looked even prettier without it. Not that he'd say anything about it, because who cared what he thought about her appearance?

"Oh, hey, Xavier."

"Hi. How was work?"

She shrugged. "It was work. But at least Frank the procrastinator had nothing for me today. And the presentation he had to give went well, so I'm told." She scooped her clothing from the washer and dumped it all, in an armload, into the dryer.

Except she dropped an article of clothing on her way.

He scooped it up, realized he held a lacy bra, and paused.

So of course she turned around to see him holding her underthings.

"You dropped this."

"Oh, thanks." She hurried to yank it out of his hand and tossed it into the dryer. "I'm usually losing socks, not bras."

"Yeah, me too." He paused. "Um, because I don't wear them."

"Good to know." She laughed at him. "Your face is pretty red right now."

"As red as yours?" he asked with a smirk.

She crossed her arms over her chest, and he had to work hard to keep his gaze on her face and not dip any lower, remembering how she'd felt against him, how she'd tantalized in her pajama top, how she looked right now, casual yet sexy as hell.

Everything about Justine attracted him, damn it. Talk about some advice he could use right about now: *Dear Aunt Truth, how do I keep my relationship casual with the new girl I'm liking more than I should?*

He realized she looked to be waiting for something. But her gaze kept dipping to his mouth, and she nibbled her lower lip.

You're killing me, woman.

She took a step closer, and he smelled something fruity. Delicious. He wanted a taste. Badly.

"So, um, I enjoyed dinner last night," she finally said, her voice husky.

"Me too." He looked down at her, some primal part of him enjoying that he was larger and stronger than Justine. "Thanks for tolerating Auggie."

Her lips quirked, and his heart raced, seeing that humor, that intelligence in her velvety brown eyes and sinking into what felt like a massive crush. So juvenile, yet there it was.

"Your sister was funny. And tough. She's pretty protective of you."

"It's a twin thing."

Her smile turned sweet. "Truth be told, I'm envious. I wish I had a relationship that close with my own sisters. But I do have Katie, and she's kind of like my own twin."

"Katie?" It took a moment, but he remembered the pretty blond who'd been with her when they'd first met. "Oh, the one who called me a dickhead?"

Justine coughed. "I think it was more along the lines of you acting like a dick."

"Semantics." He smirked. "Do you think I'm a dick?"

He should stop, because every time he heard the word "dick," his body seemed to respond, the swelling between his legs telling but fortunately hidden behind his jeans.

"Well, I'd say you were nice but left a not-so-great first impression." She winked and stared into his eyes with heat.

He'd swear she was flirting with him. So close, glancing up at him as if waiting for him to kiss her.

All the reasons why he should keep his distance faded from his mind, and he shifted closer and lifted a hand to her cheek.

Her eyes widened. "Wh-what?"

"An eyelash." He pulled his finger back to show her. "Now you're supposed to make a wish and blow it away."

She licked her lips, and he fought a groan. She blew across his finger, and the eyelash flew away.

"I guess I shouldn't ask what you wished for or it won't come true." Damn, he sounded gritty. But he was so keyed up he was proud of stringing words together to form a sentence.

Silence built between them, and he knew it had to be more than just him feeling it. Yet they waited to see who would make the first move.

Justine took a step closer.

Xavier's heart threatened to pound out of his chest.

"Oh, are the washers empty? I see the dryers going."

They sprang apart like cats doused with water. Xavier turned to see Sam holding a large bag full of laundry, the kid's attention fixed on the washing machines.

Justine cleared her throat. "No, Xavier and I just put our stuff into the dryers. You have the washers all to yourself." She smiled brightly at Sam, then at Xavier. "See you guys later." She danced out of the room in a hurry, and Xavier was left with a thirteen-year-old going on forty.

The newly crowned teenager glanced at the empty doorway. "Sorry, dude, but she's too young for you."

Amused despite his tension, Xavier raised a brow. How old did Sam think he was? "Oh?"

"Besides, I'm going to ask her out again. She likes younger men."

"Is that right?" That wacky previous moment of stress broken, Xavier felt both disappointed and relieved to be back to normal. "Well, for the record, I think your love interest is more into older men, ones who can at least drive." He looked around. "Better keep your brother away from her. He's got his permit, doesn't he?"

"I know. I've been keeping watch, don't worry." Sam sounded so serious and determined Xavier had to laugh.

"Need any help with your laundry?"

"Um, sure. That would be good."

Xavier helped the boy, listened to an earful about his uncle not allowing him to do anything fun, like jumping off bridges or hanging out after dark with his friends in the city, then left for his apartment.

He wondered if he should confront Justine about their odd bouts of attraction. But what if he'd been overthinking the situation? Could he have misread her intentions? What if she hadn't been leaning in for a kiss? He'd been the one to initiate touching her, after all.

He went back to his drafting table to color some new panels, alarmed at how he might have projected his feelings into the situation. The more he thought about it, the more he got wrapped into his head and tried to help himself out through a deeper analysis of his feelings, of what had truly happened.

By the time he readied for bed that night, he realized he must have misread Justine and that he needed to find someone else to help him satisfy his needs. Because at the rate he was headed, he was on the course to ruin things with his new friend and neighbor. Not a great situation at all. Because one—he liked living here without any drama. And two—he really, *really* liked Justine.

The thought of spending his days without the possibility of seeing her smile or hearing her confide in him hurt. Way more than it should.

So he packed away any foolish longings and weighed his feelings versus his needs.

As always, he came out the stronger for it and relegated any discomfort with distress to a healthy way of idealizing balance.

He fell asleep with ease.

And this time he didn't dream. Or at least, he didn't choose to remember.

CHAPTER 12

"I almost kissed him," Justine confided to Katie Friday night at her apartment as they watched the first episode of one of Katie's favorite series of all time. The show involved half-naked and fully-naked men fighting each other and having sex with women all over the place. Justine could see why her best friend loved the show.

Katie's eyes grew wide. She paused the television and turned to gape at Justine. "Say that again. You almost kissed *your boss?*"

Horrified, Justine shrieked, "Are you insane? No, Katie. I almost kissed Xavier. Yesterday in the laundry room. We were standing way too close, and you could cut the tension with a knife."

"Cliché, but I'll allow it." Katie held up a finger to stop Justine's retort. "No, wait. I want to hear everything. Right now."

With a sigh, Justine told her all about Wednesday evening coffee and meeting Auggie, and then the near kiss in the laundry room. "And I swear," she ended, "I can't be sure, as I was trying not to get caught staring, that he was pretty excited to be near me, if you know what I mean."

"What? No." Katie shoved a handful of popcorn in her mouth and chewed like a hungry squirrel.

"What do you mean, no? And ew, I can see your food."

"I can't believe you waited until now to tell me. How are we best friends?"

"Oh stop. I haven't told anyone else." Not that she had anyone else to tell. Well, if Aunt Rosie had been around, she might have called her. But then, probably not. Her aunt had a way of making her feel like an old cow put out to pasture, as her aunt liked to say, and Justine had yet to reach thirty.

"I'm still a little confused," Katie said. "I know you and Mitch didn't end in a good way. Well, minus any drama, it was the driest breakup ever. No screaming or throwing things. You just took a few extra weeks to get all your stuff together, slept in the spare room, and were never home. Then you moved all your stuff here."

"I thought it was a mature way to end things."

"Bah." Katie scowled. "You're an amazing person with creative ideas and a real passion for life. Except when it comes to guys. Xavier seems intelligent."

"He is."

"Nice."

"He's nice."

"And he's freaking hot. You have to admit that."

Her cheeks still felt warm as she answered, "He is."

"So what's the problem? There's no time limit between getting new boyfriends. And let's face it. Mitch was a pain for a long time," Katie pointed out. "You and he had emotionally broken up months ago. Why not see where this thing with Xavier leads?"

"That's my point. There is no thing with Xavier." But there could have been yesterday. Right? Or had she been reading into the situation? She shook her head. "No, I know he felt something. He touched my cheek."

"To remove an eyelash, you said." Katie snorted. "That's right up there with the stretch to land an arm around your shoulders. I can't believe neither of you made a move."

"Well, Sam interrupted. Or maybe I'm delusional."

"No, you know what you felt and saw." Katie added with a sly smile, "So what exactly did you see that made you think he might be super 'excited' to see you?"

Justine blushed, remembering. "I didn't mean to look down at him. I couldn't help myself. And it was just... His jeans looked pretty tight. And he was pretty, um, er, big."

"Um, er, big? Which in Justine-ese, means *huge*, right?"

"Stop it." Justine laughed. "How are you so able to talk about all this without blushing?"

"Have you met my mother? The one who's so *not* embarrassed about anything that she's actually embarrassing about everything?"

"Oh, right."

"And anyway, you're repressed. Not your fault, since your parents are always on you to conform and behave—whatever that means. But come on, sex should be fun. Adventurous. And always with a man with wonderful proportions." Katie paused. "Unless you're not into men or physical sex. Not judging, just saying."

Justine sighed. "You know I like guys."

Katie brightened. "Right. So you want 'em hung and into making you happy. Seriously, sixty-second wonders, no matter how big they are, aren't worth more than the eye candy."

A knock at the door startled them both.

Justine answered to find Xavier standing in the doorway.

"Hi, Justine. Can I talk to you?"

She pulled back, and he glanced at Katie sitting in the living room munching on popcorn.

"Oh, sorry. I can come back another time." He blinked at the TV. "What are you watching?"

She turned to see the main actor's ass hanging out as he was frozen on the screen in a wrestling hold with a larger, more muscular combatant.

"And speaking of hung and making 'em happy..." Katie murmured.

Xavier turned to her. "What did you say?"

"Nothing," Justine blurted and glared at her friend.

"No, I think this calls for a man's input." Katie motioned for Xavier to join them. "Want some popcorn? We're rewatching *Spartacus*. It's one of my favorite series."

Xavier entered, and Justine helplessly closed the door behind him. With any luck, Katie would be less "Katie" and not shock everyone in the room into awkward silence. Yet that was one of the reasons Justine loved her. Katie didn't hold back, not with what she said or how she felt. And the girl was loyal to a fault, a true friend even during their disagreements.

Xavier cleared his throat. "The Spartacus I know is based on the Thracian gladiator who rebelled against the Roman Republic for freedom. This... doesn't look anything like the movie I once saw, which was an older version in black and white." He joined Katie on the couch and took a handful of popcorn. "Thanks."

Justine sighed. "Something to drink?"

"Sure. Anything's fine."

"Ice tea coming right up."

"Top me off, Justine?" Katie asked.

"Fine, so long as you behave."

Xavier chuckled. "Uh-oh. Katie doesn't like behaving, eh?"

"Well, it's more what we were talking about before you got here that's got her worried," Katie just had to mention.

"Oh?"

Don't say it, you viper. Don't you dare. The warning in her eyes must not have penetrated because Katie looked at her then looked at Xavier and said, "What are your thoughts on size versus skill?"

Xavier paused. "Well, I'd have to have more context."

Katie pointed at the TV, where they could all clearly see hints of the combatants' packages from behind. "Take our main man. He's not as bulky as his opponent, but he's streamlined and has a nice bit of man meat the camera's teasing us with."

Justine massaged her temples.

Xavier gave a noncommittal murmur. "Ah, I see."

"I was telling Justine that I think size is important, but if you don't know what you're doing with that size, then it's all for show."

Justine tried but couldn't see Xavier's reaction, only the back of his head. She hurried over with more drinks for everyone and sat on the floor so she could observe while they talked.

His cheeks looked a little pink to her, and that naughty gleam in Katie's eyes was telling. Her friend was having a blast with the vulgar conversation.

Xavier, though, surprised her by laughing. "You know, you and my sister would totally get along. Auggie's pretty frank too."

"Sounds pretty self-confident," Katie said.

"You have no idea," Xavier answered. "But in response to your question" — he paused to glance at Justine, his growing grin wicked indeed— "then I think both are important. First, you need to fit, physically. If he's too big it could be painful. Too small, then there's no sensation for either of them, really."

"Good points."

"Oh my God," Justine muttered.

They ignored her.

"But like you said, if he doesn't know what he's doing, he's the only one having a good time. She'll likely never want to see him again. One-and-done guys are typically selfish and boring. Or just really inexperienced, but that's not an excuse."

"I agree," Katie stated. "Justine?"

"Yeah, sure. What you said."

"Isn't she cute when she's blushing?" Katie teased.

Xavier nodded. "Adorable."

She shot him the finger, surprising herself, and had Xavier and Katie laughing.

Xavier followed up with, "I'm sorry. I'm trying to be a good guest by answering Katie's questions."

"Whatever."

"No, he's got a unique point of view. Continue, Xavier."

Xavier gave Katie a warm smile, and Justine felt the wattage of it and needed to cool down. "Look, every guy wants to be thought of as larger than average, because people make such a big deal about size. But a man who's interested in pleasing his partner is more about skill than his anatomy. It's, what's the expression? It's not the size of your boat but the motion in the ocean?"

"Oh, I like that." Katie nodded.

"You would," Justine said, still not understanding how Xavier had become part of this conversation.

"You will too once you have rockin' waves."

Xavier raised a brow.

"She's in between boyfriends."

"I know. She's waiting until she's ready."

"Ha! Take that." Justine pointed at Katie. "Xavier understands all about needing space."

Katie answered, "Which is why we're hanging out here watching naked men wave their flags around instead of hanging at a bar where we could be meeting showers and growers."

Xavier choked on his drink.

"Hey, Xavier, do you want to watch some *Spartacus* with us? Or would you rather talk to Justine about whatever it was you wanted to talk about?"

Xavier got a strange look on his face as he looked from the TV to Justine. "You know what? I think watching this show with you sounds fascinating. My conversation can keep. Justine, are you comfy down there on the floor?"

Katie patted the spot between them on the couch. "Yeah,

there's plenty of room to join us. You can sit right between Xavier and me."

It would be a super tight fit. Something Justine couldn't handle just now. "Nope, I'm fine. You sure you want to watch this? It's pretty violent."

"And sexual," Katie had to add.

Xavier's grin made her want to sigh. "Sounds perfect. Besides, what could be better than watching gratuitous sex and violence with two gorgeous women? Wait until I tell my friends how I spent my Friday night."

"With two hot babes and a lot of swinging dick," Katie added.

Xavier chuckled. "Exactly."

Justine groaned. "Screw the ice tea. I think this calls for beer."

CHAPTER 13

Despite the embarrassing way the night had started, Justine ended up having a ton of fun with her friends. Katie kept saying whatever shocking thing popped into her head, and Justine knew it was her way of testing Xavier, to see how he'd respond.

He answered her with humor and some insightful commentary. The therapist in him never far from the surface, apparently. Yet Justine didn't mind. She found herself more and more attracted to Xavier's quick wit and thoughtfulness. She also liked that in some instances he very much acted stereotypical, thoroughly enchanted by the violent scenes of fighting on TV.

"Wow. That's a move. I bet he wrestled in high school, maybe college."

"Thinking about grappling for fun? Don't look at me," Katie warned. "Though Justine's been known to be pretty scrappy."

"Oh, stop." Justine's face had felt permanently warm all night. "Rolling around in the sand doesn't look appealing. Plus, you get sand in all sorts of places."

The episode ended, finally, and before a new one could get started—they'd already watched two—she paused the series.

"Good point." Xavier stood and stretched, and Katie shot a quick gaze at his crotch and gave her a subtle thumbs up.

Fortunately, he missed it.

Justine looked at the floor, trying not to laugh, and felt as if she'd left all her dignity in the other room. Katie never failed to make life fun, that was for sure.

"I feel like I've monopolized your evening. Sorry about that." He smiled down at her.

Justine smiled back, lost in his sparkling brown eyes and full mouth drawn up in amusement.

So when Katie cleared her throat, she startled.

"Time for me to go. I'm so tired." Katie's yawn was beyond fake. But she bolted out the door with a "Call you tomorrow," leaving Justine all alone with Xavier.

"Again, sorry for popping over unannounced. But I learned so much." Xavier chuckled. "Katie's hilarious. She and Auggie really do need to meet."

"I don't know if the world would survive such a cataclysmic meeting of minds," she said drily, which had Xavier laughing hysterically.

"Thanks. I needed tonight. Cataclysmic." He guffawed some more. "I had fun. I hope I wasn't imposing, but you did ask me to stay."

"I'm glad you did." Not a lie. Being around Xavier made Justine feel good. Oddly, she felt safe with him. Sure, Xavier had height and muscle, but he just radiated security. She never feared he'd make fun of her for something she said or did, or that he'd turn mean if he didn't get his way. Which was ridiculous, because they weren't dating or anything, and she didn't know him that well.

But of all her friends and family, only Katie was never malicious or condescending with teasing. And now Xavier fit in Justine's tiny trust bucket.

Xavier frowned. "You look tired. I should go."

"Wait." She stood. "What did you come over to talk about?"

"Oh. Well, I..." He studied her face, and she wondered what he saw. The pleasure of having him close? The attraction she tried to keep in check? Her growing curiosity about what a kiss against that soft-looking beard and mustache might feel like? To know the taste of him?

Xavier gave her a weird smile. "It's not important. I had a blast tonight. More fun than I've had in a while, actually."

She paused as a terrible thought crossed her mind. "Was it Katie?" she asked out loud and horrified herself for a second time. Would he want her number or something?

"Katie? She's funny, sure. I like her sense of humor. She really brings you out of your shell." He flushed. "God, I try, but I can't take the work hat off. Forget I said that."

Relieved he didn't seem into her best friend, she shrugged. "No apologies needed. You're right. With Katie, I can be me. I feel, I don't know, freer." She gave him a shy smile. "With you too. I feel like I can say anything and you won't judge me for being stupid."

"You're not stupid."

"No, I'm not." She sighed. "I don't know why I said that." She did know why. Because she often felt stupid, not enough, underwhelming. But she refused to admit that to Xavier. Fortunately, he didn't call her on it. "I just meant if I say something wrong, you wouldn't take it as a statement about my intelligence or start judging me for it."

"Well, I don't know. If you think real men are like the ones you just saw in *Spartacus,* I might judge you for being too strict about physical fitness. I don't come close to those oiled up gladiators."

She flushed and joined him in his laughter. "You're a goof."

"Yep, that's me." He seemed delighted with her mock insult.

Their gazes locked, and that thick tension that had surged between them in the laundry room came back. She wanted so badly to walk into his arms and drag him down for a kiss. *Make the first move, for heaven's sake,* she told herself. But she was frozen in indecision. What if he didn't feel anything but platonic like for her?

He stared over her face, tracing a path from her eyes to her mouth and lingering. She saw his chest rise and fall faster. *No, he's into me. Right? Or am I wrong? Being wrong about this would kill our growing friendship for sure.*

Xavier coughed, breaking the spell. "You're fun to be around. I really like you." He opened and closed his mouth, paused, then said, "I don't want to overstay my welcome. Or become a pest. So I'll go now." He slowly walked to her and gave her a half hug, not full body contact but shared warmth all the same. He quickly pulled back. "See you later."

She watched him leave, her knees weak, and had no idea why him leaving without a full hug, or even better, a kiss, made her want to cry.

♡

AFTER RUNNING into Justine only a few times during the week, by the following Friday, Xavier felt as if he'd gotten a handle on his feelings for his upstairs neighbor. A sweet, funny, yet harried woman, Justine didn't have time for a man in her life, let alone Xavier, who was still processing his past relationship, wondering how it had all gone so horribly wrong.

They way all his relationships seemed to.

To his surprise, his ex had left him a message about getting together to piece through everything, needing "closure." But he didn't think that was Christine's true intent, so he hadn't called her back. They'd had closure over a month ago and hadn't spoken in weeks. Just what the hell else could he do for her?

Plus, lately, his thoughts had been occupied by the gorgeous brunette doing her best to handle an unhappy work life while navigating rocky family dynamics. He really felt for her, but she hadn't asked for his advice, so he was doing his best to keep his thoughts to himself. Plus, he had a feeling she'd been avoiding him, which made him wonder if he'd made a mistake being so free with his opinions last Friday.

Xavier sighed and continued to watch the clock, waiting on his mother to show up for a home-cooked Friday brunch. She didn't usually make him wait, always early for everything. So when she still hadn't answered his texts ten minutes later, he grabbed his keys and left the apartment to find her.

He heard her talking to someone in the courtyard and paused at the mouth of the hallway.

His mother was laughing with an equally animated Top. The usually taciturn guy wore a smile and seemed a lot more at ease than he normally was. And Cynthia chatted as if she and Top were best friends, her smile warm, her tone a little…flirty?

No, no. Definitely not. When he took a step out from the stairwell toward them, Top turned, saw him, and assumed his usual mien. That of serial killer meets prison warden.

"Mom, where have you been?" Xavier gave her a hug and a kiss. "Hey, Top. What's up?"

"Just talking to your mom." He glanced from Cynthia to Xavier and shook his head. "Still hard to believe you have grown kids, Cynthia. Unless you had them when you were twelve."

Xavier's mom blushed. "Oh you."

Top gave her a warm smile, glared at Xavier for no reason whatsoever, then waved. "Gotta get back to work. Nice meeting you."

"You too. Are you sure you don't want to join us for brunch upstairs?"

Top quickly walked away and shot over his shoulder, "Sorry, too much to do today."

Conscious they waited until Top had departed out of sight, Xavier frowned at the bag his mother carried. "Are these groceries? I told you I was making you brunch today."

"I just brought some fruit for fruit salad." She continued to look at where Top had disappeared. "What a nice man."

"Top? *Nice?*"

She frowned at him. "He was extremely polite. I met him on the street while parking, and he was kind enough to let me in."

"Really? Because he always makes us use our keycards or the keypad to enter. And he *knows* we live here."

"I told him I was coming up to see you, and we got to talking. Did you know Max used to live in Oregon? Right near where your father and I spent a few years in the central part of the state."

"Small world." Max? He hadn't told Cynthia to call him Top? "But you're late. You're never late."

She flushed as they went to the elevator he normally avoided, sticking to a routine of using the stairs all the time. "I'm sorry. I lost track of time when we were talking. And I couldn't get to my phone buried in my purse."

"What is it you always like to tell me? Excuses are like assholes—everyone has them."

"Oh stop it. I'm a little late. Get over it." Her lips quirked. "But that is a winning line, isn't it?"

He chuckled. "Totally. I'm telling Auggie you were late."

"Please don't. That girl loves having something to hold over my head." She shot him a sly glance. "But as I understand it, you've been keeping secrets, Xavier. You said Justine was just a friend. I hear she's more than that."

He groaned. They reached his floor and finally entered the apartment. "Auggie doesn't know what she's talking about. I already told you. Justine's a very nice woman, and we get along. That's it." That's all there should be between them, at least. Friendship.

"No need to get huffy, Son. I was just curious." The gleam in her eyes didn't bode well, but she said nothing more as they worked together to make brunch. He reheated the quiche he'd prepared the night before then put bacon in the oven to cook. His mother chopped fruit and filled him in on all her friends and what she'd been up to since their dinner the week before last.

"And then Michelle told me that the girls' trip we all had planned needed to be rescheduled due to Ed's surgery. The hospital moved it up, and they decided to take it. Now next weekend, which a bunch of us had planned, is open." Cynthia sighed. "I was really looking forward to our time on Bainbridge Island too."

"Why can't the rest of you go without her? Do another girls' trip later."

"That's what I said, but then Mimi thought Michelle might get her feelings hurt. I mean, it's not Michelle's fault they keep moving Ed's surgery date. And his shoulder's in a lot of pain. He needs it done. If they don't jump on this new time, he might not get in until much later."

"I know, but it seems ridiculous Michelle would expect all of you to cancel just for her."

Cynthia frowned. "For a man who has regularly helped people handle their relationships, you don't understand. We're a tight group. It wouldn't be the same without Michelle there."

"Look, I'm not trying to mess up your girl gang."

"Patronizing, are we?"

He grinned. "Heck no. You'll kick my butt if I even think about talking down to you."

She harrumphed.

"I'm just sorry you're having to miss out on a planned vacation." He had an idea, one that would get back at his sorry twin for blabbing about Justine. "You know, this might be a terrific opportunity to bond with Auggie, just you two."

His mom brightened. "I hadn't thought about that."

"I know Auggie has been super busy lately with work and that competition that's coming up. She could probably use the break. Besides, when's the last time you guys had some good old fashioned mother-daughter bonding? She can take a weekend to be with her favorite mom."

Cynthia grinned. "Her only mom, you mean."

"Nah, I mean favorite."

They sat down to eat and continued to talk about what Cynthia and Auggie might do together, as Auggie was a little hyper on even her down days. Between the food, the idea of his sister having to calm down for a weekend, and the joy on Cynthia's face at the idea of spending time with her daughter, Xavier had a terrific time.

He wasn't at all prepared when his mom asked him to invite Justine over for their next family dinner.

"What? Why?"

"You sound a little panicked there, Xavier."

He cleared his throat and drew on his trademark calm. "Not at all. I just hadn't expected the shift in conversation. You want to meet Justine?"

"Sure. I was friends with Rosie, remember. I'd love to meet her niece."

He could swear his mother was up to something, but if he called her on it, she'd want to know why he felt so defensive over mention of Justine. And since he had a tough time acknowledging just what he and Justine had between them other than friendship, he did his best to smile and pretend a family date with her didn't bother him.

"I'm happy to ask her to join us. But fair warning, she's been pretty busy with work and her own family lately. I haven't seen her all that much this week."

"I'm sure you'll bump into her at some point. You don't have her number?"

"Well, no. If I need to talk to her, she's right upstairs."

"And now you have an excuse to get her number."

"Mom." He sighed.

"You're welcome. Now pass the fruit salad." She paused. "And tell me more about Max."

CHAPTER 14

"You're kidding. What a nightmare," Katie said as they walked out of the office building together Friday night. "When is someone going to hold Frank accountable? He's a terrible manager."

"Tell me about it." Justine's head throbbed from a growing headache after fixing her boss's problems all day. "I have my own work to handle plus his, which he never seems able to do correctly."

"Maybe because he spends all day long up his boss's ass. Hard to get work done when your sniffing ass crack."

Two guys in suits stared at Katie as they passed her, having obviously overheard her.

She just waved.

One of them grinned and waved back.

Katie turned to her and linked arms. "You need to speak up, Justine. If you don't tell him how much you hate working overtime when you have your own life to get back to, nothing will change."

"I'm not even getting paid the extra hours," she muttered,

annoyed she still hadn't had her yearly review for a raise. Frank kept putting it off.

"Wait, what?" Katie stopped in her tracks, forcing Justine to stop with her. "Are you telling me you've been doing all your own work *and* his, staying late, and you're not getting any OT for it?"

"No. It's not in the budget."

"This is bullshit, Justine." Katie softened her voice. "Look, honey, I know you're a team player. You work so hard, don't expect a pat on the back for it either, and are trying your best. But this is not at all a good fit for you."

Tears came to Justine's eyes. "You don't think I know that?"

"You're miserable. Frank is getting all the credit for your ideas. Plus he's so busy schmoozing the boss that he looks like he can do no wrong while you're holding him up and getting no respect for it."

"I'm trying to make our team look good."

"You're just making *him* look good. Not the team." Katie paused. "Why isn't Phil or John or Sarah working overtime for him?"

"They have families."

"So only single people are expected to work for no pay? No. Try again—especially since Sarah is only engaged, not married, and no kids."

"I guess... Well, Frank asked them a few times but they demanded to get paid." At Katie's knowing look, Justine hastened to add, "But they have a lot more years in the company than I do. I can't lose this job."

"Fuck that. You totally can. You're more talented than all of them—well, except me. But you're not confident enough in yourself to know you can work for someone else."

"I've looked."

"Not hard, because you're afraid word might get back to Frank."

Justine flushed.

"Besides, we both know what you really want."

"What's that?"

"To work for yourself. You're so smart, but you can't see it. You're a lot like your dad, only softer. Intelligent, talented, and driven, though you pretend you're not. You're just nice about it while your family are like pit bulls making deals."

Justine sighed. "Now you're just insulting. I'm not like my dad."

"You totally are. He's not content working for anyone but himself. He has an idea of how he thinks his business should work. So do you. But he works in finance, and you with art. Hey, they can say what they want, but our company is about making pretty art for people to gawk over, so they go and buy from our clients. We appeal to the public in an artistic medium—TV, magazines, billboards. We design it. They buy it. Your dad appeals to people's wallets directly. Spend money to make money. It's similar but not."

Justine tugged her friend to start walking again. "You've put way too much thought into this."

"I have. Because you're miserable. You're losing weight."

The one positive aspect of her misery. "Thanks."

"You have no social life. And I mean that in a nice, I'm-worried-for-you way." Katie added, "When's the last time you saw Xavier?"

An automatic blush lit her cheeks. "I passed by him the other day. I had to go back into work to fix something Frank screwed up."

"Come on. You like him—Xavier, I mean. He's amazing." Katie stopped by their cars and put a hand on her hip, her tone aggressive when she said, "If you aren't going to make a move, I might."

"*What?*"

"Look, dating is hard. Xavier's handsome, smart, built like one of the *Spartacus* guys, and he's funny. He doesn't live with his parents, has a job—I think—and have I mentioned he's built?"

Katie grinned. "The little green monster in your soul is glaring at me even though you're trying to pretend you don't care."

"I don't care."

"You are such a liar."

Justine gritted her teeth. "Not lying."

"Pants on fire, liar," Katie taunted.

"Seriously, go ahead. Ask him out."

"Fine. I will." Katie gave her a smug look. "Race you back."

Then the blasted woman got in her car and drove away. As Justine quickly followed, she kept thinking Katie must have been joking. Did she mean to ask Xavier out now? Seriously?

But Xavier was hers!

Well, not for real, but in Justine's fantasies, she and Xavier were living in a house surrounded by a white picket fence with three kids and a fourth on the way. They never argued, and Justine had her own business that was making more than her father and sisters ever would. Xavier lived for nothing but sex, spending quality time together, and cooking all their meals. It was a perfect world in Justine's tiny mind.

And Katie was going to ruin it all. Justine couldn't handle her best friend dating Xavier. Though ridiculous, because she had no claim on the man and could make no decisions regarding Katie's love life, the pair of them dating felt so *wrong*.

Once parked and rushing to beat Katie to the apartment's front entrance, she threw her body against the doors, her arms outspread, blocking the entrance.

"What the heck are you doing?" Katie laughed. "Are you seriously body blocking me from going in?" Because Katie had the codes to enter.

"It's not funny. You can't ask him out." Justine felt like a fool but had no idea how to proceed.

"Why not? You don't want him."

"Maybe I do."

"Ah-ha!" Katie poked her in the chest. "Then make a move."

"I can't," she all but wailed. "He's the first decent friend I've had since meeting you. I don't want to mess it up."

"Finally, the truth." Katie pulled her into a hug. "I was messing with you, Justine. I would never poach on your man."

"He's not my man," she muttered against Katie's shoulder.

"Not yet. But if you don't do something about that, some other smart cookie's going to grab onto him. Not me. Like I said, I don't poach. But you have to see how amazing he is, right? He liked *Spartacus*."

Justine gave a reluctant laugh as she pulled back. "Liking *Spartacus* should not be the reason you like someone."

"It's not, but it is a cool dating litmus test. He's not so full of himself he can't appreciate other strong, hot men. So he's not homophobic, he's sex positive, and he knows it's more important how to use his equipment than how big his equipment is. Although, I gotta say, his pants outlined some very, very nice looking gear."

They totally had. "Katie."

"Go home, get some sleep, and I'll meet up with you on Sunday, okay? We'll do that movie I want to see."

"The one with hot guys?"

"And magic. Yes." They hugged. Katie left, and after grabbing her things from her car and locking up, Justine went inside.

Unfortunately, on her way past the inner courtyard, water squirted her right in the face, causing her to trip over a large bucket and a teenager.

They landed in a tangle of limbs.

"Whoa, lady. Get off!" A younger boy kept pushing at her.

"I would if you'd stop pushing," she grumbled and finally got to her feet. "Who squirted me?"

She stared at obvious siblings. Sam, looking adorable and soaking wet, carrying one of those giant water rifles, and what must be his older brother, Rylan, a handsome teen with a frown and a water balloon in hand.

A glance around showed pieces of broken water balloons all over, in addition to the bucket she'd tripped over still full of the rubber water grenades.

She picked up her bag and laid it and her jacket on the nearby bench. The trickle of the fountain and smell of sweet flowers eased something inside her. As did the cautious look on both teenagers' faces.

"We're allowed to do this here," Rylan said, going on the offensive.

"Oh?" She crossed her arms over her chest. "You have a permit, I take it?"

Sam looked at her with big brown eyes full of admiration. Apparently the little guy still had a crush. "I do."

"Where is it?"

Rylan scowled "That's ridiculous. You don't need a permit for a water fight."

"Oh? Did you sign the same rental agreement that I did? It clearly states you can't have more than 500cc's of water in any recreational sport involving water." She had no idea what she was talking about, but it sounded good. "Otherwise the landlord, via the superintendent, can suspend your lease. Now, I've met Top. He'd probably only give you a warning, but I doubt your uncle would like that. He's a policeman, isn't he? They don't like breaking the law."

"That's stupid," Rylan scoffed. "There's no law against water fights."

"No, but there are codes and regulations for privately owned dwellings and apartment complexes."

Rylan seemed less certain. Sam kept his mouth closed and appeared worried.

"Look, just make sure what you're holding is less than 500cc's."

"I don't know how much that is," Rylan admitted. He still

looked at her with suspicion. "And besides, who would know we're even having a water fight? You have to prove it."

"I got hit by a water gun, first of all." She pointed to her wet, spattered blouse and hair. "And secondly, you have balloon pieces everywhere. I don't know Top well, but I know for a fact he'll lose it if he sees his garden messed up."

"We'll clean it when we're done," Sam assured her. "Please don't tell."

"Well, maybe. Let me make sure your water volume meets code." She motioned for Rylan to hand her the water balloon he still carried.

He looked unsure but deposited it in her hand. "I still think you're lying."

"I am." She threw the balloon at his chest and watched him gape as he got drenched.

Sam laughed really hard until she scooped another balloon and tossed it at him. Smack. Right in the head.

"Ha. Suckers." She grabbed two more and raced away, using part of the fountain as cover.

The boys whooped and raced away after grabbing more ammunition from the bucket. Sam started shooting at her whenever she got free, and she got wetter and wetter as their fight progressed.

Until she hit Adam—in uniform—in the chest with a balloon. Benji, behind him, got wet from Sam's water gun.

Everyone froze until Adam yelled about making arrests. Benji, to her surprise, darted for the bucket and launched a few balloons at Rylan with poor aim. Then Xavier walked out of the stairwell and got beaned in the head. Sam laughed so hard he cried, and Benji stole his gun and shot him with it.

"I am now your leader. Cry forfeit, worthless mortal!" he roared.

Xavier stood, stunned for a moment, so Justine had to hit him again. A water balloon crashed against his chest and soaked him.

He goggled at her before joining in the fight.

It only wound down when Top made an appearance, asking about all the damn noise. But Top, of course, dodged the two balloons thrown at him. He looked like a thundercloud as he saw what had become of his pristine garden.

Then Sam grabbed his gun from Benji and took a knee, sighting in on Top. "Freeze, Marine, or this breath will be your last."

"I've got grenades," Rylan warned, holding a balloon in each hand as he stood behind his brother.

Adam chuckled. "Don't worry, Top. We'll clean it all up."

"Damn right," Top grumbled and held up his hands. "Well? What are the rest of you gonna do? Put up with this insurrection or take out the enemy while I'm distracting them?"

Xavier shot a balloon at Adam while Justine took a hit from Benji, not sure whose team she was supposed to be on.

Top went down in a blaze of water, while the teenagers and Xavier kept trying to pelt each other. Xavier paused at one point to share a grin with Justine.

The moment was so perfectly fun and joyous, she never wanted it to end.

Chaos reigned.

And Justine had never had a better time.

CHAPTER 15

Justine woke up Saturday morning confused. She lay in her bed as the phone buzzed and gradually recalled an amazing water fight last night, followed by a warm bath and frozen pizza. While eating, she'd taken out her special notebook and continued doodling ideas for logos for her brand new business, one in which she'd work regular hours and have only the best-paying and most pleasant clients on hand.

The phone stopped buzzing. Finally.

It started again.

With a groan, she turned to see her boss calling.

"No. I'm not doing this with you today, asshole." She ignored her guilt in referring to her boss as such, at her core always so uncomfortable fighting against authority. But hell, she'd worked a sixty hour week and hadn't seen anything positive for doing so. Frank's attaboys had long past lost their luster.

She couldn't believe his temerity when the phone rang again, only to find the call from her mother. Justine told herself not to but decided to answer it anyway. She'd left her last conversation with her mother on a good note. Everyone had their jobs to do for the wedding, and since Justine had already done most of her part by designing the wedding invitations and website, she had little more to do than help the others with small things. Something she didn't mind since it kept her in her parents' and Mallory's good graces.

She answered, "Hi, Mom." She still felt relaxed from her fun evening. Clad in her favorite sleepshirt and tucked under her warm blankets—much needed thanks to Seattle's cool evenings—she heard birds chirping from outside and saw the sun filtering through the window, shining light onto the foot of her bed.

The world seemed right, her happiness still a fuzzy remnant making waking up less of a chore and more of a good start to two blessed days off.

"Oh, Justine. I'm so glad I caught you."

"What time is it?"

"Um, nine o'clock. Sorry, nine-fifteen."

"In the morning?"

"Very funny, dear." Her mother sighed. "I've been waiting on you forever, and I just had to make the commitment. I've added Cal as your plus-one for the wedding. We needed even numbers, you know. Now you—"

"You can't," Justine blurted, so opposed to being made to do something she didn't want to—at the ripe age of twenty-nine, for God's sake.

"Honey, we've told you over and over again you need someone to accompany you. We're all coupled up, and it would be odd if you weren't. Now, if you'd rather go with Nick, we can fit him in instead. The girls and I thought you seemed more comfortable with Cal, but if—"

"I already have a date." She couldn't stop the lie from tumbling from her mouth.

"Oh?"

Too late to take it back now. "Yes. We met and hit it off, but I was waiting to make sure he had the date free before letting you know."

"Well that's *wonderful.*" Her mother's voice warmed. "Who is it?"

Names raced through her mind, but only one made any kind of sense. "His name's Xavier. He's a really nice guy, and we've been taking it slow while dating."

I'm going to hell for this.

"Does Xavier have a last name?"

Her mind raced. "Hanover."

"Xavier Hanover. Perfect. Does he have any dietary restrictions?"

"Huh?"

"For the meal, Justine. We have to get the meals settled by tomorrow. Though I'm sure we can fiddle a bit with the catering with the prices we're paying," Jeanine muttered.

"Uh, what I had. The steak, I think."

"Okay. He will be dressed appropriately, I assume."

"A suit and tie is fine, Mom. He doesn't need a tux."

"He's not in the wedding party, so no. But I don't want him to be outshone too much by my beautiful girl."

Justine wanted to embrace the compliment, but it felt more like a warning. She could never be sure Jeanine meant to make Justine feel good or to make herself feel good for having given birth to such beauty.

"Okay, honey. That's all I needed. Have a nice weekend! I'll call if we need you to do anything else."

The call disconnected, and Justine lay in bed, aware she'd just made a colossal mistake. She went through the motions of showering and cleaning up, the mint of her toothpaste barely there as she realized the impact of what she'd done.

Now she'd have to drag Xavier into her family drama... That was if he'd even go.

So nervous, she had no idea what to do about Xavier as she

dressed in the first thing she dragged out of her closet, a pale blue tee-shirt dress, perfect to run a few errands. She worked on getting her head on straight while she dithered over how to break the news to Xavier.

Or to renege and just go with Cal.

She could always make some excuse to her mom that Xavier couldn't attend. Why did it feel like such a big deal to have her mother choose her companion for the wedding, anyway? Losing control of her life for just one day shouldn't be a big deal.

Yet that one day loomed like an eternity of hell on earth. Xavier seemed like the cure to all her problems. Her friend that she'd just thrown under the bus.

Too sick at her lie to eat, she threw on her sandals and grabbed her purse before realizing she hadn't put on any makeup. But did it matter?

Of course, because if she went without, she'd no doubt run into a bazillion people she knew. And if she put it on, she'd end up seeing no one.

With a sigh, she decided on a quick swipe of mascara and eye liner just as someone knocked.

Startled, she hurried to the front door and looked through the peephole to see *Xavier*.

Her heart raced, and nerves flooded her.

The universe had apparently decided she should confront the victim of her ugly lies.

She opened the door to see him holding coffee and pastries, like the last time he'd come to visit.

With a groan, she welcomed him inside. "Hey, Xavier."

"Oh boy. You sound terrible. But you're up and dressed. What happened?"

She plunked herself at her kitchen table and sunk her head into her hands. "I have to apologize for something, and I'm so sorry. I just need you to hear me out."

He sat with her and took one of her hands in his. "Hey, you can tell me anything."

"You're making this so much harder." She sighed. Truthfully, what she'd done wasn't that terrible. But she felt as if she'd stepped over some line, perhaps harming their fragile trust with each other in some way. "My mom just called me."

"Uh-oh," he joked. He stroked her hand, and a shiver of pleasure stole through her. When he shifted, she smelled his cologne, a subtle scent that had her body waking up when she really needed it to stay asleep.

"Look, there's no easy way to say this." She stared him in the eyes, aware his were so incredibly pretty, a light brown ringed by a darker brown, filled with care and affection. She swallowed. "I lied to my mom and told her you were my plus-one when she said she'd decided I'd go with Cal."

He didn't falter in any way. "So you were 'assigned' someone else and decided to take me instead."

"Well, I lied. I, ah, kind of told my mom I'd met someone." She tried to tug her hand from his, but he didn't relax his grip, so she stilled. "I told her your name. I'm sorry. I just didn't want any entanglement with Cal. He's nice, but I don't want a date I didn't choose. And really, I should just be able to go alone so—"

"Do I need to get a tux?"

She blinked. "What?"

"Should I get a tux? How dressy is this thing going to be?"

The sight of him in a tux would take her breath away. "Um, I think a nice suit and tie would work." After a pause, she said, "You're not mad?"

"Not at all." He tightened his hand around hers then released her to put a coffee in front of her. He bit into a pastry and sighed. "These are so good. Have a bite." He held one out to her.

She automatically leaned forward and took a bite. "Delicious." She licked off a bit of cherry filling and saw him staring at her mouth.

All at once, she remembered that full-body hug, how warm and solid he'd felt against her. How good he smelled, how big he was when aroused. Her body reacted, her nipples beading, the need to squirm and soothe the tingling between her legs yet another sign she wanted him.

"Justine, I'm happy to help in any way I can."

Why did that sound super naughty? She read all sorts of implications that he probably didn't mean. "Any way?" she heard herself asking, unable to look away from the sensual curl of his lips.

"You know, I've been fighting this for a while."

She nodded, not sure what he was talking about. He scooted his chair closer, and she caught another whiff of his scent, pure sex wrapped in smiling eyes and an amazing body.

"I don't want to make you uncomfortable."

"I'm *so* uncomfortable right now. I might die if you don't kiss me," she admitted and swallowed audibly. "I can't believe I just said that."

His gaze trailed from her eyes to her lips, then farther down. She wondered if he noted her nipples poking through the thin dress.

"Can't have you dying on me," he breathed before leaning close to kiss her.

She froze at the feel of his lips against her, the soft scratch of his mustache and beard against her face. Then he slid his tongue through the seam of her mouth, and she sighed at how much she wanted to taste more.

He groaned and cupped her cheeks, angling her face so he could get more access to her mouth.

Justine had a tough time focusing on anything but the throbbing of her lower body. She'd never been so aroused, not from a simple kiss. His hands had yet to leave her face, yet she wanted them badly all over her. Cupping her breasts, between her legs, inside her...

She moaned her pleasure when he lifted her into his arms and straddled her over his lap. The kiss grew more insistent, his hands on her ass kneading, pulling her closer.

"Hmm. More," she murmured against his mouth and kissed him back, seeing stars behind her eyes. He made her feel tiny in his arms, the dichotomy of the careful way he held her yet the demanding nature of his kisses and caresses making it unbearable to sit still.

Before she knew it, she was grinding against him, the big bulge seated at the core of her making it impossible to not move. His kisses deepened, and his hands began to roam. But not fast enough.

She took his hand and plastered it over her breast.

At first he paused, then he squeezed, riding her nipple with his palm and causing her to rock faster over his lap. He pulled back from her, panting. "Fuck, Justine." He looked into her eyes and kissed her again. "Bedroom?"

She wished he hadn't paused, hadn't given her a chance to think. She needed him so badly...

"I want inside you," he growled and nudged up against her. "I'm ready to come right now."

The thought turned her inside out. "Yes. Yes, bedroom." Well, hurray for her managing to string a few words together. She groped his chest, so in lust with the muscle under palms. She rubbed against his nipples, saw his eyes darken, and pinched them.

"Condoms?" he asked, his voice hoarse. But he didn't let her answer, kissing her again, his hands pushing up the hem of her dress while he caressed her thighs, his thumbs achingly close to her panties yet not close enough to do her any real good.

She widened her legs, but still he kept teasing, kissing and petting and driving her wild with need. "I have condoms," she reminded him and was rewarded when his fingers moved under her panties, gliding between her slick folds.

She shuddered, and so did he. Then he removed his hand and sucked his finger clean.

"I hope you have more than one. Because we're going to need them."

CHAPTER 16

Xavier followed Justine on unsteady legs toward her bedroom. It was a struggle not to stop her, throw her up against the wall, and fuck her senseless. If he'd had a condom on hand, he would have. The woman felt like a dream and tasted like perfection.

In all his years, he'd never been so damn hard for a woman. And not just any woman. Justine did something to him he couldn't explain. He'd been a horny teenager. He'd been obsessed with sex in his early twenties. Always safe, always respectful. But he'd had enough intimate encounters to know when something was off.

And he was about to *go* off if he didn't get inside her soon.

That she was leading him made it all worse, because between those slender thighs, Justine was so wet and hot, so ready for him. He wanted this to be perfect but had a terrible feeling he was going to come too soon and prove himself a total douche.

He focused on his breathing, on needing to make it good for *her*. To hopefully not mess up anything between them, because his affection was growing. And this sharing of intimacy would no doubt make it much worse. Deeper.

God, need to get deeper in her...

They made it to the bedroom, which to his surprise remained as red and gaudy as it had been when Rosie had once given him a tour of the place. But he didn't have any time to indulge in his study because Justine shut the door behind them and pushed him against it, then kissed him senseless.

Her hand found its way down his pants, and his eyes rolled up his head. "No," he moaned, "not yet. Gonna come to soon."

She grinned against his mouth, and he turned them around so that her back was at the door. She yanked his shirt off while he toed off his shoes then pulled off her dress, leaving her in a lacy bra and panties. Not enough, not even close.

He knelt, pulled her panties to the side, and closed his mouth over her.

Heady with her scent, he licked and sucked her into an orgasm that had her yelling his name as she clutched his hair. Shivering, she gradually stopped gripping his head, pushing her fingers through his hair with urgency.

He kissed his way up her body after pulling her panties off. When he got to her bra, he unfastened it with shaky hands, so full of Justine that nothing else mattered.

Once her bra dropped, he feasted on her full breasts, sucking her nipples and wanting to get closer.

"Xavier," she pleaded and urged him to kiss her again.

While they kissed, she unsnapped his jeans, but he stilled her.

"Get them off," she insisted.

"Bossy, hmm?" He smiled, and she smiled back. He pushed down his jeans and underwear, not surprised to find it sticking to him, his arousal evident.

Before he could get to his socks, Justine pushed him to sit at the edge of her bed and knelt.

The sight of her between his legs had him aching, so ready to come. She took her time removing his socks, and when she kissed her way up his calves to his inner thighs, he nearly lost it.

"Justine, I'm not going to last. You are so fucking hot."

She smiled at him, and he noticed a dimple that should have made her cute and instead made her adorably sexy. "I like you hot. You and I mesh."

"I want to mesh with you so much," he said with a fervency that made her laugh.

"Don't come yet."

"I'm trying not to." He stared at her breasts, her long hair waving over her shoulders, offering him teasing glimpses of her nipples. Her hips ideal for him to hold onto while she'd ride him.

Then she pushed his legs wider and kissed his inner thighs, eventually licking her way to his balls.

"Yes, oh yeah, please," he urged, not sure what he was asking for.

Justine sucked his balls then ran her clever tongue up his shaft and licked him so that a burst of fluid shot into her mouth. Not an orgasm, not yet, but so close...

"Yum. Salty sweet," she said from between his legs.

He closed his eyes to slow down, the fantasy of her making it difficult to hold back. The pleasure-pain of having to wait the sweetest agony.

Then she slid the condom over him, and he tensed all over and opened his eyes.

She moved behind him, lay back on the bed, and spread her legs wide. "Do you need an invitation?"

He pounced, making her laugh then groan when he slid inside her in one big push, her swollen sex tight and wet and as close to heaven as he'd ever get while alive.

He kissed her while he moved, unable to keep still.

"So good," he crooned as he thrust in and out. He wanted to say they were making love, but at this point it was all about fucking. Taking. Her moans and breathy cries, the friction of their bodies, her sex gloving him with wet heat—all of it overwhelmed.

With a primal need, he moved faster, deeper, and heard her

cry out as he reached his end and jetted into her, coming so hard he couldn't think.

"Yes, Xavier, yes," she whispered and clenched her thighs tighter around him, her legs up around his waist, her ankles locked, as she drew him deeper inside.

He groaned and continued to come until he feared he'd black out. When he finally stopped, he blinked down at her. She wore a lazy grin, her eyes dark with passion, her smile wide.

"That was..." He had no words.

"Right? It really was..."

They both laughed. Xavier was moved by a wealth of affection for her, Justine's warmth and giving nature a balm to a man who constantly gave all of himself.

"Thank you so much for having condoms," he said.

"You, um, think we'll need more?" The blush on her cheeks enchanted him.

"For sure." He rotated his hips once and closed his eyes, still half hard and super sensitive. "I think you about killed me."

"Oh, yeah. Back at you." She lifted her arms to twirl the hair at the back of his neck. "You're still in me."

"Yeah. I need to take care of this." He slowly withdrew, left her to dispose of the condom in her bathroom, and cleaned up quickly before returning to her with a warm washcloth. He found her buried under her covers, a blush staining her cheeks.

"What's that for?"

"For you." He whipped the covers back.

"*Xavier.*"

"Hey, I've already seen you. No fair covering up all the goods."

"I still see your goods," she murmured. "I guess fair is fair." She put her hands behind her head on the pillow, trying for casual and failing badly.

"I can't imagine why you'd be embarrassed. You have the best body I've ever seen."

"Oh, stop." She bit her lip then laughed. "I do?"

"Yeah." He gently cleaned between her legs, wanting to take care of her. Wanting another taste of her... "So, um, I'm usually a big talker. Taking things slowly, being safe, you know the drill."

She tensed.

"But you got me so hot I couldn't think," he admitted. "We should probably talk fast before I forget myself and get inside you again. Justine, I know you just wanted to be friends. I'm trying, but..."

"Oh man. This is not how I wanted to talk about this. I'm still sorry for using your name with my mom." She cringed. "I'm naked and mentioned my mother. This is not going well."

He laughed. "See why talking can sometimes be overrated?"

She gave a slow smile. "Yeah."

"Quick chat—I'm clean."

"Me too. We always used condoms. Always."

"Yep. I didn't always with Christine, but totally did at the end. And I've had a checkup since then. All good from the doctor. I take my health seriously."

"I do too."

Justine's face had turned beet-red. She lay still, naked, while they talked. He knew it had to be killing her.

So after joining her in bed, he pulled the sheets over them. He lay on his side, watching her, and pushed her hair behind her ear. "Justine, I consider you a friend. I really don't want to mess up our relationship. You make me laugh, and I like just being with you."

She sighed. "You too. I feel the same."

"I can't help feeling attracted to you. I tried not to be, because sex can complicate things. But, well, I think it just made everything better between us."

She blinked. "You do?"

"Hmm. I must not have been doing it right." He leaned forward to kiss her and got lost in her taste, her touch. So that when he pulled back, he had her under him, rocking his half-hard cock against her belly and getting harder. "You are so sweet." He kissed her lips, her cheek, and whispered in her ear, "I want to lick you all over again. Swallow that cream and then fuck you so hard. You get me all worked up without even trying." He moaned when her fingers curled around him and squeezed. "Keep it up and I'll come all over your pretty sheets."

She kissed him back and teethed his ear, causing him to jolt. "You're pretty good at the dirty talk."

"I'm good at everything involving your body. Let me show you."

"I guess you really aren't mad at me for inviting you to the wedding."

"Not at all." He pushed deeper into her fist. "But if you don't want a mess, find me a new condom."

"Oh, quick on the trigger, hmm?"

He laughed, surprised at her humor since she seemed so shy with him. "With you, yeah." He sighed. "You taste good."'

"So do you."

"Hmm. I have an idea." He pushed the covers aside and kissed her. "Want to race?"

"Huh?"

He pulled her to get on top of him then urged her to her hands and knees. "Turn around."

She faced his erection while he stared up at her pussy, her legs spread wide.

"Oh, a race," she said before taking him to the back of her throat.

He jerked and arched up before doing his best to ease back. Then he yanked her hips down, her sex to his mouth. "Winner gets a shower. Loser has to do all the washing."

Her answer was to suck harder.

Needless to say, he ended up cleaning her when they finally made it to the shower.

Because his Justine was such a dirty, dirty girl.

CHAPTER 17

The Sunday movie made her laugh, and it took Justine's mind off yesterday's unreal time with Xavier.

After the amusing horror-comedy, she and Katie sat in their favorite diner for an early dinner when Katie said, "Okay, spill it. Something happened. I can tell. You're being weird."

"Define weird."

"It's not something I can put my finger on. You seem preoccupied."

"Um, yeah. With that movie we just saw."

"No, it's more than that. Tell me."

The server stopped by their table. "Ladies, can I take your order?"

After he left, Justine said to Katie, "Well, yesterday, ah, Xavier came over." She glanced around and lowered her voice, leaning toward her friend. "We had sex."

"*Yuss!*" Katie pumped her hand in the air.

"Shh." Justine frowned, and Katie hunched a little in her seat.

"Sorry. Well? I need specifics, woman."

Without going into too much detail, Justine confessed what had happened.

Katie just sat there for a moment. "Holy bananas. All morning long? Like, for *hours?*"

"Yeah." Justine sighed. "It was like a dream."

"Or a porn movie."

Justine flushed. "Indoor voice, Katie."

"Sorry, sorry. It's just... *Xavier.* Wow. I knew he had the hots for you. Obviously, you felt it too. So now what?"

"That's the weird thing. Our chemistry was crazy. I've never been with anyone like that before. Like, we were made for each other." She groaned. "That sounds so stupid, but I can't explain it."

"I get you. The hard part is when you have physical chemistry with someone but nothing else. So you think the great time between the sheets should equal a great relationship, and it doesn't." Katie huffed. "Although at this point, I'd settle for some great between-the-sheets action."

"Oh, so your last date didn't work out?"

"Work out? He was rude to the servers, drank too much, and insisted I split the bill, of which I really owed maybe a third. Needless to say, I told him never to call me again."

"You told him that to his face?"

"Of course not. He was obnoxious and drunk. After I shoved him into an Uber, I waited until the next day. Then I texted him and told him to lose my number. Haven't heard from him since."

"Ouch."

"Yeah, so if you have something golden with Xavier, why not go for it?"

"That's the weird thing." Justine paused while the server brought their food. As they ate, she continued, "We hugged and hung out for a while after all the sex. Then we talked about what happened. I swear, it felt surreal. I wasn't embarrassed or anything. Somehow, we agreed to continue being friends and not let what we did affect that."

"So he friend-zoned you after he got what he wanted?" Katie looked disappointed.

"Nope. He asked me what *I* wanted. We're staying friends and just friends because *I* want to."

"Really? You don't want to date him?"

"I do, but I don't." Justine sipped her drink and thought about it. "I mean, I'd love a relationship with someone who put me first for once. But I don't want to tempt fate by losing the first guy friend I've had in... Well, in forever. Xavier's so great. He doesn't push me for anything I don't want to give. But maybe that's because we're just friends right now. And yes, before you're skeevy little mind can add 'with benefits,' fine, with benefits. But I think maybe we should just keep it to that one time."

"You mean that one morning."

Justine grinned. "It was a morning I'll always treasure."

They ate in silence for a bit before Katie said, "I see your point. I mean, you and Xavier are vibing as friends. You need more friends, and guys give you a perspective we just don't have. I have to say, I like the guy. He's pretty funny and seems self-confident. He held his own with you on Friday night, and apparently on Saturday."

"Katie."

Katie laughed. "You know what I mean. I'm happy for you, really."

After a pause, Justine nudged her. "But...?"

"But I think you're letting fear of failure stop you from maybe having a kickass boyfriend. Before you come at me, I know you just got out of a mess with Mitch. And you really should have quality me-time before hooking up with someone else. Normally. But how many Xaviers are there? He's handsome, smart, independent, funny, and likes you for you. I'm just saying. Friendship is great, but so is the possibility for more. Just think about it."

"I know. You're right. But it feels..." Justine didn't know how to explain it. Her sexual marathon with Xavier had been idyllic.

Almost unreal. Then she'd floated back down to earth to have a mature conversation with a man who wanted to let her set the pace. Xavier hadn't pressured her or made her feel awkward for having been with him. She'd never experienced that kind of liberation before, and she wanted to see where that feeling took her.

Plus, he'd been adamant that he didn't want their friendship to change. Knowing he valued her for more than her boobs gave her all the warm fuzzies.

Katie put a hand over Justine's on the table. "I'm not badgering you. I swear. I only want my best friend to be happy."

Justine glanced at their hands and smirked. "Does this mean I'm on a higher tier of best friend than Jon?" Katie's other best pal and a really funny guy. Unfortunately, Justine and he never seemed to be in the same place at the same time. He had a very odd schedule.

"Yes, but don't tell him that." Katie looked around, as if Jon would pop up unexpectedly. "Besides, he doesn't need me as much. He's got a fiancé now."

"No kidding?" Justine blinked. "Who? When did this happen?"

"It just happened, like, yesterday." Katie frowned. "I want to be happy for him. I really do. But I have some reservations. He's so smart and funny. I don't know about Alan. He seems a lot more needy than is healthy. But he's buff and famous—he models—and I think Jon's blinded by all that."

"He was pretty handsome." And a bit narcissistic, in Justine's opinion. Having met him and Jon two weeks ago at the bar, she hadn't been overly impressed with Jon's boyfriend. "I think you might be right. Jon can do so much better."

While they continued eating and Katie gossiped about Jon and his many exes, Justine considered the state of her own personal life. She still couldn't believe she and Xavier had hooked up, that it had been so good, and that she felt comfortable where they'd left things.

Normally, Justine dated men who liked to make the rules. But this time she was in the driver's seat. And not because Xavier was trying to control her in some weird way or make her feel responsible for the totality of their friendship. She genuinely liked the fact that he respected her.

Huh. Had she ever been friends with a guy before dating him?

She didn't think so. Most of the guys she'd dated she'd first met through friends or dating apps. The whole point of meeting each other had been to gauge a potential love interest. But Xavier had been a friend first. Not had been, *was still* a friend.

She felt good about her choices and paid more attention to Katie's complaining, hoping she and he could make their odd friendship work.

♡

Tuesday, Justine's boss from hell pulled her into his office for her yearly review.

Finally.

"Justine, I so love working with you. Your drive and dedication to the company are what make Mayze Creative such a great place." Frank beamed with enthusiasm. "Now let's talk about your projects."

Frank appeared especially slick today, his dark hair styled just so, the wattage of his bright white smile and the approval in his light eyes shining. He had his *Best Boss* mug turned to face her, and even that didn't make him look like a putz. The guy could sell anything to anyone. Charismatic yet incompetent at the same time. Why couldn't she have that same gene? Instead, Justine came across as pleasant and smart but weak. A pretty doormat, she'd once heard her father say of her.

Trying to push her father's voice away, she focused instead on the paper file Frank read from.

They poured over her positive client feedback before

touching on several projects of Frank's she'd helped with. He had nothing but glowing praise for her, and her excitement over her pending raise grew.

"You are a wonderful addition to the team, as I said before. So I wanted to extend Laura's role to you. She recently left the company, and it was a minor position, but you're so capable, we think you're a good fit for it. And of course, there's that raise we promised you." He mentioned a figure lower than she'd anticipated.

It took her a moment to understand what he'd said. "Wait. So I'm moving into Laura's job?"

"In addition to the one you have now."

He must have seen her confusion, because he explained, "The company is going through a restructuring, and you know what that means." A fake laugh. "Fortunately, you have no worries about staying on. You're a team player, and I made sure to let the higher-ups know that."

"Thank you." *For stating the truth.* But she had to make sense of his words. "Just to be clear, I'm getting a raise lower than I was promised when I signed on. And you're giving me another job as well?"

"What? No, no. That's not what I'm saying. I'm sorry for the confusion."

She nodded, glad to have been misinformed. Then Frank told her exact same thing but in different words. He called Laura's job important but low effort, and they needed someone smart to take over the responsibility. A team player who would serve the company's needs without a problem.

Without the pay.

"I'm sorry, Frank. I just keep hearing that I need to do more work. The work of *two* people, yet I'm only getting paid for one position, and at much less than our competitors'." She knew because she'd looked.

Frank appeared disappointed. "I'm sorry if I'm not explaining it to you correctly."

Oh no, I understood you perfectly.

"It's just... A lot of our people were let go. I fought to keep your position. But not because I'm a great boss or anything," he said, trying to downplay his ability that didn't actually exist. "But because you deserve it. You've been nothing but a help to me and this department."

You need to earn your place, she heard her father say time and time again. *We Ferreras have always had to work twice as hard as others because we don't come from money, but we manage to rise to the top. Adversity is just an obstacle, Justine. Quitting gets you nowhere. Keep working on* you *and you'll see.*

She did know that several people had left the company, but from what she'd heard, it was to take better employment—with a commensurate salary—elsewhere.

Frustrated and let down, she felt on the verge of tears. Not at all how a professional would handle a meeting with her boss.

She swallowed down her disappointment. "Thank you for the meeting, Frank."

He smiled, relief clear on his face. "Good. Well, why don't you take off early today?"

She glanced at the clock on his wall. She only had another fifteen minutes before her day ended. What a guy.

"I'll have Rebecca send over Laura's workload, so you should have it first thing in the morning."

With nothing more to say, she stood, nodded to him, and left.

Her drive felt empty, her thoughts and feelings all over the place. Needing to take the edge off, once home, she dressed in running clothes and made herself more miserable by running to exhaustion.

She returned home as the sun set and sat on a bench in the inner courtyard, trying to let the soothing sounds of the fountain wash away her worries.

All the comebacks she should have shot at lazy-ass Frank came to her, some more vitriolic than others. A lot of cursing, slurs on his parentage, his laziness, and those bleached teeth fighting for prominence.

But worst of all, she sweltered under a terrible self-loathing, her inability to stand up for herself a mire of self-disgust that threatened to drown her.

"Well, neighbor. Fancy meeting you here." Xavier slid into the bench next to her. He looked her over and frowned. "Hey, Justine. What's wrong?"

She burst into tears. Not only had her boss made her feel like a submissive retriever, but her recent lover was now seeing her at her absolute worst.

What else could go wrong?

CHAPTER 18

Xavier wanted badly to offer comfort, but Justine held herself distant, hugging herself while trying to scrub away her tears.

Looking at her sadness tore his heart out, but he did his best to offer what *she*—not *he*—needed. "Talk to me, Justine. What happened?"

She sniffled and wiped her nose on the back of her arm. "Sorry. Bad day at work."

"Want to talk about it? I swear, I'll just sit here and listen."

She wiped her eyes, and even with lids lined with red and her face splotchy, she looked lovely. "I, well, I feel like an absolute loser."

He just nodded, turning his entire body to face her, and waited.

Justine let out a breath. "God, I'm so sorry. I feel like a pathetic asshole." The swearing only emphasized how frazzled she must truly be. "I just had my yearly review at work."

Ah, professional and not personal issues. He felt better about possibly being able to offer comfort without seeming like he was shoving advice at her. The poor woman already had enough on her plate with her sister's upcoming wedding.

"And?" he prompted.

She let it all out, a deluge of opinions and a recap of her conversation with her pathetic team manager. Her boss sounded like a horse's ass, using Justine all the time without offering the pay for her hard work.

"And you know, he would have been demoted so many times if I hadn't helped out. All when *he* needed to take personal time or just schmooze it up with the bosses while *I* did all the work." She sniffed. "Well, not just me. But a lot of it was me. I had to help my own clients in addition to Frank's work. And now, not only do I get a subpar raise, which to be honest, is just keeping up with inflation. It's not what I'm worth at all. Then he has the gall to dump Laura's job on me without pay! Sure, her gig was part-time, but that's not the point! I'll be working two jobs for less than what one of them should be." She tugged at her hair. "He's such a fuckhead."

He nodded. "A dickwad."

"A real shit for brains." She added several other insults.

Then a younger voice added, "How about a fart-knocker?"

She and Xavier paused as Sam joined them.

Justine's face turned bright red.

"Hi, Justine. You look pretty today." Sam flirted for all he was worth and managed to squeeze between her and Xavier on the bench. "I'm sorry you had a bad day."

"Sorry I cursed. I didn't know you were around."

"It's okay." Sam patted her knee. "I hear a lot worse at school."

"When's your last day?" Xavier asked, amused at how Sam tried to cut him away from Justine.

The boy turned to him, subtly sliding closer to Justine. "This Friday, actually. Uncle Adam and Rylan and me are going on vacation for a week in Hawaii."

"Wow. That's awesome." Justine gave him a smile. "I bet you'll have a great time."

"You should come," Sam said.

"Ah, that sounds more like a family vacation. Plus, I have work."

"You should quit. That Frank guy sounds like a real dickass."

Justine covered her face.

"That's pretty good," Xavier said, doing his best not to laugh. "What else you do you have?"

"Douchenoggin is pretty popular at school. Or deadshit. Then there's assclown."

"What grade are you in again?"

"Ninth. Almost. In two more days, actually." Sam puffed up his chest. "If you want, Justine, I can talk to the dickass for you."

"Um, no, that's okay." She patted him on the shoulder, and the kid looked like he'd been knighted by the queen. "For being such a nice guy, how about the next time I go for ice cream, I grab you a cone? Xavier, you too."

Sam shot him a dirty look but was all smiles at Justine. "Sounds good. I like chocolate with sprinkles."

"Vanilla with sherbet," Xavier said. "Though if you wanted to be fancy, rainbow jimmies are the best."

"What's a jimmie?" Sam had to know.

Xavier explained the difference between jimmies and sprinkles. They were different names for the same thing, but it gave Sam something over which to argue.

"Sam, where..." Adam sighed as he walked over. "Boy, did I not tell you to at least leave a note if you go out?"

"Hey, Uncle Adam." Sam nodded to his uncle, who was still dressed in his uniform and looked beyond tired. "Can you believe this douchnozzle calls sprinkles jimmies?"

Xavier noticed that Justine seemed much happier than she'd been when he joined her, and he had to hand it to Sam for distracting her from her terrible day.

But after the boy left with his uncle, Justine's expression drooped.

"Hey, tell you what." He shouldn't. He'd been doing his best to give her space, to let her come to him on her terms. It had been a hellish two days. Three counting today, but she needed a distraction. "Why don't you go clean up and come on down to my place? We can watch whatever you want, and I'll make you dinner or snacks if you already ate."

"You don't have to do that."

"I want to."

She gave him a slow smile. "I'd like that." Her stomach rumbled. "And I guess I'm hungry after all."

"Fish okay?"

"Perfect." She leaned close and kissed him on the cheek. "Thanks, Xavier."

"Don't thank me yet. The last time I baked fish, Auggie said I overcooked it."

She laughed and walked away. "I'll see you in twenty minutes."

"Bring it, Ferrera."

TWENTY MINUTES later on the dot, as Xavier put together a nice medley of veggies to go with the fish, a knock came at the door. "It's open."

Justine entered, her hair damp and long, wearing shorts and a cropped sweatshirt. She still looked tired but not as downtrodden.

"I have wine, beer, water, and lemonade. Pick your poison. Glasses are to the left of the sink." He nodded to the cabinet. "Once you have what you want, just sit pretty and compliment me."

She helped herself to a glass of wine and sat at the kitchen island, watching him. "Nice ass."

He couldn't help laughing. "Thanks. By compliment me, I

meant about my cooking. Though I'll take a 'nice ass' any day of the week."

She snickered and drank her wine. "Thanks for letting me vent. I swear, I wanted to punch my boss the minute he mentioned my 'raise.' He was so nice about what a great worker I am, only to smash my soul under his Paul Stuart knockoffs."

"Should I know what those are?"

"They're nice shoes. My dad owns a few pair. The Giordano dress shoe is a thousand bucks. I doubt Frank can afford the real thing. Although, he does kiss up a lot. Maybe he did buy Paul Stuarts. Who knows?" After a pause, she lifted her head to sniff. "That smells fantastic."

"Fresh caught salmon in a teriyaki glaze. We'll also have rice pilaf, a Caesar salad, and some veggies."

"I'm drooling already."

He smiled. "How have you been since Sunday…not counting today?"

"I saw the latest horror-comedy at the movies with Katie. It was really funny." She mentioned one of his favorite actors, and they discussed the guy's films while he finished putting dinner together.

The conversation felt so effortless. He laughed and bantered, plated their meals and watched her set the table without being asked. They worked well together.

He kept telling himself not to make more out of their relationship, a weird mix of friendship, lust, and companionship he wanted more of. Breaking out of bad patterns—rushing affection—could only help him grow as a person.

But it was difficult, sitting across from a beautiful woman he didn't want to leave. *Stop being a tool. Cherish your time together and don't be so damned weird about the future.* He pledged to do better and made a conscious effort to only focus on making her feel better.

After dinner, he convinced her to sit with him on the couch

and watch some TV. She chose a dark show about a vigilante killing people in all manner of ways.

"Should I be worried about this bloodthirsty streak of yours?"

She snuggled into his side, and he let his arm fall over her shoulders, saying nothing, not wanting to jinx the moment. She poked him in his ribs. "Yes, be very worried. If you even think about giving me someone else's job without pay, I'll find a way to blow up your brain."

He chuckled. "Hell, all you have to do for that is to get me in a room with clients who keep repeating the same mistakes and refuse to change because they know better."

"Yet they keep coming to you for advice."

"Which they don't ever take. I typically have to ask what they want out of our therapy sessions and eventually refer them to other people. Because I'm obviously not helping them and I feel guilty about taking their money."

"Aw, a nice guy." She snuggled deeper into him, and he swallowed a sigh of contentment.

"I really am. Super nice." He hovered his hand over her head, then said screw it and stroked her hair. The caress soothed him as well, despite the swearing and decapitations on the screen.

After a brief silence between them, Justine asked, "Is it weird how relaxing this is? Even though our hero just cut through another dozen people?"

He laughed. "I was just thinking that." He let himself fully unwind and sank into the sofa. "I'm feeling pretty mellow as well."

Two hours later, he blinked his eyes open and realized they'd both fallen asleep.

"Xavier?"

He glanced down at Justine. "I think we fell asleep."

"I know. Sorry." She mumbled something as she pushed up to a sitting position next to him.

"What's that?"

She blushed. "I just said I hoped I didn't drool on you."

"Hey, what's a little drool between friends?"

She chuckled and stood. Then she stretched, and he did his damnedest not to stare at her flat, toned stomach. "Guess I'd better get home."

"I'll walk you up."

They left without any of the awkwardness he kept waiting to settle. At her door, she turned and gave him a brief kiss on the mouth.

"Come over tomorrow," he blurted as she entered her apartment.

"Tomorrow?"

He nodded. "Auggie's coming over. We're heading to Benji's for a game night."

"You sure Benji won't mind me coming over?"

"Nah. He likes you. You converted him with all that gaga talk about *Arrow Sins & Siege*."

She grinned. "Sounds like a plan. And thanks for listening to me."

He wanted to know what she had planned in regards to her job. But she seemed so relaxed now, he didn't want to ruin her mood. "Anytime. I mean that."

"Thanks." She looked as if she wanted to invite him inside, but she didn't.

He took a step back and waved. "Tomorrow night at seven, work? I'll text you."

"Sounds good. Bye." She closed the door.

He walked back downstairs and went to bed early.

He slept soundly, though his bed felt empty without Justine next to him.

CHAPTER 19

Justine expected her day to go terribly.

It didn't disappoint.

She spent the morning doing her best to catch up on all her work so she could take the time to look over her *new* job. All the while, she tried to figure out how to explain this to Katie without Katie having a meltdown.

She grinned, remembering her time with Xavier the previous night, where people had literally melted down and spazzed in gory ways on TV.

What an amazing guy. A true friend. He'd listened, not making any moves at all while accepting her need to cuddle. She wondered why just being with him, minus all the hot sex, felt as intimate as time with Xavier without her clothing. So odd, yet exhilarating. Xavier remained a bright spot while in her dungeon of an office she shared with other prisoners. Heck, no one looked all that happy today, all of them hunkered behind cubicle walls.

At least the day passed swiftly, probably because she did her best to avoid facing Frank. The two times she'd spotted him she'd deliberately walked the other way. She didn't care if he knew she was upset; she just couldn't face him yet.

Couldn't face her own disappointing behavior at letting him step all over her.

By the time the day ended, she'd promised to join Katie for a quick drink at a nearby coffee shop.

She met Katie there. To her surprise, an old friend from design school sat with her.

"Oh my gosh. Kenzie?"

Kenzie stood and smiled. "Justine Ferrera, still hanging out with this one?" She nodded at Katie. "You poor thing."

Justine laughed and gave her old friend a hug. "How the heck are you?"

As Kenzie filled them in on her life, now married and eight-weeks pregnant, she admitted to still working with her best friends, who, in Justine's opinion, were even wackier than Katie.

"I know. It's incredible that I'm still with those same idiots." Kenzie snorted. "And 'idiot' is a compliment. You should hear what they call me."

"So a husband, a kid, your brother who still lives with you, and your business, which just got a huge mention?" Katie pulled out a copy of a popular trade magazine and showed it to Justine.

"Oh yeah. I read that. I can't believe how great you're doing! I mean, I can. You're super talented. But you have just taken off."

Kenzie nodded. "We got an account with a new vegan place that has gone viral. My peeps are hot on several social media platforms, and it shows. We're busier now than we've ever been."

Katie looked from Kenzie to Justine. "You looking for any employees?"

Justine wanted to throttle her friend. "Katie."

Kenzie laughed. "Not quite yet, but we're getting there. I still don't know why you never went private, Justine. You know how to engage clients and their customers. Katie and I were talking about the company. We did some freelance work for Mayze. It was, well, it was interesting."

Katie snorted. "That's business-speak for sucky."

"You said it. Not me."

Justine shrugged. "What can I say? I'm stuck in a job I hate but not sure where to go if I leave. And no, that's not a poke to see if you're hiring, Kenzie." She shot Katie a look.

Her friend cringed. "Sorry. I'm just putting a line out there for you."

"Never a bad thing to do." Kenzie agreed. "Look, if I hadn't needed a flexible schedule due to raising my troublesome teenage brother, I would probably have taken the offer a prominent PR firm gave me way back then. But I had to do things my own way. I'm not saying that's better than working for a company."

"You mean working for 'The Man,'" Katie said.

"'The Man,' right." Kenzie chuckled. "I'm just saying working independently fits me and my friends. But it's not without its own problems. Finding and keeping clients, having your own insurance, no paid sick or vacation days."

"But you're happy," Katie said.

"Yeah. Like I said, it works for me. Have you guys thought about doing your own thing?"

Katie nodded, to Justine's surprise. "I have. I ended up getting a great boss at Mayze or I would have quit. I keep telling Justine she needs to branch out on her own."

"But it's scary," Justine said. "Just as you said, no more benefits, no more schedule, no more clients." She sighed. "All the freedom of being my own boss and all the risks."

"That's the truth." Kenzie paused to drain her water bottle. "I totally had—and still have—those same fears. But the more work we do, the better we get." She studied Justine. "We're overflowing with needy clients. If you want to start freelancing, I can totally divert some work your way. Just let me know." She checked her phone. "Dang it. I have to go. Evan's freaking out about dinner."

Justine had a pang of envy, that her friend seemed to have everything Justine wanted. But Kenzie had gone through a lot of negative experiences to get there. Her parents dying, raising her brother on her own. Friends but no family... Except it seemed like Kenzie had a family in her friends.

Kind of like Xavier and Katie. My friends who feel like family.

At least, Katie did. Justine still wasn't sure what to make of Xavier.

Kenzie left them with promises of a future lunch date, and Katie turned to Justine. "Okay, woman. Tell me exactly how your review went. I heard from Rebecca, who said you didn't look happy after leaving Frank's office."

"I'll tell you, but only if you promise to just listen and not tell me what I should have said or done after my review."

"Oh boy. I'm going to need something stronger than tea for this." She left and returned with a plate of sticky buns. "You eat too, or I'll feel guilty."

"You don't have to twist my arm." Justine took a bite of sugary goodness and explained how awful her review had gone.

After, they sat in silence while Katie drew a finger through the leftover cinnamon sugar from the plate and licked her finger clean. "Am I to understand you now have two jobs for less than the price of one?"

"Yep." Justine tried to keep a straight face.

Katie studied her. "Oh, Justine. I'm sorry."

She teared up, though she'd been doing so well throughout her day. "Me too." She blinked to clear her vision. "I'm still thinking about how to handle this."

"So you're not just going to take Frank's bullshit. Good." Katie glared. "I'm so done with that asshole. He treats you like crap, and everyone knows he's only golden because of the work he gets others to do for him. The senior staff on the team know he can't bully them, while you're their punching bag." Katie took a deep breath then let it out. "Sorry. I got carried away."

Justine patted her shoulder. "Don't worry about it. I got carried away yesterday, trust me." She finished off her latte. "I cried when I got home. Then guess what? My thirteen-year-old neighbor gave me a list of insults to use on Frank, and Xavier made me dinner."

Katie sat up straighter. "Oh?"

"It was awesome. The food was incredible. I ended the night by falling asleep on him after we watched *Retribution III*."

"I love that movie!"

"I know."

"All that gore and violence. Five stars, totally." A funny comment coming from a perky blonde who took *cute* to new levels. "Xavier's quite the friend, hmm?"

"Stop it with that look."

"What? What look?"

"We're just friends." At Katie's smirk, Justine grumbled, "Yes, with benefits. But I'm calling the shots. In fact, I'm heading to his place tonight for game night with his twin sister and our neighbor. Want to come?"

"Nope. I have a hot date with Jon." Katie's eyes sparkled. "He broke up with Alan. I'm so happy but sad for him. So I have to practice looking as if I'm upset Jon ended things. How's this?" She made a few faces, none of which looked genuine.

"I'm not believing any of those. But I'm confused. Why did they break up? They just got engaged."

Katie frowned. "Yeah, well, apparently Alan got an invite to a fashion week in Venice. And he didn't want Jon to come with him. They argued, and it turns out Alan likes to sleep around with fellow professionals. He calls it networking. Jon calls it cheating. But Alan can't bother to be tied down right now when his career is skyrocketing." She paused. "Poor Jon. He's acting all mad, but I think it's more that he's hurt."

"Oh man. Want me to cancel and come over to offer moral support?"

Katie squeezed her hand. "That's so sweet. But it's okay. I'm picking up Jon's favorite pizza and beer. We're going to bond over sucky men. You go have fun with game night. And Xavier." Katie wiggled her brows.

"Well, if you're sure."

"I love, ya, kid. But you have your own bullshit to deal with. You go have fun with Xavier and his friends. And don't forget to contact Kenzie about some freelance work. You need to figure out your job situation. The sooner the better."

"I know, and—" Her phone buzzing interrupted her. "Hold on." She answered. "Hello? Mom?"

After a few minutes, Justine hung up and just stared at the empty plate in front of her.

"That didn't sound good." Katie stacked their dishes. "What's this about dinner Thursday night?"

Justine groaned. "My mom wants to meet Xavier. She invited us for a family dinner."

"Like I said, you have your own bullshit to deal with." Katie shook her head. "I'm so glad my parents are low-middle class with only one kid who will probably never get married."

"That's you."

"Duh. And I'm on the outs with relationships. Between your sisters, Jon, and my handful of one-date exes, I'm taking a break from the peen."

Justine burst into laughter. "God, Katie."

"Yep. Just me and the job. I'm only allowing myself one piece of trouble in my life at a time. You, girl, are juggling three."

"Three?"

"Don't forget, you're only in your aunt's place for the next two and a half months, unless she extends her vacation. So you have to deal with your sister's wedding, your job, and finding a new place to live."

"Thanks so much for reminding me." Justine swallowed a sigh.

"Keeping it real for you. Enjoy game night with the hottie from 2C."

"I think I will." Justine stood and glared down at her friend. "After all, the rest of my life really sucks right now."

"Exactly what I said. So if you're smart, you'll ride any part of the happy train and not look back. Now get out of here. I have to go comfort my other BFF about a loser ex-fiancé. Be grateful you get to go see Xavier and enjoy life while you can."

"You have a point."

"Don't I always?"

CHAPTER 20

Justine arrived home, cleaned up, and changed into comfort clothing. As if taking off her work clothes could divorce her from her work problems entirely.

She texted Xavier about game night and received an invite to pop down whenever she was ready. He seemed so relaxed all the time, and she wondered about his lifestyle as she made her way to his apartment. Though Xavier had said he was on a hiatus from his job, surely he'd need to go back soon. Would he still have the free time to meet with her? And what about when she left the Tuscan Cosmo Apartments? Would they see each other then?

Alarmed at the prospect of losing him, she knocked and let herself inside when he yelled for her to come in.

She wasn't prepared for the sight of him without a shirt on.

He smiled, holding a shirt in hand. "Hey, Justine. How was today? Good, I hope." He tugged the shirt over his head, and it took her a moment to gather her thoughts.

Xavier had a broad chest sculpted with muscle. He didn't have so much chest hair that he looked like a rug, but he had enough to look just her type—manly but not furry. Muscular but not pro weight-lifter muscular. And that smile... His eyes shone like bright pennies, and right at her.

"I, ah, today was okay. Not great, but I met an old friend after work. It was good seeing her." She meant that. She'd liked Kenzie back in college, and it made her feel good to know that Kenzie was seeing real success, especially in their shared field.

"Nice. Nothing better than seeing old friends. Unless you hated them. Then that's not great unless they've gotten ugly and divorced seventeen times."

"Ha. Yeah. But no, Kenzie's super great. She's married, pregnant, and running a successful business." *Everything I want,* she realized. To include the pregnant part. "I'm already twenty-nine."

"What's that?"

"Oh, nothing." She felt silly for thinking of babies around Xavier. Though thoughts of mentioning the B-word, just to see his expression, made her laugh.

"I'm missing the joke."

"Nah, just me being a goof. So what are we doing tonight? *Arrow Sins & Siege* or another game?"

"I don't know. Whatever Benji picks. Truthfully, I'm only invited to keep things smooth between him and Auggie. My sister is tough on the most extroverted of folks."

"That's true." She cleared her throat and hastily added, "But in a good way."

"Nice save." He laughed with her. "Look, I love Auggie, but I'm not blind to the fact she's a bit much to take in large doses. And poor Benji. So smart but so stuck in his own head all the time."

"How is it you always sound like a therapist but you never make me uncomfortable when you do?"

"We're not all pushy, trying to *shrink* everyone, you know."

"I know." She caught his teasing and eased into a smile. "I'm just... Do you miss working with patients?" A different way of asking if he intended to get back to work.

"I do, actually." He sounded surprised and stroked his jaw,

making him look like an academic despite the shorts and tee-shirt. "I'm on a break because I needed to regroup and wanted to work on a side project. But I'm probably going to head back to the office in July. But not until after the wedding, so no worries."

"Oh, about that. My mom called me today."

"Uh-oh."

"Ha. Yeah." She sighed. "We're invited to a family dinner tomorrow night. You can say no."

"I'm dying to meet your family. Heck no. I want to go."

"Oh man. Xavier, they will be annoying and intrusive. My dad's a snob, which is weird because he never had money growing up. Most of what he has now he earned before I hit high school. I didn't grow up being rich or anything, though we were always comfortable." She grimaced. "Sorry to ramble. Money is not a taboo topic with my family. They talk about it constantly."

"Hey, don't worry. I'm great with parents. They'll love me."

"Ugh. They're so annoying."

He frowned. "Would you rather I didn't go?"

"Huh? Oh, no. Not at all. I just don't want them to put you off. I like you."

He looked her over and smiled. "I like you too. Especially when you dress like this."

"Like a slob?"

He laughed. "I guess. I meant without makeup or anything fancy. I like regular, funny, slobby Justine."

"Slobby. Very funny." She snickered.

The look in his gaze heated her up and had her heart racing.

He stalked her until she had her back against the wall in the hallway.

"Xavier?"

"Justine." He gave her the whisper of a kiss, and her body tightened all over. "I can't stop thinking about you." He planted his hands on the wall on either side of her head. "I missed you last night when you went home."

"You did?" So it wasn't just her.

"Yeah." He kissed her again, the pressure firmer but still not enough. "Sorry. I know I shouldn't do this, but—"

She yanked him closer and kissed him breathless. So much for taking things slowly with him. She wanted him now. *Right now.* And in case he didn't get the message, she kicked off her shoes, shorts, and panties and dragged his shorts and underwear down to grip his cock.

"Oh, damn." He groaned and kissed her back.

She kept pumping him while his hands sought the heat of her, gripping her breast in one hand, her pussy with nimble fingers.

He let her go, took a step back, and dragged a condom out of his shorts pocket. Then it was on. He picked her up, her back against the wall, and shoved inside her.

The rush of sensation had her coming soon after, and he took her with speed and intensity, coming right after she did.

She could only breathe, still awash in pleasure, as he held her against the wall, pinning her there with his body, his big cock buried inside her. They panted as if they'd run a marathon, and she let all her cares go, replete in being wanted and satisfied by her lover.

"Justine, sweetheart," he murmured as he kissed her, his hands hot against her ass. "You're amazing."

She kissed him back, loving their relaxed play, now that the urgent need had been taken care of. "You too, studly."

His laugh turned into a groan. "Uh-oh, shouldn't have laughed."

She could feel him falling out of her.

"Be right back." He left for the bathroom but quickly returned, his clothes straightened, to find her all put together as well. "Aw, you got dressed."

She tried not to blush but couldn't help it. "I didn't want to chance your sister showing up and getting an eyeful."

He blinked. "Hell. I hadn't even thought of that."

"Well, I did. And I'm going to take a pass on game night." She pulled him close and kissed him, reveling in his scent and taste. "Not because I don't want to, but because I'm so relaxed I'm going to just enjoy it. If your sister sees me, no matter how put together I am, she'll know what we did."

He groaned. "She will, and she'll give you the third degree about it."

"Great minds think alike."

He kissed her back and hugged her. "Great minds. Great bodies. Great sex."

"Yeah." She let him hold her, and she didn't want to move.

His phone buzzed. "That's probably Auggie."

"My cue to leave."

"Are we..." He followed her to the door. "Are we still okay?"

"We are perfect." *For now,* she thought but didn't say, starting to feel more for him than she was comfortable with. "Go have fun with Benji and Auggie. I'll see you tomorrow night at six, and we can rehearse before dinner with my family."

"Now I'm worried."

"You don't look worried."

He gave her a wide smile. "That's because I can't forget that you called me studly. And you came all over me. That will live on in my mind forever."

"Xavier." She shook her head, her cheeks hot. "Tease. I need to go if your sister is coming."

"Run away. Escape while you can." He stopped her at his door and kissed her again, his hands cupping her cheeks with care and making her so very, very pliant. "Get home before I forget myself and fuck you all over again."

"Hold on. I'm thinking."

He winked and opened the door. "Might want to run. I can sense my twin coming up the stairs."

She hurried away, ignoring his laugh and enjoyed her evening doing nothing.

Until she thought about what awaited them the next night and allowed herself a mini-freakout.

♡

Ensconced in Benji's gamer cave—what he called his living room—Auggie took one look at her brother and knew he was a lot happier than normal. And for such an upbeat guy, that was saying something. She glanced at Benji, looked at Xavier, and raised a brow. Benji gave a subtle shrug.

She should have known better than to try to get an opinion from the tall nerd, but come on, anyone with a brain could see her brother practically glowing.

Had to be the chick upstairs.

Justine in 3D, who had been invited but backed out of game night at the last minute.

Hmm.

Even without the naughty neighbor, Auggie enjoyed game night at Benji's, especially because he seemed to finally be thawing in her presence. She didn't know what she'd done to annoy him, but for the past few months, he seemed to freeze up whenever she came around.

And that was a shame, because she saw a lot of cuteness under that godawful hair.

"Justine canceled because her parents are getting under her skin," Xavier announced after they'd spent an hour eating pizza and playing a few rounds using all new characters in Benji's new game-test design.

"I know the feeling," Auggie muttered, not pleased with her mom lately. "Mom not only had a mediocre date with your guy, but she stood mine up. Although, I guess Mike wasn't the best with his hit or miss plans. Still, she made no attempt to get together with him after their last cancelation."

"Huh?" Benji looked confused.

"Our mom is out on the dating scene again, and Xavier and I are helping find her a man."

"Oh, that's nice." He easily defeated an ogre king with nothing more than a poisonous vine.

Auggie leaned toward his big screen monitor, approving his home decor more than she'd thought she would. Though a bachelor, Benji had nice, comfy furniture that he kept organized and clean. Or at least, he'd cleaned up before company arrived.

She liked his style, a mix of contemporary and futuristic accents. A lot of neon against black and white. It was fun—the opposite of what nerd-guy projected. Benji in the wild didn't fit. He always seemed stressed or unhappy. Here, in his home, he had relaxed and let himself be seen as a fun-loving guy with a surprisingly muscular build.

She'd been subtly eyeing him all night, still surprised to realize that without the bad and baggy clothes, the guy was seriously ripped. He also had pretty, dark-blue eyes. Huh.

"How are you killing everyone with vines?" she asked, annoyed to be losing. "I thought this game was brand new."

"It is. We're demoing it." He shrugged those broad shoulders she wanted to measure. "Hey, can you grab me another slice?" he directed to Xavier.

"That's like a whole pizza pie," she grumbled, which had her brother laughing.

"Don't mind her, Benji. Auggie doesn't like to lose." After handing Benji another slice, her brother excused himself for the bathroom, and she fled the couch to corner Benji in his chair.

"Hey."

"What's up with Xav and Justine?"

Benji flushed and tried to peer around her at the screen. "No clue."

"Liar." She yanked the game controller from his hands and tossed it on the couch behind her.

"Hey."

"You already said that." She invaded his personal space by straddling his lap, standing on her knees so that the only place they touched were knees to thighs. To her surprise, even on her knees, she had to look up to meet his gaze.

She'd managed to mute him, and he stared at her in shock, which was an improvement from avoidance or the stammering he normally engaged in.

She nodded. "Now quit stalling, nerd-boy. You know something. Tell me, Benji."

He remained quiet, his gaze glued to her lips.

A funny flush of heat filled her, one that typically didn't exist when confronted with hairy, nerdy giants.

"Y-you are really pretty," he said in a low voice and put his hands on her shoulders.

The shock of desire stole her voice.

Then the giant leaned close, smelling of beer and sandalwood, oddly enough, to whisper in her ear, "I peeked out my peephole and saw her leave his place before you got here. She, um, looked a little like maybe they kissed."

"Or maybe they did a lot more." She pulled back and met his gaze, startled at the forest of lashes surrounding such dark-blue eyes.

Then Benji being Benji, he glanced away from her face. Except he chose to look at her shirt. At her boobs, to be more specific.

She frowned. Was Benji putting on an act or was he as awkward as he'd always seemed?

"What the hell?" Xavier boomed from the hallway.

Which had both her and Benji yelling in fright as the giant jolted upright, tossing her ass on the floor. "Be right back." Benji raced down the hall and slammed the bathroom door shut behind him.

"What did you do to him?" Xavier asked, his tone accusing.

"*Him?*" She stood and gingerly rubbed her butt. "He dumped

me like a sack of potatoes." Her eyes narrowed. "I wonder what he benches."

"Be nice," Xavier warned.

"Or what?"

He had her in a headlock when Benji returned soon after, and though they continued to play and tease each other, she caught more than a few of Benji's glances her way in addition to her brother's suspicious looks.

"Whatever," she said to them both and proceeded to beat them into submission in the game.

Before they left, she tugged Benji aside and whispered, "Keep an eye on him. I'll be back in a few days for a report."

Expecting him to stammer or avoid her gaze, she was further surprised when Benji gave a solemn nod...and a wink before he closed the door behind them.

What to make of that?

CHAPTER 21

Thursday evening, Xavier tried not to laugh at his anxious dinner date. "Relax, Justine. I heard everything you said in your apartment. I understand the players and the game. I'll be respectful and courteous. I'll also refrain from burping or slapping your mom on the butt for cooking such a fantastic dinner."

"Xavier," she snapped as they got out of her car.

He followed her up the long walkway to the front door of a stately home with a manicured lawn that screamed "big money" without being overblown.

They'd parked in the driveway behind a Mercedes and an Audi. Justine's Camry seemed a little scared behind the shiny behemoths. If he hadn't before sensed the odd disconnect between daughter and family, he sensed it presently. A small part of him was glad to have worn a nice pair of trousers with a button down shirt, although he wore sliders, not Paul Whatevers on his feet.

She knocked, and while they waited, he murmured, "I'm kidding. Don't worry. I'll be the perfect boyfriend. Trust me." He kissed her cheek just as the front door opened.

A tall woman in a flowy, knee-length dress and heels stared at them with a growing smile. "Justine, Xavier, I'm so glad you could make it."

Justine didn't look much like her mother, though something in the shape of the older woman's mouth seemed similar. Soft jazz came from the house in addition to the low hum of people inside. A party he looked forward to attending, more than curious to meet Justine's family.

"Hi, Mom. So yeah, this is Xavier. Xavier, my mom, Jeanine."

Jeanine held out her hand, and he gave her a gentle shake, not sure if he was expected to kiss the back of her hand or not. She held her hand as if she expected more.

After a moment, she withdrew and moved aside. "Please, come in. Everyone's here."

"We're early," Justine said, and to Xavier, she sounded slightly annoyed.

"You're five minutes early. Which is late in this house, young lady."

Justine rolled her eyes.

Xavier chuckled. "Sounds like my mom."

"Oh?" Jeanine took him by the arm and walked him in, leaving Justine behind. Then she introduced him around.

Justine and her sisters looked alike, the older two more physically similar to each other. Angela, the oldest, appeared dressed to impress, all lean lines and sharp eyes. Mallory, the middle daughter, gave a shy smile. He could see the softness, that eager need to please Justine had previously mentioned, in her greeting.

"So nice to meet you, Xavier." Mallory smiled at Justine. "It'll be so much fun to have you with Justine at the wedding."

"I can't wait."

She beamed.

Angela gave him a subtle onceover but was pleasant all the same.

Then he got to meet the head of the family. As Jeanine led him toward her husband, he could feel the dynamic shift. The man could totally command a room. He had a powerful presence, one used to being acknowledged.

Jeanine put her hand on her husband's arm, and he leaned in for a kiss on the cheek. A sweet yet perfunctory gesture. "Honey, this is Xavier, Justine's new boyfriend. Xavier, meet my husband, Lyle."

"A pleasure to meet you, sir." Xavier held out his hand and met Lyle's gaze, conscious Justine might as well have been his mini-me. They had the same features, the same smile, yet where Justine projected warmth, her father did not.

Lyle gave a charming smile, at odds with the calculation in his eyes, and shook Xavier's hand. "A pleasure, Xavier. Please, call me Lyle."

"Sure thing." Xavier waited for Lyle to release him before pulling away. A classic power move on the man's part, but Xavier had no intention of making problems by trying to challenge Lyle's authority and finally dropped his hand by his side. "Thank you so much for the dinner invitation. I've looked forward to meeting all of you."

Lyle nodded to the liquor bar. "Would you like something to drink?"

"A beer, if you've got one."

"I'll get it," Jeanine said. "Justine, come help me."

"Okay, Mom."

So much for not abandoning him to the wolves. Yet Justine offered an apologetic glance as she followed her mother into the other room.

Xavier took a subtle look around him, noting the grandeur of the home. Everything looked polished, from the formal dining area to the luxurious living room full of high-end, light-colored leather furniture and hand-carved wooden tables. The area looked professionally decorated—that or Jeanine had a flare for design. He didn't note one speck of dust anywhere, and the sophisticated artwork around the house gave the space a museum-like quality. It didn't help that the living area, where one would expect to kick back and relax, had been filled with neutral and light colors. He swore not to sit down on the pale couch for fear of leaving a smudge of dirt behind.

Not a place where he'd ever feel comfortable enough to relax. And definitely not a place for kids or pets, not that he'd noticed either around the house.

Still, he couldn't deny the place was a masterpiece of style.

"You have a gorgeous home," he said to Lyle when he noticed the man watching him.

Lyle smirked. "We only have nice things now because all our kids are grown and gone."

Xavier had to laugh. "That's what my mom says about her place."

"Does she live in Seattle?"

"Yeah. She's in Queen Anne, in the same house my sister and I grew up in."

"I loved our old home in Fremont, but we needed the space. We bought this house oh, about fifteen or sixteen years ago. It was a huge step-up for us."

"How big is this place?"

"A little over four thousand square feet. It's actually too big for Jeanine and me, but we like it. It's not far from work, and we finally have it just the way we want it. My wife recently remodeled the front room." Lyle took Xavier on a tour around the house.

When they returned to the living area, he saw Justine waiting for him with a beer.

She looked relieved when she spotted him. "There you are."

"Thanks." He took it from her and casually slung an arm around her shoulders. "Your dad was showing me the house. It's amazing."

"Told you."

"Almost as nice as your current digs," he teased.

Her dad watched them and sipped at a new Scotch his wife handed him. "You've been to Justine's *temporary* apartment?"

"I have. I live right below her. I was surprised to hear Rosie was going to be gone for so long."

"That's Jeanine's sister for you. Rosie's still wild and unpredictable," Lyle said with a fondness Xavier wouldn't have expected. Lyle seemed very cut and dried, yet he had a sense of humor Xavier often heard mirrored in his daughter. Sly and smart, Justine's father had thoroughly entertained Xavier on the simple house tour.

"I miss Aunt Rosie." Justine frowned. "I haven't heard from her since she left. I think she's ducking my texts."

Xavier chuckled. "I doubt that. She's probably so busy juggling admirers she hasn't had time to talk."

"You're probably right."

Jeanine interrupted. "Dinner, everyone. Please join us in the dining room."

Xavier found the table covered. Dishes and plates of food had been placed neatly on a table runner the length of the table. Each place setting had been set with a pretty set of matching plates and cups.

"Bone china from Tiffany & Co.," Jeanine said with a smile. "Only the best for company."

"No kidding. You never set this out when I come alone," Justine said.

Mallory snickered while Angela and Lyle smirked and whispered something to each other that made them laugh.

Xavier's mom would love this set up, like something out of a home magazine.

The mahogany wood table and chairs leant to a more formal feel, as did the chandelier sparkling overhead and candelabras on the table. All the platters and bowls matched the place settings fitted out with differently sized silverware.

He hoped he wouldn't embarrass himself by using a dessert fork with his salad.

Justine nudged him under the table, and he glanced up to see Angela staring at him. "I'm sorry, I missed that."

Across the table from him, Angela took the platter of meat from her father, speared a few pieces of filet, and passed it on. "I said I'm sorry my husband isn't here to meet you. He wanted to come but something came up at work."

"Scott's a hard worker. A good man." Lyle nodded from the head of the table.

Next to him, his wife sighed. "We don't want our son-in-law to be a carbon copy of you, do we? Working too much. Not when we're due for a few grandbabies."

Angela smiled. "We're working on that, Mom."

"Oh good." Jeanine turned to Mallory. "And once you and Ted tie the knot, I'm hoping for a few from you too. Then we just have our lost little duckling left." Jeanine winked at Justine.

"Ugh," Justine said under her breath before putting on a big smile. "For once, I'm following Dad's path. I'm focused on work, not babies."

Xavier felt it prudent not to comment on procreating and put some veggies on his plate. The casserole dish smelled divine, and he noted a cauliflower medley covered in a light sauce that made him salivate. Perhaps an extra helping of that…

"Tell us about work, Justine," Lyle said with a smile, but his words came out like a directive. "Did you get that raise you expected?"

Xavier could feel her tension, though Justine didn't show it.

After a pause, she said, "I did not."

Her dad frowned, and he looked just like Justine when she was irked about something. "Why not?"

"I'll tell you why not. Because my boss is a jerk." She recounted her conversation with Frank the Ass in detail, and Xavier felt for her.

"That's not fair," Jeanine said.

"I'll tell you what you should have said." Angela launched into a verbal diatribe against Frank and his weak character.

Mallory offered sympathy and a few minor pieces of advice, like talking to HR or a peer about her issues. A less direct approach than Angela's.

Jeanine reiterated how terrible Justine's company was and how she'd do much better working with the family at her father's company.

Through it all, Lyle ate and watched Justine, who did her best to ignore her father's stare.

When she looked at him, he took that as his cue to speak again. "Do you see why you aren't going to advance there?"

"Because I'm a doormat?"

"Exactly."

Xavier blinked, having expected a bit more support from her father.

"You don't stand up for yourself, so you're constantly trampled by those who aren't better than you but who are more assertive than you. How many times have I told you to speak up when you disagree with something?"

"It was my yearly review, Dad. I listened to Frank because I was trying to show that I respect my boss."

"And where did that get you?" He stabbed his knife in the air at her as he made his point. "Now you're working two jobs for the price of one."

"Less than one, but who's counting?" Angela felt the need to add. "Come on, Justine. You can do better than that. Why do you let them step all over you?"

Justine seemed to sink in her seat as her family continued to berate her. Xavier tried to keep his opinion to himself, but the poor woman would end up sliding right under the table if their badgering continued. He couldn't take it anymore.

"I think Justine did what was right for her in the moment."

Everyone stopped talking and looked at him.

"It's not as easy as it seems to disagree with one's boss when you've been trained to respect authority your entire life, as is clearly the case here."

Lyle raised a brow. "Oh?"

"You're a strong parental figure. You and your wife are the boss at home. You raised all three of your daughters to respect authority. So it's no surprise when Justine acts true to form at work. She's smart, does her job well, and is a team player. Unfortunately, her boss is taking advantage of her assets."

"Assets?" Lyle took a sip of wine, mulling the word. "I suppose you're right. She's clearly intelligent, organized, logical—for the most part."

Justine remained quiet, focusing on her plate while she pushed her food around. She acted like a completely different person with her family than the funny, assured person he knew her to be.

Her father continued, "She seems to have missed the advice we gave our girls about standing up for herself."

"Seriously, Justine." Angela nodded. "That was the first thing I learned at Ferrera-Hind working for Dad. Especially working with men."

"That's so true," Mallory chimed in. "I mean, I'm still learning." She glanced at her father, saw his nod, and continued. "But I never let anyone talk down to me or treat me like less than I'm worth."

Considering what Justine had said of Mallory, Xavier knew that to be less than true. He glanced at Justine, but when she remained focused on her food, he spoke up for her. "She did question Frank about her new job. I think she gave him the benefit of the doubt by waiting for him to admit she wasn't getting a raise. When he didn't, she decided to take the time to consider her options. Which, if you asked me, is much smarter than flying off the handle in rebuttal to some jackass who can't lead his way out of a paper bag."

Incensed on her behalf, he added while looking at her, "Justine is worth ten Franks any way you look at it. Eventually she'll get where she's going. Sometimes it takes a little time to get there, is all." He looked over to see her father's slow grin.

"Fired you up, eh, Xavier?"

"I don't like to see her upset. And you all seem to be piling on." He paused and couldn't help adding, "If I'm being *Frank* about it."

They laughed, even Justine. She squeezed his knee under the table and started eating once more.

Fortunately, the conversation turned to Jeanine's latest home project for a friend. Apparently, she didn't get paid to design but played around with home design for fun. Talk then eventually centered around everyone's significant other.

Lyle summed it up, a succinct kind of guy. "So we have Scott, who's a financial investor. Ted, who invests as well, though he's more an advisor for our smaller clients. And you, Xavier. Justine hasn't said much about you other than that she has a new boyfriend. What is it exactly that you do?"

Xavier had been surprised they hadn't given him the inquisition after he'd stepped through the front door. But perhaps Lyle had been softening him up before going in for the kill.

From the intense scrutiny her father was giving him, he thought he might not be too far off the mark. "I'm an LMFT, a licensed marriage and family therapist."

Lyle brightened. "Oh, so then, *Doctor* Xavier Hanover?"

"Nope." Xavier smiled, having been asked that question more times than he could remember. "I was eager to get into the work and didn't want more years of schooling. Or debt."

Lyle clearly approved. "Smart. You know, our firm is big into the psychology behind investing and how companies decide their futures. Investing is so much more than numbers and percentages."

"Oh?"

The conversation turned even more stimulating as Lyle, Angela, and Xavier discussed leadership and values within corporations, and how that led to increased productivity and sales. Justine, her mother, and Mallory talked about Aunt Rosie's apartment, comparing Rosie's eclectic sense of style to Jeanine's.

Xavier engaged but kept half his attention on Justine, aware he'd defended her though he hadn't been asked to do so.

He could only hope he hadn't stepped too far.

Or that she'd be angry with him because of it.

CHAPTER 22

The moment they sat in Justine's car, Xavier turned to her and apologized.

He spoke in a rush. "I'm *so* sorry for overstepping. Then I dominated the conversation until we left. I don't know what happened. I only meant to defend you when they all jumped down your throat. And then I found myself explaining about my schooling and my practice with your father." He paused. "He's a little scary."

Justine had been relieved Xavier had been there to take the heat off her. "There's nothing to be sorry about. My dad has a tendency to run right over you before you know it. You held your own. I appreciate you standing up for me."

He flushed. "I feel like I talked for you. And I hate that."

She clutched his hand in hers. "You defended me. No one does that. Well, Mallory will sometimes. But usually they just steamroll over me. It's easier to let them. I still do what I want in the end; I just have to suffer a whole lot of unasked for advice before I do."

He groaned. "Still, I'm sorry. I was a hypocrite, doing exactly what they do. I respect you, Justine." He opened his mouth and closed it.

"Go ahead." She started the car and drove them back home.

"It's not my place."

She laughed. "Xavier, I can feel you humming with the need to offer advice."

"It's like you really know me."

She couldn't explain how good it had felt, knowing he'd supported her with her family. Not cowed by her father at all, he'd answered questions while having her back. That arm around her shoulders had not gone unnoticed, and the gesture had gone a long way toward making her feel encouraged.

"You know what? You had enough people telling you what to do about your work life over dinner. How about we get home and go on a walk? It's a gorgeous night tonight. We'll walk and talk, and you can rake me over the coals about anything you want. Just so we're even."

His broad smile had her pulse picking up, though Justine told herself not to ask for too much from Xavier. Bad enough he was roped into going to her sister's wedding with her and acting like her boyfriend.

"Well, if you insist."

They made the drive back to the apartment in no time and decided to walk away from the center of town, taking in the cute neighborhood filled with a diverse mix of homes. Apartment complexes, Craftsman-styled bungalows, Midcentury modern houses, and of course, the Fremont troll keeping watch from under the Aurora Bridge.

The waning moon offered some light, and the cloudless sky allowed the stars to sparkle overhead. The breeze smelled of honeysuckle, and as they walked, Xavier took her arm and tucked it under his. Trying not to find it all overly romantic proved impossible. Heck, she was only human.

"Ask me anything. Anything at all," Xavier insisted.

"Such a grand gesture. You must feel totally guilty about dinner."

He groaned. "You have no idea."

"Fine. You asked for it." The question she'd been wanting to ask since she'd met him came to mind. "Tell me about your relationship with your ex. You know, the one with the brother you nearly fought."

"Ah, Christine." He glanced down at her. "Are you sure you want to hear about her?"

"You bet." She hugged his arm. "Come on. You said you owe me."

"Fine, fine." He leaned into her as they slowed their pace, caught up in the late spring night and, if she wasn't mistaken, each other. "I first met Christine a year and a half ago at a Christmas party. Through Auggie, actually. Someone at the gym hosted a huge get-together, and I went along. We hit it off right away."

"So she's pretty."

"No, she's a beast with missing teeth and different sized feet."

"What?" Justine blinked.

"Of course I found her attractive."

"You don't have to get snippy about it."

He chuckled. "Where was this Justine when we were at your parents'?"

"Hiding so they couldn't devour my soul."

"Ha. They nearly got mine, but my LMFT background saved me."

"My dad is really into psychology. You got lucky."

"I'll take lucky any day."

"Right. So...Christine?"

She didn't examine her interest in his love life too hard. Not that it was any of her business. But she liked him sharing, liked knowing what turned him off and on.

Turned him on...

Try as she might, the thought of tangling in the sheets with him refused to leave her mind. *Gah. Get it together, Justine.*

"Christine is a lovely woman. She just wasn't right for me. I told her from the beginning I only wanted a casual relationship. I never wanted to lead her on. I was going through a tough time at work and helping to cover another therapist's patients, and the need to help everyone was getting to me. I was burning out and just wanted a friend, nothing deeper."

"You told her what you wanted from the start." Xavier would do that, honest to the core. "And she was okay with it, I take it."

"Yes, at first. Then she and I grew closer. We never moved in together, but we spent a lot of time at each other's homes. We functioned as a couple. I guess it got confusing."

Justine could well imagine. She and Xavier weren't even dating and she'd come to think of him as hers. *Totally not cool, girl.*

Xavier continued. "And then, well, Christine started to get clingy. We had to do everything together. Now look, I like people, but I also like my own space. I like to think I straddle the line of extrovert and introvert. But needing me-time used to hurt Christine's feelings. After we'd talk about it, she'd be okay. Until the next time she got hurt feelings."

"Ouch."

"Yeah." Xavier sighed. "I did like her at the beginning. But at the end, I started to not like her so much. And in her defense, she said I counseled her all the time instead of just listening and being a good boyfriend."

"Huh. You do tend to get a little preachy."

He stopped and glanced down at her. "Really?"

"I'm kidding, Xavier. Geez. I can tell you're a super-great therapist. You're easy to talk to and you really listen. You're the most positive person I know. Heck, you felt overwhelmed and took time off for your own mental health. That's like, *super* healthy. I avoid stuff that makes me uncomfortable." She frowned, wishing she had a sturdier backbone. Frank would never take advantage of her father or Angela. They'd eat him alive.

He scowled and protested, "I'm in no way a super-therapist. But I'm flattered you think so."

"Hey, you survived my family and came out without a scratch. I'm impressed."

He laughed. "Your family wasn't so bad. Though it helped that you coached me before we went. I knew what to expect of your parents and sisters. And yes, before you ask, Angela is desperate to be your father's clone, and Mallory just wants approval. Your mother loves everyone but dances to your father's tune. And she's happy to do that. You, on the other hand, are not."

"That caps it. See? Super-therapist. But I got sidetracked. We're not done the Xavier-Christine story. So how did you break up? You tell me your story and I'll tell you about me and Mitch."

"Deal." He launched into his breakup, apparently eager to hear all about hers. "It was coming for months. Plus, Auggie kept riding me about her. She never liked Christine. Said we didn't fit. And Christine never understood my bond with my sister." He looked into Justine's eyes, and she encouraged him to continue by quietly listening. "I love Auggie. She's my sister. My twin. We obviously don't do everything together. But we do spend a lot of our free time hanging out."

"I don't understand why that's a problem."

"I didn't either. I guess Christine took my closeness with Auggie as some kind of slight against her." He shrugged. "I don't know I only knew I had to call things off. I thought she'd be on board since she'd seemed so unhappy. Except she burst into tears. When she saw that didn't move me, she left after calling me a lot of not-so-nice names."

"Oh, now *those* I want to hear."

"I'm sure." He chuckled. "I had no idea I'd see her again after that. But not a few days went by before she was calling and begging to get back together. Her desperation made it all worse."

He grimaced. "That sounds terrible, but it's true. She came across as shrewish and nasty, a total one-eighty from the woman I'd dated. It made no sense. She's a beautiful, intelligent woman who could easily be out dating someone else."

Justine squelched the irrational jealousy that surged. Xavier had had a life before meeting her. And he'd broken up with Christine after all. Not that it should matter, since Justine and Xavier were only pretending to date. How sad she had to keep reminding herself of that.

"She managed to come over to pick up something she thought she'd left behind."

"Nice gimmick."

"I know. Auggie read me the riot act about it. She's really into the phrase 'I told you so.'"

Justine liked Auggie even more.

"Then you managed to see me and Dan, her brother, nearly fight. Great first impression, huh?"

"Well, it could have been worse. He could have beaten you up."

"Good point. He tried to get me to go back with her. As in, she sent him over to convince me I'd made a mistake." He looked baffled. "I hate that she was hurting, but all her actions after the fact showed we weren't right together." His arm around Justine's shoulders tightened, hugging her to him.

He stared at the road while she studied his profile.

"What about you and Mitch?"

Her turn. "Mitch? Talk about a fiasco." She snorted, remembering how Dr. Mitch Dunderhead had first snared her. "We met through my mother, believe it or not."

"Oh, I believe it. Your mother is as shrewd as your father."

"She totally is. She tries to disarm you with a bubbly smile, pretending she's the nice parent. All while she subtly maneuvers you until you're doing exactly what she wanted in the first place."

"Like dating Mitch."

"*Doctor* Mitch," she corrected. "She met him at some fundraiser and insisted I attend the next one with her. Then I was out on a date with him without being sure how it happened." She still couldn't remember if it had been Mitch's idea to take her out or her mother's. "He was charming and smart. Totally handsome."

"Oh, please. Tell me more," he said with the the least amount of enthusiasm, which had her snickering.

"Don't worry. His personality offset all the good stuff he had going for him. He was nice at first. But when we started dating, after I moved in with him, I realized our lives would always be centered around Mitch and Mitch's needs." She paused in thought and added, "I should have seen it so much sooner."

"Oh?"

"He was nowhere near your skills."

"My skills?"

She gave a sly grin. "In the bedroom."

Xavier tripped and hurried to right himself.

"That crack in the sidewalk get you?"

"You can't just say stuff like that without a little warning." Xavier's warm smile made her heart flutter. "Although if you want, you can—you should—say it again."

"He sucked in bed."

"Again."

She laughed, pleased when he laughed with her.

He stopped her in front of someone's showstopper of a garden just as the moon speared through the clouds, illuminating them as if on stage. "Beautiful."

"Seriously. Are those poppies?"

"Not the flowers, doofus. I meant you."

CHAPTER 23

In retrospect, "doofus" probably wasn't the most romantic name Xavier could have called Justine, but a heavy wave of lust and affection blindsided him, making it difficult to do anything but stare.

The moonlight cast a glow over Justine's already pretty features, and as she glanced up at him, the moon reflected in her eyes. Her smile lit as if from within, and he thought he'd never seen a more gorgeous woman in all his life.

He leaned down to kiss her just as she reached to pull him down toward her.

Unlike the other kisses they'd shared, this felt more intimate, filled with a heady warmth under all the passion that convinced him they were more than just friends. A pair of people so in tune with each other that they would be crazy not to seek more.

He slowly pulled back, his entire body alive with excitement, lust, and lo—a healthy dose of *like*. "Wow."

"No kidding." She blinked up at him and caressed his chin. "Your beard is so soft, not scratchy at all."

"I condition it. Yes, I'm vain like that."

She smiled.

"Justine, I like you."

"I like you too."

He needed the words that refused to come. "I like you a lot. A lot-lot."

"I get that sense, yes." She squirmed in his hold, obviously feeling the erection pushing through his jeans into her.

"I—" He'd said she should set the pace of their relationship, and yet it was all he could do to hold in his new feelings. This excitement might be due to their newness or to the explosive chemistry they shared. But he'd never been so bowled over by any other woman and had no idea how to classify them as a unit. Friends? Lovers? Something more?

She kissed him again. "You what?"

"I can't think when you're in my arms."

"Oh, wow. That's poetic."

"And true. We need somewhere private so I can show you what I mean." Before he lost his mind and started doing a lot more than kissing in public.

"I know just the place." She laughed with him as they ran together back around the corner to the apartment complex.

He had her hand in his as they brushed past Adam and Max talking in the courtyard.

Max frowned at them and shook his head.

Adam shot Xavier a thumbs up and grinned.

Despite feeling like a cliché, Xavier was pleased Adam knew Justine belonged to—*with*—him.

"You have me acting like a caveman," he muttered and kissed her on their way up the stairs.

The sound of a door slamming shut from the floor below had them springing apart.

"Hurry." Justine flew up the stairs, Xavier hard on her heels.

All talk of relationships and letting her make decisions for them both fled from his mind. The moment the door closed behind them in Justine's apartment, Xavier had her in a kiss against the back of the door.

Her lips moved over his, inviting, seducing, and he was happy enough to go where she led. Helpless to follow, he raised his arms when she tugged at his shirt and stepped out of his socks and shoes while she kissed him.

Somehow, the quiet Justine from dinner had transformed into a woman who could make Xavier beg without even trying. She spun them when Xavier was finally naked, putting his back to the door, and went to her knees.

He stared down at her shiny hair, watched his dick disappear into her mouth, and laid his head back, his eyes closed as she sucked him close to orgasm in no time.

"Justine, oh yeah. God, baby. Please." He rambled, not sure what he meant by anything except to never stop this moment with her.

As he closed all too quickly on that pleasure, he didn't want to go over alone.

He pulled her to her feet and kissed her, swallowing down her moans of pleasure. He stripped her naked and lifted her in his arms.

"Oof. You better not drop me," she warned. "That's not sexy. But you holding me? That's totally hot."

He pretended to bobble her, and she shrieked with laughter.

Until he reached the bedroom. He paused and looked down at her.

Her laughter dried up, that sexual tension between them present and growing.

Along with other things.

"What are we doing, Xavier?" Justine asked, her voice soft.

Was this a trick question? "We're getting ready to have sex?"

"Yes, I know." She paused while he set her down and flushed when his sex brushed against her belly. "But… I really like you. I guess I'm confused, because this is better than any relationship

I've ever had, and it's fake." She wrapped her hand around his dick and gently squeezed.

He closed his eyes, not needing to see her touching him. Bad enough he felt it. If she kept it up, he'd come too soon. He put a hand over hers to slow her when she started pumping him. "Easy. I'll come too soon." Xavier swallowed around a dry throat. "Condom?" *Please, God.*

"I just…" She continued to hold him, but at least she'd stopped jerking him off.

Which meant she actually wanted to talk.

He shouldn't have stopped her from blowing him earlier.

No, no. Rein it in. She wants to… talk. No matter how much it hurts, hear her out.

"Inconvenient timing," he had to say. "But talk. I'm listening." He swallowed hard. "I'm *trying* to listen."

She gave him the sweetest grin, and his heart felt like it fell at her feet, waiting for her to pick it up. "Do you know how sexy it is to know how much you want me?"

"Justine, I'm trying really hard to concentrate and not come all over you. But you keep touching me and I won't be able to help myself."

She let go, and he cursed himself for being honest. "I like…" She paused, looking both confused and aroused. "I like having sex with you. Being with you. Having you with me around my family made dinner almost fun."

"Almost." He cupped her cheek, taken with her softness, and had to kiss her. Once he pulled back, he noted her lust-filled gaze, Justine clearly distracted, which hadn't been his intention. He wiped a thumb over her lips and nearly lost it when she nibbled on him. "Talk faster," he rasped.

"I just want you to know how much I—"

"You—?"

"How much I appreciate you. All of you," she said and boldly squeezed him again.

"I appreciate all of you too." He kissed her, unable to help himself. "*So much.*" A little too much, he thought but didn't say, worried about how fast he seemed to be falling for her, no matter that he'd been trying to be mature and responsible and—

She rolled a condom over him and cupped his balls, rubbing lightly.

It was enough to make him lose control. He yanked her into his arms and kissed her breathless before tossing her on the bed.

She bounced and gave a breathless laugh, soon cut off as he followed and devoured her mouth, losing himself in her taste and touch. She felt soft everywhere, and the berried pebbles of her nipples begged a bite or two. He nibbled and sucked, gratified when she hissed his name and ran her fingers through his hair, holding him while he drew on the hard nubs.

But when he kissed a trail farther down, she let him go, stroking his hair until he found the wet, hot center between her legs.

"Xavier, yes, oh yes." She arched up into his mouth, and her pleas made him that much harder.

It didn't take long for her to come so sweetly, but then she was urging him up her body. "In me," she commanded, breathless and needy.

He plunged into her, sliding easily through her slick, tight sex. The viselike grip of her body had him pumping harder, fucking her to own her, so that she'd experience such pleasure and let go.

Xavier felt his end nearing, his balls tight, the pleasure almost unbearable. "Coming," he warned and shoved one final time, seizing in an almost painful rapture. He poured into the condom, thrusting as deeply inside her as he could go while she pressed kisses into his chest and shoulders.

"Fuck, Justine," he swore, so sensitive after that obliterating climax.

"I know," she murmured. "You feel so good inside me. Like you're supposed to be there."

"Yeah," he agreed and kissed her while swirling his hips and shuddering, jetting the last of his seed into the condom. After some relaxing petting, they both came down from their sexual euphoria and settled into a warm hug.

"You're still in me," she announced.

"Um, I know. I'm the one with the dick."

She laughed. "I like this."

He leaned his forehead against hers, doing his best to ignore the irrational fear that admitting to enjoying their relationship might jinx it somehow. Could Justine possibly be this much fun all the time? So lovely and kind, even when she didn't get her way?

Like Christine, May, Johanna. The relationships had all started out so wonderfully then gone downhill. He didn't want to imagine losing Justine in that same way.

"Xavier?" She frowned. "Are you okay?"

"Hold on. My brain hasn't caught up yet." He felt her relax and sighed. "I'm an idiot."

"Why?"

"Because I should give you space and not pressure you to be together. But I don't want to." *I want to snap you up before someone else does.* He pushed deeper inside her when he started to fall out. "And I want to come inside you over and over again." Just the thought made his dick twitch. "Justine, my fake girlfriend. I'm putty in your hands."

"Ah, I see. I can get you to do anything I want if I let you inside me."

"Anything, yes. Everything. Whatever you want. Anytime, anywhere."

She laughed. "So easy."

"I'm really not. It's you."

She smiled into her eyes. "No, it's you." She kissed him.

"Before this conversation gets any more cloying, let's just

agree to disagree so we can have sex again in another few minutes."

She chuckled. "Yeah, okay. Now let's go take a shower together. You like me wet."

"I really do." He withdrew and grimaced, missing her heat. "We could always wait here until I slide inside you again."

"But I wanted to swallow your very clean, very wet cock."

He couldn't help a groan. "That's it. I'm going with you to every family dinner from now to eternity so you can reward me with your steel-trap lady parts."

She burst out laughing. "Let's get clean, my not-a-doctor hero."

"I'm no one's Mitch, that's for sure. Get it? Not bitch. Mitch. Heh."

"Keep it up and I'll Mitch-slap that fine ass all the way to the shower. Or would you rather forego my tongue cleaning?"

He'd never moved faster to the bathroom in his life.

CHAPTER 24

The phone rang early the next morning. Justine couldn't get it because Xavier was taking her from behind, her hands braced against the dresser while he plowed in and out of her.

"More, yes," she hissed as he shoved faster. She touched herself, her orgasm looming like a storm cloud that suddenly released.

She cried out as she came, and he followed soon after, shuddering as he jetted into the condom.

He sighed her name and hugged her to him, his hands roaming from her belly to cup her breasts.

A surge of heat made her shiver, the feel of his large hands as he caressed her one more point of intimate contact between them.

She felt his kisses along her neck. He pushed her hair aside and kissed the shell of her ear then whispered, "You make me lose all sense."

She smiled and clenched him tightly inside her, stifling a laugh as he gave another groan.

"Damn. If this keeps up, I might die of sheer exhaustion. Or dehydration."

He withdrew and turned her around to hug her. "Not to be gross, but I don't think I have anything left inside me to fill any more condoms."

She flushed and kissed his chest. "Not to be gross."

He snickered and left her for the bathroom.

Tingly and happy to her core, Justine fell back into bed. They'd been like rabid bunnies for hours last night, using up a lot more condoms than she'd needed the last six months. Fortunately, she had the day off as a flex day, giving her a three day weekend she hoped to continue with Xavier.

Last night had been spectacular. They hadn't been able to get enough of each other, and the sex had been both intense and fun. Xavier made her laugh, made her moan, made her come.

Every. Time.

That never happened. Or at least, it hadn't with her past lovers. Maybe because she was too inside her own head while with those men. Unable to turn off her thoughts that she might in some way be disappointing them. That she wasn't smart enough. Or that she wore that extra ten pounds in a bad way. But with Xavier, nothing but sensation took over her mind. Feeling his large, hot hands stroking her, listening to his moans and demands she take her pleasure first. Xavier refused to come until she'd been pleasured, and that unselfishness was both shocking and refreshing.

She stretched and smiled, feeling more than satisfied.

Truth to tell, she felt a little anxious. Last night, she'd almost asked him to date her for real, using labels like boyfriend and girlfriend. Only a faint sense of self-preservation had stopped her from blurting out how much she'd grown to care for him.

A man who saw himself as her friend, her lover, and her *fake* boyfriend.

Thus far, the sex they shared hadn't soured the relationship.

She'd be an idiot to seek more when he was already giving her so much.

Right?

He returned, still naked, and she watched him crawl under the sheets to join her. She loved looking at him. For a man with a sedentary job sitting behind a desk talking to patients, he sure had an athlete's build.

"How are you so muscular?"

He turned on his side and flexed his free arm. "You think I'm big, you should see my sister."

She laughed. "I have seen her. But I haven't seen her flexing."

"We'll have to change that." He leaned in for a kiss. "Have I told you yet how glad I am that you have the day off? Got any plans?" He moved to her neck and took a big sniff. "Ah. You smell so good."

"Eu de Sex?"

He pulled back and tugged her on top of him, then forced her to sit up and stared at her breasts now bared by the sheets pooled around her waist. "Yeah." He wiggled his brows.

She laughed. "Lech."

"That's me. Hannibal *Lecher*."

"Very funny."

"I aim to please." He ran his thumb over her left nipple. "I've gotta say it. I love your breasts. They're the perfect handful."

"Oh stop." Yet she leaned into his touch.

He smirked. "Perhaps I'm not the only one who's putty in your hands."

"Huh?" She deliberately misunderstood, teasing him. "How am I putty in my own hands?"

"Smartass. I meant you're kind of melting in *my* hands." He shifted under her. "Melting on my stomach, actually. You get so wet for me. It's so sexy."

"You love making me blush, don't you?"

"I do." He chuckled. "So you didn't answer. What are your plans for the day?"

"I—" The phone rang, reminding her she'd missed a call earlier.

"Crap. Hold that thought." She reached over him to grab for her cell and froze when his lips closed around her nipple.

He sucked and kissed, nibbling.

She clutched his head.

When he pulled back, she couldn't help being disappointed. Every time they touched she felt closer to him. Despite the danger to her heart, she couldn't help wanting more with Xavier.

"We'll get back to that later." He winked. "I hope. Since you have some time off, I was thinking we could spend the day together." He paused. "I mean, unless you have stuff to do."

"I think that would be nice." A day spent with Xavier, just hanging out together. No terrible boss, no pushy family, just a sexy man at her disposal. "Although, I was hoping to go get myself a massage today as a reward for surviving the family dinner."

His eyes sparkled, his grin wide. "A massage, eh? I can give you a massage." He looked her over and stroked her ribs and belly. "In fact, I can't wait to oil you up."

"Sounds perfect."

"But maybe after some breakfast? I'm starving. It takes a lot of energy to keep up with you."

"Me? You're the one with the stamina." Was he ever.

"I am, aren't I?" He sounded smug, and she laughed.

Before she could respond, the phone rang again. As did his.

They reached on opposite nightstands.

"Hello?" They said at the same time to their respective callers.

"Well it's about damn time," Justine's aunt said in a raspy voice. "Where the hell have you been, girl?"

"Me? You're the one not returning my calls." Warmth

unfurled, her aunt's familiar voice a soothing balm where her family had rubbed her raw.

"Sorry, Mom. I meant to call you last night," Xavier was saying.

"Hmm. Is that Xavier I hear?" Aunt Rosie asked. "Exactly what time is it there?"

Justine glanced at her phone. Seven a.m. "Er, what time is it there?"

"It's four o'clock in the afternoon, and I'm sharing wine and antipasti with a handsome Italian count." A man's deep laughter, then words in Italian, followed.

"Oh, nice. How's Tuscany, Aunt Rosie?"

Xavier tiptoed out of bed and grabbed his underwear before darting out of the room.

"I know that was Xavier," Rosie muttered. "Fine. Don't tell your aunt about the man in your room at—" more low Italian rumbling "seven in the morning. And I know you, Ms. Not a Morning Person. So if there's a man there, it's because he was sleeping in your bed." Trust Aunt Rosie to sound both smug and happy about that fact. "It's about time."

"What?"

"Wait. Oh no. It's not Mitch, is it?"

"No, we broke up. That's why I moved in here, remember?"

Rosie sighed with relief. "Good. Just making sure you didn't backslide into boring-ville. So. That was Xavier, wasn't it?"

Justine sat up and pulled the sheet over her chest, as if her aunt could see and know all from abroad. "Uh, maybe."

Rosie burst into laughter. "I knew it."

"I told you so."

Justine paused, that voice she'd overheard not her aunt's. "Hey, that sounded like Kai."

"You mean, amazing, must-read, bestselling children's book author, Kai Strand? Why yes, yes it was." Rosie added in a lower voice, "She's currently teasing Guillermo's cousin and brother. Kai's quite the hussy."

Kai laughed, and more male voices joined her in the background.

Then Rosie said, "I'm pleased for you, kid. So tell me what's been going on. I miss you."

Justine smiled. Aunt Rosie had always been on her side whenever Justine needed a friend. Someone not intimidated by her parents or ruled by a need to earn millions, despite being savvier than Lyle Ferrara when it came to investing, though on a much smaller scale.

Justine cleared her throat. "Well, I've made a great friend in Xavier. I convinced him to be my plus-one for Mallory's wedding, which saved me from having to go to the wedding with one of dad's cronies."

"Oh boy. Lay it on me."

Conscious that Xavier was in the other room, Justine didn't want to talk too long. But she did miss her aunt and ended up telling the woman a bit of everything. What Katie was up to, about the terrible boss and unfulfilling job, her new neighbors, and her "fake" boyfriend, Xavier—minus the sex parts.

"I knew you two would hit it off."

"Really? You never mentioned him before I moved in. And then you only said he was a decent enough neighbor who didn't make too much noise below you."

"All true." Her aunt chuckled. "Didn't hurt that he's handsome, intelligent, and well-off financially."

"Oh? He's on a break from work, from what I know." She lowered her voice. "But he's an LMFT. He can't be a bazillionaire." Not working as a therapist.

"Still on a break? I figured he'd be back to work by now. Talk about slacking."

"What?"

Rosie laughed but didn't answer. "I'm glad you're doing well, socially. But honey, that boss and the extra job you're not getting paid for need to go."

"I know."

"Speaking of needing to go… Your mother. Is she still being a pushy bitch?"

"Aunt Rosie," Justine said, sputtering with laughter.

"That's a yes, then."

"Kind of. I just… I wish Mallory wasn't marrying Ted. She's too good for him."

"But it's her choice. Just like it was Angela's to follow your dad into business and marry the man he approved of. Good old Scott. What a gem," Rosie said dryly. "And now they're trying to procreate, you say?"

"Yep. And Mallory will be soon enough. She's getting married next week, you know. Eight more days."

"I wish I could be there." Pause. "No, I really don't. But I'll get her a nice wedding gift and celebrate it when I get back. But enough about your idiot sister."

Justine tried but couldn't quell her wide grin, glad no one could see it.

"What do you think of the other tenants? That Adam in 1A, he's a cutie, isn't he? And Benji? Geeky but sweet."

"Everyone's actually really nice. We had the most amazing water balloon fight."

It was some time later before she realized she'd been talking to Rosie for a good half hour. "Oh shoot. I need to go. Send pictures of your handsome Italian men, and call me next week, would you?"

"For my favorite niece, anything. *Ciao, bella!*" Her aunt made a kissy sound and disconnected.

Justine rushed out of bed and threw on an oversized shirt and shorts. She found Xavier in his boxer briefs drinking coffee in her kitchen.

"I'm so sorry. Aunt Rosie was on the phone."

He gave her wide smile. "How's Rosie doing? I miss her."

"She's great. Breaking hearts left and right, I'm sure. And giving everyone unasked for advice."

"That's the Rosie Gallo I know." He chuckled and sipped his coffee. "Want a cup?

"Sure." She watched him move around her aunt's kitchen, amused. "You sure do know your way around this place."

"Rosie and I have spent many a morning drinking coffee and realizing how people should be living their lives."

"Oh?"

He cleared his throat. "Um, yeah, you know. Gossiping about our neighbors."

"Aunt Rosie has opinions and she's not afraid to share. She could give Aunt Truth a run for her money."

He just stared at her. "Aunt Truth?"

"You know. Aunt Truth? The big syndicated advice columnist? I follow her. She's always helping everyone with their problems."

"What about you? Ever written in to ask for advice?"

"Nah. I usually have my family to tell me what to do," she said with no small amount of sarcasm.

"That I can believe." He snorted. "Man. Your family dinner was tough." He sipped his coffee. "Sorry. That sounded pretty judgmental. I'm sure they only mean well."

She lifted a brow.

He grinned. "Or not. But they're your family. And though overwhelming, your parents clearly love you."

"Do you think?" Sometimes she wondered if they only approved when she did what they wanted, not sure unconditional love was a thing in her family.

"Yeah. I do think so. Now when you end up meeting my mom, you'll see she's different but the same. She's sweet and open and shows her affection freely. But she also has a way of trying to manipulate her children into doing what she wants. I think it's a mother thing." After a pause, he added, "I'd actually love for you to meet my mom. She's great with all my friends."

Friends. Not girlfriends. Justine had to refrain from jumping in with a *heck, yes, I'd love to go.* It wouldn't do to appear so eager to meet his mom. That was a total couple move, introducing each other to the parents. She'd only done so under pretense.

Now she was second-guessing Xavier's part in her mess with the wedding.

"Are you sure meeting my folks was okay? I didn't want you uncomfortable. I mean, we're only pretend dating."

"We sure as hell aren't pretend fucking," he said bluntly.

She blushed. "Xavier."

"Sorry." He didn't look sorry. He looked a little peeved, to her surprise. "I mean, well, we're friends, Justine. More than friends, obviously." He looked her over, lingering on her breasts clearly unbound beneath her overshirt. "I'm trying not to make anything weird. But hey, I met your folks. It's not a big deal unless you wanted to hide me."

She matched his slow smile with one of her own. "Hide you? Why would I want to do that?" She looked him over, in lust with his strong frame.

"Now that's better." He flexed for her, making her laugh. "And just think. We might get to the point I'll need you to get my mom off my back. She's been suspiciously quiet about me getting married, and it's because she assumes I'm going to start dating again. So save a date for me if I need a fake girlfriend. Deal?"

"Deal." Justine felt better about last night's dinner. If she ever did need to meet his mom to help him out of a jam, doing it as a favor was a lot easier to digest than wanting to cozy up to the man she wanted to claim as her own.

"I'd be happy to help you. Together, we can Mitch-slap anyone who gets in our way," Justine teased.

Xavier laughed. "Mitch-slapped is totally now added to my lexicon."

"Oh my gosh. What a word nerd. 'Added to my lexicon,'" she said, imitating him.

"Word nerd?" He chortled, sounding like a cartoon villain, which had her chortling with him until they both broke down laughing and hugging each other.

Which soon turned back to kissing.

"You have too many clothes on," he said as he nuzzled her neck.

"I do, don't I?" She asked as she pushed down her shorts and whipped off the extra large tee-shirt. Then she hooked her fingers into the hem of his shorts and tugged them down, kneeling in front of him.

To her pleasant surprise, he was already half-hard. And when she put her lips on him and sucked, he thickened immediately.

"Justine…" He held her by the hair and started fucking her mouth.

She moaned, lost in lust and affection, needing more than they shared.

But she'd take the hot sex for now.

Because Xavier was nothing if not an equal opportunity pleaser.

CHAPTER 25

Saturday morning, when Xavier was trying to sneak back into his apartment, Benji happened to be standing out in the hallway, locking up his door. The sly grin he gave Xavier seemed out of place. Typically, Benji avoided interaction. Then again, they were friends, and he'd been a lot more open at Wednesday's game night.

Benji smirked. "Walk of shame, eh?"

Xavier couldn't exactly hide his bedhead or wrinkled clothing. He and Justine had shared the most remarkable Friday together. Mostly in bed, doing all manner of things. They'd gotten takeout, watched movies, and made love all day and night.

Tired but sated, he didn't have the energy to do more than hold up his hands in surrender. "Busted."

"I have a feeling you're walking down from the third floor. Am I right?"

Benji's smug expression only made Xavier laugh. "Maybe."

"Nice. But you might want to be careful. From what I hear, you have some tough competition for the lady upstairs."

"Oh?" Xavier started to come down off his Justine-high.

"Yeah. I bumped into Adam last night, and apparently Sam has a real crush on Justine." Benji grinned. "Kid's got it hot for an older woman. Better watch yourself."

Relieved Adam wasn't looking at Justine for himself, Xavier nodded. "Good to know. Thanks."

"No problem."

"So where are you off to? It's Saturday. Don't you normally game all day?"

Benji looked away, fiddling with the door he'd just locked. Now *that* Benji Xavier knew. "Um, usually, yeah. But I've got a few errands to run today. Bye." Benji took off as if his shorts were on fire. In sneakers, not his customary sandals.

Hmm. Something seemed off about that, but Xavier had a tough time focusing when all he could think about was Justine, naked, on her knees, her back, her belly, while he thrust inside her. In and out, over and over.

And like that, though he should be too tired to function, he wanted her all over again.

He let himself into his apartment and took a long shower and nap, needing to rebuild his energy and regroup. He'd lost himself in Justine, wanting nothing more than to be with her, in her.

Consumed by her.

He had a feeling she felt the same way, a bit overwhelmed by it all. They'd mutually agreed to spend the day apart, taking care of chores and odds and ends. Fortunately, instead of their separation turning awkward, it felt natural, and he didn't sense that he'd offended her at all by agreeing to part ways for a while.

Xavier knew that made sense. He'd been so wrapped up in Justine he hadn't wanted to leave. *Must be in the new, obsessive phase of this relationship.* He tried to convince himself it would pass, but after waking several hours later, he missed her even more.

And that wasn't good at all.

He tried to distract himself by getting in a decent workout, going for groceries, and cleaning up his already spotless apartment. Then he worked on a few more panels for Aunt Truth.

As he drew and answered advice questions, he wondered if he'd ever answered one of Justine's. Most of those inquiring never used their real names or email addresses, but every now and then someone did.

He wondered why Rosie hadn't confided in her favorite niece that she was in fact Aunt Truth. But since she hadn't, he hadn't felt comfortable telling Justine about her aunt's secret identity. Or his part in Aunt Truth's columns. He needed to talk to Rosie to ask why.

After another hour of work, he figured to go downtown and grab a drink or ice cream. He wanted to ask Justine to accompany him, but he didn't want to seem pushy. Plus, anytime he thought about her, he recalled how good she felt wrapped around him, how she tasted of sex and sweet cherries, a lingering aftereffect of her shampoo and soap.

He had it bad for her, no doubt. But as much as he fixated on her looks, it was her smile, her joy with life, that had him truly enchanted. So intelligent and compassionate, yet Justine was less than perfect with her insecurities and vulnerability.

It was that imperfection that drew him to her. She was perfect because she *wasn't* perfect.

No, Justine was the whole package—personality, smarts, and looks.

A woman he could easily envision a forever with.

But he knew better than to think of happily ever after.

Worried when he'd previously been so happy, he hurried out of his apartment and downstairs, on the hunt for ice cream, when he saw his mother and Top laughing near the fountain. He stopped at the foot of the stairs and watched, not liking all the closeness he was seeing.

"Oh, wow. How'd you get to be so handy, Max?"

Xavier gaped at the surly Max Dixon grinning like a kid at

Christmas. Holy shit, was that a dimple? And had she called Top by his first name? The guy had allowed that?

"Ah, just lucky, I guess. I used to fix everything around the house for Lydia. Then after she passed, I needed something to keep me out of trouble. When I wasn't out in the field or overseas on a float, I'd have too much time on my hands at home. So I started fixing things. Taking classes about electric and plumbing work. I planned on building my own home someday."

"Did you?" Cynthia leaned close, looking way too attentive.

Hold on. Had his mother just batted her lashes? Was she *flirting?*

"I did not, but I did help my brother build his place." Top shrugged, the nice, collared polo making him look somewhat polished, his short hair gleaming under the evening light.

"Oh? Where's that?"

Top broke into an animated description of a house in the Midwest. Cynthia, bless her, looked captivated by his every word.

Xavier stared at the pair, hidden in the stairwell though he might as well have been sitting right next to them. It wouldn't have mattered. They seemed totally enrapt in their conversation.

And in each other.

Huh. Did Auggie know? But really, did Xavier? Just because his mother and Top seemed to be overly friendly didn't mean much. He'd seen them chatting before. No, they were just being sociable.

Oddly relieved, he walked out of the shadows, determined to see for himself, and watched as his mother's eyes grew large when she spotted him.

Top drew back with a smile that to Xavier, seemed forced. "Hey, Xavier. Just chatting with your mom."

"I see that." He looked his mother over, sensing nothing odd in her appearance. She looked pretty, as always, dressed in a casual tee-shirt and shorts, a spot of makeup enhancing her beauty. But she wore jewelry today, not something she always did.

"I was just coming up to see you." His mom smiled and turned back to Top. "Thanks for keeping me company."

Top shoved his hands in his pockets, looking discomfited. "Ah, it was nothing, Cynthia. Great to see you again."

"Hey, Mom. I was just heading out for some ice cream." He studied Top but saw nothing but the man's poker face. Had Xavier imagined his unease? "Feel free to come with us, Top."

"Nah. You and your mom enjoy. I think I might take some time off today."

Cynthia nodded. "You totally should. Maybe see a movie. The latest action thriller has been getting decent reviews. There's a six o'clock showing I might see."

Top nodded, hanging on Cynthia's every word. "Huh. Maybe I'll check that out."

The way he looked at Xavier's mom, Xavier thought the guy would do more than check it out. No doubt he'd be there early, entrenched in position, waiting for Cynthia to show.

His mom flushed. "Great seeing you. Bye." She walked with Xavier toward the front of the building.

Top watched them leave until he saw Xavier watching him. Then he gave Xavier an indecipherable look, turned, and walked away.

"Mom, what is going on with you and Top?" Xavier asked the moment they left the building.

"Who? Oh, Max? He's such a nice man."

"Top?" His voice came out louder than he'd intended, and he deliberately softened it. "I mean, yeah, he's a decent guy. A real hard worker. In fact, I was telling Auggie that he's probably a softie on the inside." Buried very, very deep.

"Exactly. I think he acts tough to keep others away. I get the sense he still misses his wife. She died fifteen years ago, you know. Cancer."

"No kidding. I knew he was married but not that she passed away." That explained a lot about the gruff older man. "So you're going to a movie later?"

She nodded. "I need a break myself. I've been helping Jane with her online craft store, and a bunch of us have been putting in hours with Pets Fur Life, that animal charity that's been pretty popular."

"You're getting a pet?" Was his mother having some kind of midlife crisis?

"Um, no. I'm helping animals get adopted and working to schedule a few events since their coordinator is out East helping sick family."

"You're such a nice lady. Trying to get yourself into heaven with good works." He patted her head.

She slapped his hand. "Don't be a jerk, boy."

He chuckled. "I still think you're nice." Too nice for Top.

"I am nice. So nice that you're buying me a rocky road ice cream cone."

"Sounds good."

"And while we're eating, you can tell me all about this new woman who has you hooked. Apparently, you're eating out of the palm of her hand, and it's embarrassing and amusing."

"Freaking Auggie," he muttered.

Cynthia hugged his arm as they walked. "She likes the girl. Kind of. But of course, she thinks it would be best if I met her too. How about inviting her to dinner tomorrow night?"

Xavier had called it with Justine earlier. A need to use the fake girlfriend. He smiled, pleased he could rationalize the need to spend more time with her. Not because he was falling for her, but because his mom wanted to meet her.

The lie scoured his brain, but better discomfort than a broken heart when the relationship ended.

He paused in thought. *Is that what I'm afraid of? Grief?*

"Xavier?"

"Sure, Mom," he hurried to say, bemused at his inner demons. "I'll invite her. Tomorrow, what time?"

"Six sounds good. Anything she doesn't like?"

"Nosy women prying into her life, I'm sure."

His mother popped him in the back of the head. "Ow."

"You're not so old that I can't take you down a notch."

"Yes, Mom."

She smiled. "Good. Now tell me about Justine Ferrera and what's going on with Aunt Truth. Any new advice letters that have you stumped?"

"Not so far. Although there was one from a harangued man in his thirties dealing with a demanding mother."

Her eyes narrowed. "Is that so?"

He smirked. "Yeah. Aunt Truth told him to give his mother whatever she wanted and she'd leave him alone."

She gave a harrumph. "For that smart comment, I'll get two scoops instead of one. And I'm definitely getting chocolate sprinkles."

Xavier laughed. "Whatever you want, Mom. I am but your humble servant."

"You remember that." She patted his arm. "Now tell me about Justine."

He sighed and gave in. "You're going to like her. I'm sure of it." He found himself running at the mouth about all of Justine's finer qualities. When he'd finally wound down, they stood outside the ice cream parlor, and his mother was smiling at him in a weird way.

He added in a mumble, "Oh, and from what I know, she's not allergic to anything. But I'll doublecheck."

"That's my boy."

♡

Saturday morning, while Xavier napped...

"You're sure he was coming from the third floor?" Auggie asked him again.

Benji didn't pause in his repetition, finishing the set. He dropped the weights and wiped sweat from his brow. To Auggie's surprise, he'd met her this morning at the gym without protest.

Of course, she had promised him breakfast afterward, but still. The shy guy actually showed. It helped that the gym wasn't too crowded on a Saturday morning. She loved it, having already run three miles to warm up.

He nodded to the bench. "Want me to spot you?"

"Nah. I'm doing legs today. You keep going. We adding twenty-fives?"

He nodded.

She watched him settle back down and added the weight to his bar. Lost in the rhythm of his workout and what Xavier's new connection with Justine meant, it took a minute to realize he'd finished and was sitting up, staring at her. "What's wrong?"

He swallowed, his expression hidden behind a lot of a hair over his eyes. "You're pretty defined. Nice arms."

She looked down at herself. "Oh, yeah. Got a summer competition coming up." Not nearly as important as this news about Xavier. "So my brother. You're sure he was coming down from Justine's?"

"Since Kai's in Italy with Rosie, yeah. Unless he's getting it on with Top or Adam, I'd say he was coming from Justine's place."

"Oh my gosh. Was that sarcasm I heard, Wolf Man?"

"Wolf Man?" He frowned. "Oh, a crack about my beard, right?"

"Beard, hair, all of it. You're almost furry. Get a haircut, why don't you."

He shrugged. "I hadn't thought about it."

"But don't you get all sweaty under that mop?"

He wiped his face again with a towel. "You get sweaty, but I'm not complaining." He gave her tank top an appreciative look.

Shocked, Auggie stared. "Are you on drugs?"

"What? No." He flushed and stood.

Auggie had to look up to make eye contact. "I'm teasing. It's nice to see that you have a sense of humor up there."

"Ha ha. First I'm hairy, then sweaty. Now I'm too tall?"

She was teasing, but he didn't seem to understand that. "I'm just messing with you, Benji. Geez." She turned to walk away, but his large hand on her shoulder stopped her.

He squeezed. "I'm messing with you right back, Auggie. Geez," he said in a higher voice, poking fun at her.

She turned back and grinned. She caught his return smile and felt something inside her shift. Seeing Benji in a whole new light as a fellow gym enthusiast passed by and gave him a onceover startled her, and she coughed to cover her confusion.

"You know, you owe me."

"I do?" He crossed his arms over his broad chest.

Huh. Benji has muscles and a broad chest. How have I never seen this before?

"Yeah, you owe me. I helped you with that video game demo. You're slacking on the intel, buddy."

Benji frowned. "What are you talking about?"

"You haven't given me much on Justine. The pretty lady my brother's boning."

He flushed, as she'd known he would. Man, he was cute when he was flustered. How about that? "How would I know about her? I've talked to her maybe twice."

"And? What do you think? Is she pretty? Nice? Smart?"

He flushed even redder. "She's okay, I guess."

"You guess?" She tightened her ponytail.

"She's not prettier than you."

"Aw, Benji. Just for that, I'm not going to make you do burpees. Goblin squats instead."

He groaned.

"Then we'll go to breakfast for our first official date."

He tripped over a barbell sitting nearby but righted himself quickly. *"Date?"*

Man, who knew his voice could pitch that high and still sound masculine? She winked. "Grab that kettlebell and let's get to it."

His shy grin had her pulse racing, doing a workout all its own.

CHAPTER 26

Sunday night, Xavier did his best not to laugh at Justine's nerves. Just as she'd been at her own parents, she turned on the anxiety while waiting outside the door to his mother's home.

"I swear. She'll love you. Now, remember how much you *like* me, my lovely girlfriend."

She blushed. "Not love?"

"Well, not yet. That kind of feeling takes time."

He felt all kinds of weird about the L word with Justine. Mostly because he was scared he felt that raw, untamable emotion for her despite doing his best not to feel anything but mutual admiration and a healthy dose of *like*.

But hell, after their weekend of marathon sex and spending time together, he couldn't help himself. He'd done his best to leave her alone yesterday but had caved by eight last night and asked her over to watch a movie.

Except they spent their time on the couch doing anything but watching the TV for entertainment. Several orgasms later, she slept in his arms, and he didn't have the strength to wake her to see if she'd rather go home. Instead, he'd carried her into his bedroom and curled up next to her.

He'd never slept so well. As if he'd finally found home.

Which freaked him the hell out. As a therapist, he knew he should delve deeper to find out why he'd panicked. But the cowardly side of him wanted to enjoy his time with Justine without thinking too hard about it.

And now, standing in front of the home he'd grown up in, he was about to introduce his fake girlfriend to his mother, when everything about his relationship with Justine felt more real than anything he'd ever had.

"Ha. Now who's looking stressed?" She was even cute when smug.

He leaned down to kiss her, and of course his mother opened the door just as their mouths met.

"Ah ha. The mysterious Justine is in fact real." Cynthia sounded way too pleased with herself. "I knew it."

Xavier hastily tore his mouth from Justine's but kept his arm around her shoulders. "Hey, Mom. Meet Justine. Justine, my estimable mother, Cynthia Hanover."

Cynthia pulled Justine in for a hug. "I'm so happy to meet you."

Justine was flushed when she pulled back, but her shy smile told him she liked the embrace. "So nice to meet you too."

She let Cynthia tug her inside. Xavier followed and shut the door behind them. "Are we waiting on Auggie, Mom? I don't see her car."

"Oh, your sister is busy. It's just the three of us tonight."

"Is that so?" What was his sister up to? He had a tough time believing she wouldn't have wanted to interrogate Justine at a family dinner. For that matter, his sister had been surprisingly quiet lately. He'd chalked that up to her ramped up training, but now he wasn't sure…

His mom started pestering Justine about all sorts of details, taking her attention. But Cynthia did it in such a nice way Justine immediately seemed at ease. She helped his mom prepare the salad while Xavier had been tasked with firing up the grill.

He compared dinner with Justine's parents to dinner with his mom and noticed the difference in his date. Here, she laughed and was at ease. She answered honestly, well, with the exception of their fake dating.

Unfortunately, his mother was all over that. "So, you're Rosie Gallo's niece. Xavier's a big fan of your aunt. I only met her once, but she made an impression."

Justine laughed. "That sounds like Aunt Rosie. She has definite opinions about everything and lives her life the way she wants it."

"I respect that." Cynthia slanted a glance at Xavier. "That's what I'm trying to do."

"My mother is on the dating circuit," Xavier reiterated for everyone's benefit. "But it's slow going. She hasn't had much luck with the guys my sister and I have chosen for her."

"Wow. I've never met an actual matchmaker."

His mother snorted. "He's a bad one. Between the men he and my daughter have mentioned, I might be single for the rest of my life."

Xavier might actually be okay with that and immediately felt ashamed for thinking it. "Mom."

Justine laughed.

"I'm just glad to see my boy with a girl *I* like for once." Cynthia looked pleased. "Even Auggie likes you."

"She does?" Justine asked.

"From what I could tell, yes."

Xavier immediately turned the conversation to his sister, and Justine chimed in with various stories about her siblings.

All in all, the dinner went very well.

Until his mother asked a few questions about Max Dixon.

"Why do you want to know about him?" Xavier narrowed his

gaze. "You seemed friendly enough yesterday when you two were chatting." He didn't know why it should bother him that his mother had hit it off with Top, especially with he and Auggie trying to get her to date. Yet something about Top felt wrong to him.

"Wait, Max? As in, Top, our Super?" Justine asked, looking as poleaxed as he felt.

"Yes. He's really a sweetheart."

"Um, okay." Apparently aware her response seemed half-hearted, Justine rallied. "He was a great part of our water fight. Last week, I got revenge on our teenage neighbors by water-balloon bombing them back. Then everyone got in on it." Justine paused in thought. "You know, for an older guy, Top's not bad looking. He's in pretty great shape, actually."

Xavier didn't appreciate that she'd noticed Top's assets. *Oh my God. I'm jealous of Top?*

"Older guy, ha." Cynthia grinned. "I'll have to tell him that."

Flummoxed, he went on the offensive. "Tell Top that? Why would you tell him Justine thinks he's hot?"

Justine flushed. "I didn't say hot. I said he was fit. And yeah, he's good-looking in a tough guy kind of way."

Cynthia nodded and said to Xavier, "You might as well know he and I met yesterday for a movie. Then we shared dinner. He's a great conversationalist."

"*Mom.*" The other men he'd had in mind for his mom had been nice. Safe. Maybe even a little boring. Top would be anything but.

"I think it's sweet." Justine smiled. "Xavier, just think. Your mom may have met her prince charming, and all because of you."

He felt a little ill. "Prince Charming? More like Beauty and the Beast."

Cynthia scowled at him, though he could see the twinkle of amusement in her gaze. "Xavier, honestly."

"But which one is the beast, that's the question," he said, causing his mother and Justine to laugh. "You know I'm kidding, Mom." *Come on, sound like you mean it.* He cleared his throat. "I like Top. *Max.* But if he treats you wrong, I'll break his kneecaps." He could never forget how much she'd cried after his father had died. Heart wrenching sobs that had made his own grief even worse.

Justine sighed and batted her lashes at him. "My hero. A guy who takes care of his mom."

"Don't encourage him, Justine. He's a little bully." Cynthia snorted. "I mean, I'd expect that kind of talk from Auggie, but not my sensitive son." She looked him over. "As if you could take Max down. That man looks pretty solid to me."

"Me too," Justine said in a loud whisper, glanced at Xavier, then tried to hide her laughter. "But not as handsome or in shape as *my* man."

Xavier shouldn't have flushed at hearing her call him that. But that easily, she flattered and pleased him with little effort. And if he happened to start buying into the fiction of his and Justine's relationship, it was just two friends having some fun.

Right?

MONDAY AFTERNOON, Justine received a text from her friend, Kenzie, about some contract WORK if she was interested. After spending most of her day learning about the scope of her new duties at work—talk about a headache—she replied right away.

SIGN ME UP!

Kenzie sent back a laughing emoji and gave her the details for the job.

Justine worked two hours overtime, for which she wouldn't be paid, just trying to catch up on all the work of her own she'd missed while learning her new duties. And no, according to

Frank, Justine would not be getting any help. She needed to learn to manage it all herself.

Hurray.

She returned home, exhausted, only to see a bouquet of flowers left at her door. The note with them read, *I know today must have sucked. Was thinking of you. XO. Your Man.*

She grinned from ear to ear as she brought the lovely arrangement inside. After fixing a dinner and relaxing, she texted Xavier a big thanks. She debated on whether or not to add a big heart then said to heck with it and sent it.

He hadn't communicated at all except for an early message to have a nice day. She appreciated him giving her space, but her thoughts still crept to him and what he might be doing while she worked.

She felt warm and fuzzy, staring from the TV to her flowers. She moved them to her bedroom and set them on her dresser.

And fell asleep staring at the fragrant blooms.

The next two days followed a similar pattern, until she was frothing with rage by the end of Wednesday. Katie met her three hours after she should have gone home, and Justine vented over beer and brats at the local German pub while Katie nodded and listened, adding an occasional "Frank's such an ass" where needed.

When Justine finally wound down, she noticed Katie studying her. "What?"

"You haven't mentioned Xavier at all, so I'm waiting to hear you roast him too."

"Xavier? No, he's awesome. Supportive yet distant enough he's not overbearing."

Katie frowned. "There has got to be something wrong with this guy. No one is this perfect. Let's face it—he's got the hot part, the smart part, and the magic peen part down pat." Of course Katie added the bit about the magic peen as two handsome mid-thirties guys passed.

They heard and laughed out loud, winking back at Katie.

She returned the wink before turning to Justine. "Well? What is rattling around in his closet, do you think?"

"He hasn't been working lately, but he's going back to therapy soon."

"Being in therapy is a good thing though, right?" Katie asked.

"No. He's not getting therapy. He gives it. I told you he's an LMFT."

"Oh, right." Katie tapped her lip. "And we're sure he's not dating anyone while being your personal massage toy?"

Justine felt her cheeks heat up again, but this time she laughed. "You're such an ass."

Katie stuck out her tongue. "You know you love me. Besides, you're too pent up. You need a breather. The beer with me is great, but maybe some magic Xavier time would help."

"Yeah, maybe." And that, right there, was her other problem. "Katie, I…"

She meant to admit how much Xavier was coming to mean to her when Dr. Mitchell Ascot, her annoying ex, walked into the pub with a gorgeous brunette on his arm. Justine intended to pretend she hadn't seen him and hoped he'd do the same.

Unfortunately, he saw her and redirected his course, his gorgeous date in tow. As he approached, his smile widened.

Katie gave a soft groan. "Man, with you, when it rains, it pours. Is Dr. Dickhead coming closer?"

"Yep." *And now my day is complete*

CHAPTER 27

Justine met Mitch's smile with a bright one of her own. "Hey, Mitch. How are you?"

"Great, thanks." His enthusiasm died a little when he looked across the table. "And Katie. Hi."

"Hey, there, Dr. Feet."

He frowned.

Justine did her best not to giggle. The beer—make that *beers*—seemed to be going to her head.

"Dr. Feet?" His date asked. "Oh, because he's a podiatrist? Funny." She smirked at Katie and gripped Mitch's arm with more than little possession.

"Don't mind Katie." Justine forced herself to remain pleasant, aware Mitch seemed eager to stand around and rub his date in her face. "I'm Justine."

"Mikayla. It's nice to meet you. Mitch, I'll go grab us a table." She gave him a peck on the cheek and walked away. More like flounced away with an ass that could bounce quarters, but whatever. Mitch liked his women fit, as she recalled.

"What are you up to?" Mitch asked.

She saw Katie texting like a fiend and realized she'd get no help there. Instead, Justine did her best to act as if seeing Mitch wasn't beyond irritating after the day she'd had. Not that she harbored him any ill feeling, but he'd always acted as if his needs were more important than her own. Kind of like standing around, using all her oxygen when she was busy bitching to Katie and reveling in friend-time.

"Not much, actually. I'm still working for Mayze Creative and enjoying my aunt's place. It's terrific and right near downtown Fremont."

"Nice." He paused. "Seeing anyone?"

"How is that your business?" Katie asked without looking up from the phone or stopping her fingers from flying.

He sneered. "Was I talking to you?"

"She's seeing someone else, yeah. Someone who values her opinions and doesn't treat her like she's beneath him." Katie gave him a wide smile. "Now why don't you skedaddle back to your date before her boobs deflate."

"They're real," he denied then flushed. "And that's a real nice way to talk about another woman."

Personally, Justine didn't care. "Mitch, it's been a long day. I'm glad you found someone to date. She looks lovely." *Though those boobs do look a little* too *perfect,* came the catty thought, causing her to grin.

"What the hell is so funny?" he asked, looking livid.

Your stupid face. No, not what she should say, no matter how much she wanted to. She wondered how Xavier would calmly and maturely handle the situation. "Look, I've had a bad day and a little too much to drink. I'm sorry if Katie offended you."

"I'm not," Katie muttered.

"Please accept our apologies and enjoy your evening. Mikayla seems really nice."

"She is." He seemed like he had more to say, then shook his head. "I just wanted to say hello." He ignored Katie. "And to let you know I'll be at the wedding this weekend. Mikayla is friends with Ted through his sister. I'll be her plus one."

Katie looked up.

Justine blinked. "Huh?"

"It's lucky we ran into you tonight. It doesn't sound like your sister told you I'll be there." He paused. "I don't have to go, if that would be easier." Mitch seemed to be sincere about not wanting to make her feel bad. Despite being a little selfish, he was a nice guy.

"Thanks, Mitch." She gave him what she hoped was a sincere smile. "That's not a problem. I hope you enjoy the wedding. I'll look forward to seeing you there."

He didn't seem to know what to make of her response. Honestly, she didn't either. She felt like she was channeling Xavier, acting all mature.

After a moment, Mitch gave a hesitant nod. "Sounds good. See you." Still ignoring Katie, he turned and left to join his date several tables away, his back to their booth.

"What an ass." Katie ordered another round of beers. "I never liked that guy."

Justine snickered. "Dr. Feet."

They burst into laughter, and Justine felt much better as the night progressed.

To her surprise, the next time a handsome man stood at the side of their table, it wasn't their server but Xavier looking sexy as usual.

He looked them over, focusing on Justine. "Well, well, what do we have here?"

"Hey, man. Take a seat." Katie scooted over and patted the spot next to her. "Sit by me so you can moon properly over your cutie."

He snorted. "How many have beers have you had, Katie?" He shook his head at Justine. "And you. I'm surprised. It's a work night."

"Screw work." She drank some more. "I hate Frank."

"And Mitch," Katie added, toasting bottles.

"I'll drink to that." Xavier grabbed a glass of water neither of them had claimed.

It took Justine a moment to process. "Hey, what are you doing here?"

"Katie texted. Said my girlfriend needed me. So here I am."

"Wait. Girlfriend?" She turned to Katie, who didn't look nearly as innocent as she pretended to be, even after several beers. Justine asked in a hushed voice, "Uh-oh. I told you about the fake boyfriend thing, didn't I?"

"You did," Katie whispered loudly back. Then she laughed. "I texted him and here he is. A superhero with a big package."

Xavier blinked. "What?"

She pointed to the hat he'd set down next to him. "Did I say a big package? I meant hat."

He flushed, and Justine thought him just the cutest. He smiled. "The cutest, huh?"

"Crap. I said that out loud." She had a bad habit of saying whatever popped into her mind aloud when drunk. That would not be good with Xavier. He couldn't possibly know how much she liked him or was attracted to him. "Don't want to scare you off."

He looked smug. "No chance of that." He glanced around and whispered to Katie.

She nodded in the direction Mitch had gone.

"Ah. The dark-haired guy with the pretty date in red?"

"That's Dr. Douche."

Justine sighed. "Katie, if you had a jar for every time you swore, you'd have a lot of nickels."

Katie and Xavier just looked at her.

"What?"

Xavier shook his head. "I think you two need to lay off the beer and start downing water. Tomorrow probably won't look so sunny at work. Oh, and I'm driving you both home unless you want to call for a ride."

Katie pouted. "You're not nearly as fun as you were when we watched *Spartacus*."

"True." Justine agreed.

"Well, someone has to take one for the team." He looked up when Mitch and Mikayla stopped by their table. "Can we help you?"

Wow. Xavier sounded so polite.

Mitch frowned. "Who are you?"

"Her boyfriend," Katie said before Justine could answer. "And he's got a big package. I mean, hat." Katie gave an exaggerated wink.

Justine slapped a hand over her face, but not before she saw Xavier's shit-eating grin.

"I'm Mitch. Justine's ex-boyfriend." Mitch stared down at Xavier.

Xavier, always the mature, sensible guy, remained seated and courteous. "Ah, the doctor ex-boyfriend. Nice to meet you. I'm Xavier, Justine's current boyfriend."

Justine drank water, trying to sober up before she admitted to Mitch that Xavier was just pretending…and that her brief, fake boyfriend was better than Mitch had ever been.

"This is Mikayla, my girlfriend," Mitch introduced while looking at Justine.

She watched the woman, not pleased to see Mikayla's subtle interest in Xavier.

Xavier nodded. "Nice to meet you both. I've heard a lot about you, Mitch." He said nothing more, just smiled.

Everyone stared at one another in silence before Mikayla prodded Mitch to break eye contact with Xavier. What Mitch thought he was doing with all the male posturing was anyone's guess, but Xavier didn't look impressed.

"See you at the wedding," Mitch tossed out before leaving with Mikayla on his arm.

After they left, Xavier turned to Katie and said, "And that's how you Mitch-slap Dr. Douche without saying a word."

Katie laughed so hard she cried, which had Justine snorting and laughing as well.

Unfortunately, she wasn't laughing an hour later as Xavier carried her into TCA's elevator and they rode up to her floor. "Oh man. I feel dizzy."

"What happened to you two? Katie texted that Mitch had arrived with some woman on his arm and that you needed backup. So I came."

She sighed into his chest and snuggled closer. "Thanks."

He chuckled, and she heard the vibration through his body. "You're slurring, sweetheart."

"Aw, I like when you call me all the mushy names."

"You're going to regret this in the morning, aren't you?"

"Am I late for work already?"

"Huh? It's just a little past eleven, but I doubt you drink so heavily when you need to be at work the next day. When do you get up? Six? Seven?"

"Six-thirty. Do you ever work? How can you take so much time off? Are you a secret billionaire?" She yawned. "It doesn't matter. You're too pretty to work. You just need to find a sugar-momma to keep you."

"Oh? Know any?"

"Well, if I'm not tired for hating my job, I'll do it. Although I'm kinda not rich." She stroked his beard, loving the soft texture that could feel kind of scratchy in all the right places. "This feels so good between my legs."

His grip tightened. "You really have the worst timing."

"Come on, sexy. Let's go to my place and Mitch-slap each other." She giggled, snorted, and laughed so hard she nearly fell out of his arms.

"God, you're cute even when you're drunk. How much did you have to drink, anyway?"

"Four beers. But I didn't eat much today." She groaned and snuggled closer. "You always smell so good. Why can't we fuck until we drop?"

He bobbled her in his arms but managed not to drop her as he gently set her down. "You're killing me, you know that? No way I'm taking you to bed until you sober up."

"What a Boy Scout."

"Not quite. I'll take a kiss." He gave her soft peck on the lips.

When she would have extended the kiss, he pulled back. "No teasing. Keys?"

She grumbled and handed him her purse. A moment of sobriety returned. "I'm sorry Katie called you. We would have called for a ride, you know. We might be a little drunk but we're not stupid."

"I trust you. But no reason you had to deal with your ex alone. I mean, Katie's great, but it's always nicer to have a fake boyfriend to make your problems go away."

He smiled, his eyes clear, his gaze soft. This close, she could make out the striations of amber and brown in his gorgeous eyes.

"I like you so much, Xavier." She let him tug her into her home and followed as he prodded her toward the bedroom.

She lifted her arms when he told her to and let him take off her clothes, leaving her in a bra and panties and feeling like a toddler. But the look he gave her made her feel very grownup.

She grinned and cupped her breasts.

"I swear, I should be getting some big karmic boost for this." He groaned and helped her out of her bra and into her favorite sleep tee. "Go on." He nodded to the bathroom. "I'll wait out here."

She sat down on the toilet and relieved herself, forever it felt like.

A knock at the door revived her. "Justine? You okay in there?"

"Yep. Be right out." *Man, I almost fell asleep on the toilet with Xavier right outside! Talk about getting a little too familiar with the boytoy.* She laughed out loud and hurried to finish. After she washed up, she rejoined him in her bedroom.

The bed looked ultra inviting. As did Xavier.

She slid under the covers and patted the spot next to her. "Just for a little?"

"Twist my arm." He laid on top of the covers on his side, looking at her. "I like you a lot too, Justine." He leaned forward to kiss her. "You're sweet and smart. Your body is amazing, and you're fun to be around."

"Yeah, all that. About you, I mean." She closed her eyes, still seeing the curl of his full lips.

"Sleep tight, Justine. Want me set your alarm?"

She didn't know what she said. She only knew the feel of his arm over her and the scent of Xavier seeping into her made her feel at home.

CHAPTER 28

Thursday morning, Xavier stood next to the bed and stared down at a sleepy Justine.

Something had to give.

All this pretend nonsense had turned into something real he wanted more than anything. So much so that he'd dropped everything last night just to help out his "friend" with an ex. And she hadn't really needed the help. Katie had thought his presence might make Justine feel better.

So of course he'd gone.

It struck him that he'd do pretty much anything for her. And no, he hadn't liked that dickass Dr. Douche, as Katie had called him, being anywhere near Justine.

Jealousy, affection, lust, care, worry—he had it all for the adorable woman currently drooling on her pillow.

"Justine? Time to get up."

She moaned and rolled over.

He turned off her phone alarm. He'd been up since six, unable to help his healthy habit of being early to rise and getting a ton done before most people went to work. "Up and at 'em, killer."

She mumbled what sounded a lot like, "Fuck off." Which added yet another dimension to the usually soft-spoken woman.

"Excuse me?" he asked in a deep, authoritative voice to screw with her.

She turned and screeched when she saw him. "*Xavier?*"

"You were expecting Mitch, maybe?"

"Oh, my head." She sat up and clutched her temples, her hair mussed, her shirt rumpled, yet she still looked gorgeous.

He handed her a pain reliever and apple juice, anticipating her troubles. "Take it. I got the pill from your medicine cabinet."

"Oh, man. I love you for this." She swallowed the pill and closed her eyes as she downed her juice, fortunately not seeing what those three little words had done to his state of mind as she left the bed.

Secretly freaking out because he had a bad feeling he'd fallen in love with her *for real,* he took a moment to bury his panic before following her into the kitchen, where he had coffee brewing.

"I'm going to take a quick shower, okay?"

He nodded, watching her over the brim of his coffee cup. "You remember everything from last night?"

"Most of it, I think." She finished off her juice and placed the cup in the sink. "I can't thank you enough for helping us. You didn't have to come."

"I wanted to."

She gave him a sincere smile that gave him *all* the feels. "Thank you."

What would Aunt Truth say about that? Something about Cupid hitting him right where it counted.

He cleared his mind, or at least, he tried. "Oh, Justine. If you only realized I'd move mountains for you." He winked to show he was—mostly—teasing. "That's not just fake boyfriend sentiment. We're real friends, in case you didn't realize."

"I know. More than friends, though, huh?" She looked him over. "You spent the whole night with me."

"I did. You have a nice bed."

"Very funny."

He leaned back against the counter. "What? It's true."

"I…" She groaned. "I'm going to go get clean and get myself together. Then we need to talk."

"Whatever." *We need to talk.* The four words a man rarely wanted to hear from the woman he'd fallen in love with. *Jesus, I'm in love. Hadn't expected* that *to happen.*

The shower turned on, but he didn't make much of it over the thread of panic weaving through him. Xavier was supposed to be recuperating from his breakup with Christine. Taking time to mentally heal from all the stresses in his life, both professional and personal.

He also knew Justine had no intention of dating. Hell, they were just friends who'd had sex. He was her fake boyfriend—emphasis on the *fake.* The smart thing would be to stay away from her and put a respectable distance between them. To help her out with the wedding then back off and return to his regular life. Work, the gym, his family, maybe find a woman to date once he felt whole again.

The problem was he felt whole when with Justine, and he didn't know what to do about it.

"Xavier," she called, sounding anxious.

He raced to the bathroom and knocked. "You okay in there?"

"I need help."

He pushed through the door and saw her form blurred behind the shower curtain. Knowing she was naked turned him inside out. He cleared his throat and told himself to behave. "Justine?"

She ripped the curtain back and yanked him by the arm into the shower, a lot stronger than she looked.

"Oh, no. You're getting all wet." She had him naked and plastered to the tiled wall in seconds.

"Justine?" Confused and in lust, he tried waking himself from a scenario straight out of his X-rated fantasies.

"I just wanted to thank you for being such a sweetheart." She moved closer and kissed him, and he tasted minty toothpaste. A fact that had him seeing stars when she went to her knees and took him in her mouth. The pressure of her lips was heavenly in addition to the tingle from the mint, but thank God not overpowering.

"Oh, *fuck*."

She grinned around his cock and started blowing him, the suction drawing him deeper while he tried not to ram down her throat.

"Justine, oh, yeah. Baby, you don't have to..." He couldn't think as she cupped his balls and deep-throated him. When the hell had she learned *that*? But when he neared his end, he grabbed her by the shoulders and edged her back. "Get up."

She licked her lips and smiled at him, a woman sure of her power. "Like it?"

"Love it." He kissed her, changing positions as he lifted her in his arms and set her back to the tiled wall, wrapping her legs around his waist. He leaned close to suck her nipples, gratified by her moans for more. When he stopped, she kissed him and ground against his dick, which nearly slipped inside her a few times.

"In me," she insisted.

He nearly pushed inside her then froze. "I don't have a condom handy."

"We don't need one." She kissed him again. "I'm on birth control and safe. And you are too, right?"

"God, yes."

She didn't let him wait and shifted, taking matters into her own hands. He slid up into her, bombarded with pleasure as he seated himself balls-deep.

"Oh, Xavier." She kissed him and angled her pelvis to grind against his.

The angle left no space between them, and he let himself go, pumping inside her while they kissed, rubbing against her clit while she cried out and humped him even harder.

"Xavier, yes, I'm coming," she moaned and clamped down on him.

He was lost, pouring into her before he could blink, the orgasm all-consuming.

The water continued to pour over them, but Xavier couldn't process more than the feeling of her warmth surrounding him while he filled her.

"You feel so good in me," she whispered and stroked his wet hair. "I'm sorry I took advantage of you. Last night and today."

"No, I'm good. It's all good," he managed as he got his breath back. "Technically, Katie texted me last night, not you."

"I feel like a helpless idiot around you sometimes."

He stared at her in shock. "Justine, I can barely remember my own name right now. I'm the idiot." He wiggled his hips and pumped once more, the feel of her incredible. "Or not, because I came so hard inside you." He kissed her, unable to help himself. "I know I should let you get ready for work, but if you give me a little time, I can go again."

"How much time?"

It didn't take him long to get ready for more of Justine. When they managed to leave the shower, the water had turned lukewarm but not yet cold.

"Want something to eat?" he asked a few minutes later, leaning against the doorjamb of the bathroom. He wore a towel around his waist, his clothes in the drier.

"Oatmeal?" She'd dressed and was applying her makeup.

"Coming up." He left for the kitchen to scrounge, in a fine mood, and made her a bowl.

She soon joined him in the kitchen. "You're not eating?"

"I'm meeting Auggie for breakfast later." He frowned. "If I didn't know better, I'd say she's been avoiding me." When he saw her concern, he waved it away. "That's typical Auggie, being dramatic. Are you going to be okay today?"

"I guess the cure to a hangover is an ibuprofen and two orgasms. Oh, and oatmeal." She winked.

He laughed. "Good to know I'm useful and not just a pretty face."

Justine flushed. "I said a lot of nonsense last night. I hope I didn't make a fool of myself."

"Not at all. You're cute when you're drunk. But Katie... Not a great singer after a few beers. The acoustics in the car didn't help."

She laughed. "Oh boy. We really do owe you."

He let her eat before asking, "I have one question for you. What was all that about Mitch coming to the wedding? Your sister's wedding?"

She grimaced. "I thought I'd dreamed that. Ugh. Seems Mitch is coming with Mikayla, who was invited. So not only do you have to be my date, you might have to deal with my ex as well." She eyed him with hesitation. "It's not too late to back out."

"No way. I'm in." He paused. "Unless you'd rather I didn't go?"

She brightened. "Heck no. I want you right there with me. Fake boyfriend or not, you're the best thing that's happened to me in a long time." She blushed. "I, uh... I just meant, um. No pressure or anything."

Justine sounded as unsure about them as he was, and for some odd reason that made him feel better. "Well, *girlfriend*, then I'd suggest we make a game plan. Let's get our stories straight and have the best damn time we can at your sister's wedding. And hey, if we're lucky, everything will go smoothly. Right? I mean, what's the worst that can happen?"

CHAPTER 29

Xavier had to wait an extra twenty minutes after Justine left for his clothes to dry, but he appreciated the extra time, certain Benji would have been at work before he made it to his apartment.

"Didn't you wear that yesterday?"

Xavier nearly jumped a foot as he turned to see his neighbor staring at him from his open door across the hall. "Dude, warn me next time."

Benji frowned. "Am I wrong?"

"Why do you keep track of what I wear each day? And shouldn't you be at work?"

Benji shrugged. "I'm home today. They switched me this week with Owen." He looked Xavier over and smirked. "I don't know what you wear every day, but I'm pretty sure I saw that shirt on you yesterday." Something fell behind him in his apartment. "Gotta go. Later." Benji disappeared in his apartment.

"Weird." Xavier shrugged and let himself inside. After throwing on some fresh clothes, he picked up his cell phone and saw two missed messages from Auggie, so he called her back. "Hello?"

"Hey, dumbass. Answer your phone once in a while."

"Well, look who took the time to call. Ms. Drama."

"Up yours."

He grinned. "We still doing breakfast?" He heard a deep voice in the background. "Auggie, are you calling from a boy's house?"

"You are such a pain." Auggie snickered and must have muted her phone, because after a lengthy silence, she said, "Yeah, yeah. I'm here. I'll meet you at Roxie's at eight-thirty."

"Okay, I—"

She disconnected.

"Rude." He snorted and gave himself extra time since his sister had bumped their breakfast by half an hour.

After looking over his *Aunt Truth* work, he emailed it off to the editor and sat back, staring at an email from a friend from the office. Ava always made him smile, the psychologist both funny and amazingly balanced with a happy home and work life. He wanted to be more like her.

Apparently, they needed him back because another of their doctors planned on a month-long vacation while their other family therapist took a much-needed break. The nice thing about working at MYM Counseling was that the staff all worked hard to be mentally healthy themselves. And they all treated each other like equals, doctors or not. Something not every clinic could brag about.

He'd interned at one place where he'd been treated like dirt because he didn't have a DR in front of his name. But Xavier had never aspired to that much schooling. He loved what he did, helping people. And he found more value in on-the-job learning. Plus, his peers and the doctors with so much experience had been invaluable in his practice.

"I've got to get back to it," he admitted aloud. Enthused about the prospect of seeing clients again instead of stressed at the thought, he knew he had taken the right amount of time to relax himself. But now he worried about work cutting into his time with Justine.

Between his stint stepping in as Aunt Truth, his new "fake" girlfriend, and jumping back to MYM, he'd have his hands full handling everything. But Xavier thrived on challenging himself. He just hoped he could convince Justine to give them a real chance after the wedding was over. What if she only wanted him for a wedding date, after which they'd go their own way?

Part of him felt saddened, another part devasted, and just a slight bit of him felt relieved. Because if she pulled away, then he wouldn't need to deal with the eventual drama when they parted. So why did that make him mourn what he didn't even have?

BY EIGHT FORTY-FIVE, he and Auggie sat at a back booth. He waited while his sister ordered the latkes and eggs before choosing the super deluxe homefries. Their server poured them both more coffee, flipped Auggie off with a grin, then left.

"Back at ya, Hermione!" Auggie called after her.

"I thought her name was Hetty."

"She changed it the last time we were here. Didn't you see her name tag? Just because she's serving you doesn't mean she's not a real person, Xavier." She shook her head. "Do better, Bro."

He flushed, aware he let his sister get under his skin. "Sorry. *Hermione.*"

"Better." Auggie smirked. She loved nothing better than turning the tables on him, because it was usually Xavier holding "the world"—according to Auggie—accountable for supporting people instead of tearing them down. Not that his sister would ever try to demean anyone, but she had the old USMC attitude of "suck it up, princess," whenever anyone voiced a complaint.

He snorted. "Nice job correcting me when I had no idea she'd changed her name."

"Not my problem, Dr. Do-Little. Do. Little. Two words. Ha.

Get it? Because you do so little?" She looked way too pleased with herself. Yet, she seemed to be hiding behind forced laughter.

"You're not that funny." He stared at her, aware something felt off about Auggie lately. "Why have you been avoiding me?"

"Avoiding you? Please."

He stared at her, aware she couldn't meet his gaze. "Who was the guy on the phone?"

"Which guy? There've been too many to count." She gulped down caffeine as if it could save her from his interrogation.

"And why did you ditch me and Justine at Mom's Sunday night?" He narrowed his gaze. "It's the guy. You're into him."

She huffed. "Whatever. I like men. That's no secret. And I will not be slut shamed."

He groaned when a woman from another table shot him a dirty look. "Would you stop? I've never shamed you for being a slut. Not that you are one. Hell, I don't even like the word."

"Because I wear the name proudly?"

"That's right, honey. Be sex positive," said a person from behind them.

Xavier could almost feel the daggers being shot into his back. "Happy now?"

She snickered. "Yeah."

They looked at each other.

At the same time, they both blurted, "I know you're boffing Justine." "I know you're into this new guy, whoever he is."

They paused, glaring at each other. "Go ahead," Xavier said. "You first."

"Pearls before swine," Auggie said in a snooty voice and laughed at the face he made. "Fine. I know you and Justine are getting hot and involved. Mom liked her. I like her. I think. I don't know her all that well though."

"You should go out with her and get to know her better. Or would that get in the way of your new man?"

They waited while *Hermione* dropped off their food.

"Eat it, bitch." She turned from Auggie and gave Xavier a huge smile. "Hey, sweetie. I haven't seen you lately. Just the loudmouth with her shaggy boyfriend."

"Hermione," Auggie growled. "Go. Away."

"I'd better get a big tip," the server warned, flipped Auggie off, then waved at Xavier. "Let me know if you need more coffee." Pause. "Or anything else, on or off the menu."

He winked, and Hermione sighed before barking at the next customer.

"Hermione sucks," Auggie muttered and stuffed her face with potato pancakes.

"Shaggy boyfriend?" He frowned, wondering who that might be. Benji immediately came to mind, but his sister would never go out with him. Too nerdy, according to Auggie when they'd discussed his neighbor upon first meeting him.

"Because he's someone Hermione wants to shag," Auggie said. "Just give me ten minutes in the gym with her and she'll be sobbing with apologies." Auggie glared at the perky server.

"The gym is supposed to be about making people fit and healthy. Not a place for punishment."

"Keep it up and the next time I have you in there, I'm gonna hurt you."

He rolled his eyes. They concentrated on breakfast before talking again.

"So what's up with you?" Auggie asked.

He filled her in on the dinner with their mother and helping Justine out with Mitch.

"And?"

"And what?" he asked.

"Just admit you're hitting that."

"Oh my God. 'Hitting that?' It's like you're not even trying to be offensive, which I find even more offensive."

Auggie snorted. "You're so repressed. Fine, Mr. Uptight. I

mean, just admit that you find her attractive and you're making sweet, tender love whenever the mood strikes. Better?"

"You're so annoying."

She grinned. "But am I wrong?"

"No." He sighed.

"Hot damn." She clinked her cup with his. "Congrats. Now what?"

"Now I pretend to be her boyfriend at the wedding." He ran a hand through his hair, stressed about a lot more than what came next. "Then I have to figure out how to start dating her for real." *Or do I? Should I just let this end naturally? Why am I acting so indecisive? What's my problem with all this, really?*

"What's to figure out?" Auggie slurped her coffee. "You're already making hot monkey love and moon eyes at each other. You like her. She obviously likes you. Ask her on a real date. With real words."

"That's so…" Reasonable. Trust Auggie not to overthink things, a quality he actually admired about her. "Fine. Maybe I will. And maybe you can tell me who's making you blush, because not just anyone can make my sister turn red in the face." He recalled his mother's blush over dinner. "I need to tell you about Top."

"What about him?" Auggie had a soft spot for the older guy. He was crabby, a Marine, and still benched an impressive set of weight. Her ideal man if he had been a few decades younger.

"Well, I'm not sure, but I think he and Mom might have something going on."

She paused, her cup halfway to her mouth. "What? *Top?* The guy who hates most people just for existing?"

He nodded. "I know. Mom asked about him. She went to the movies with him."

"Well, talk to him."

"I can't do that."

"I sure as hell can." Auggie looked indignant. "I want to know what his intentions are regarding my maternal unit."

Xavier groaned.

Auggie continued, on a roll. "I mean, do they use protection? Should I expect another brother or sister any time soon? And what should I call him? Dad? Father? Daddy?"

Xavier tried to contain a laugh but couldn't at the thought of Top's reaction to his sister's questions. "Please let me be there when you have that conversation."

"Oh, no. We're *both* going to be there. I mean, this is our mom we're talking about."

"Fine." He thought about what he knew of Top. "Apparently, Top was married before. His wife died of cancer a while ago."

"That's awful." Auggie blinked. "I'm still not going easy on the guy, but no poking into his past, I guess."

"How magnanimous of you."

She shook her head. "You try to act all smart—"

"I *am* smart."

"—but we both know that's obviously today's word."

He frowned.

"Remember who bought you that word-of-the-day calendar for Christmas, dumbass."

"Now you're just being truculent."

"Huh?"

"Obstreperous. Refractory." He gave her a smug look. "Obnoxious."

"Ah. Okay, yeah. All that. But still. You're so much smarter thanks to me."

"Bugger off."

She smirked. "With any luck, I'll be doing just that while you're at your girlfriend's wedding."

"It's her sister's wedding."

"Ha. You admit she's your girlfriend. Now quit being a wanker and make it real."

"And you can thank me for that urban dictionary calendar. Wanker is new."

"My word of the day, jackass."

They glared at each other before Xavier sighed. "You win."

"Don't I always?"

"For now." He warned, "But don't think I won't find out about you and your shaggy boyfriend."

She shrugged. "Meh. Give me a few more days and he'll be right where I want him. Under me in chains, begging to serve his dark mistress." She gave a dark laugh and wriggled her brows. "Now where did I put that riding crop?"

"I think I need my brain cleaned out." He gagged. "Must. Get vision. Out of. My head."

"Detoxify, you mean. Yes, you should. Right after you get the check."

CHAPTER 30

The wedding was lovely. Justine did as she was told and walked with Ted's cousin down the aisle. Her sister made a lovely bride. Ted, keeping his mouth shut except to exclaim over his beautiful wife, made a decent enough groom.

Mallory was now Mrs. Ted Cochran. Their parents beamed, the handsome newly married couple basking in the crowd's adoration as the party got underway.

"They sure do know how to throw a party," Xavier said from beside her and handed her a glass of wine.

The reception was in full swing, the music a soft jazz that added to the classy ambience and guests. Though she'd recognized many of her father's associates from work from the many parties her parents hosted, she also saw several of the city's wealthier movers and shakers comingling under her mother's watchful eye.

And of course, at the groom's cluster of tables sat Mikayla and Mitch, looking debonair in a tux.

"Thanks." She drank a sip of a smooth, red wine and gave her date a looksie. "Just who are you and what have you done with Xavier?" She leaned up to kiss him on the cheek, amused when he flushed. "You look so handsome, man of mine." Every time she called him her boyfriend or acted possessive, everything in her settled.

He's mine. Mine. Mine. Mine.

She smiled, pretending she wasn't secretly freaking out about how much she'd come to like him. He helped when needed, supported her, and had been there from the beginning with a gorgeous smile and a sense of humor that made her feel as if everything in her life would be okay.

And now, here, surrounded by people he didn't know at a wedding where he was supposed to act loving and endearing to her family, he acted naturally, going so far as to convince her he meant all the complimentary things he said. It was enough to shove a girl headfirst into love.

She swallowed a sigh, knowing she cared for him a lot more than she should. Again, she felt terrible for taking advantage of his nurturing personality. All he'd wanted after his breakup with Christine and a departure from his job was time to heal, and Justine came barreling into his life asking for favors.

"Hey, are you okay?"

She sighed. "Yeah. You're just so great. I want you to know I appreciate you so much." *I think I love you.* She wanted badly to tell him how she felt, but what if she did and messed up their friendship? She didn't want to lose him just because she had no self-control.

He smiled, the curve of his lips not hidden by that soft beard and mustache. "Well, I'm pretty sure you're going to show me your appreciation later, aren't you?" He leaned close and kissed her on the lips, sending tingles down her spine. "You promised."

She shivered. "I never break a promise. And I am *sooo* going to appreciate *all* of you." She kissed his cheek and patted his strong chest.

He leaned closer and growled, "Stop it before I embarrass myself in front of your family."

She bit back a grin. "A shower and a grower. My favorite kind of man."

He laughed and hugged her before putting a bit of distance between them. In her tight-fitting dress, she could feel everything easily, and Xavier definitely liked holding her close.

She tried not to keep looking at him, but she failed, meeting his gaze each time. "Why do you keep staring at me?"

"Because you're the most beautiful woman in the room."

Stop saying stuff like that! "Xavier."

"Besides, you keep looking at me. Relax, Justine. I swear I won't embarrass you."

"What?" She gaped at him. "I never thought that. I just..." She felt her cheeks heat. "You're the best looking guy here."

His slow smile warmed her all over. "Even better than Dr. Douche?"

She laughed, as he'd no doubt intended, and relaxed. "Dr. who?"

"Oh, now there's a conversation we could have. Dr. Who versus the evil that is this wedding. Look there! It's Mitch, obviously an Auton. Oh, and I think I see a few Daleks pretending to be tables over by the wall."

"What's an Auton? What's a Dalek?"

He stared at her, agog. "I just... I think we need to break up. Autons were introduced to the show a long time ago, but a Dalek? Everyone knows what they are! Have you no shame, woman? That's it. When we get home, after you appreciate me, we're watching a marathon of *Dr. Who.*"

She groaned. "A closet geek. I should have known you'd have something wrong with you." She was teasing. She'd seen her share of the sci-fi show and had enjoyed it, though not as much as the horror movies she and Katie liked.

Before they could delve into Time Lords and all their glory, the emcee asked everyone to take their seats for dinner.

She and Xavier sat at the head table with Angela and Scott,

Justine's parents, Ted's parents, and one of her fathers' close friends and his wife. Too bad Aunt Rosie couldn't have been there, but then, her mother wouldn't have wanted to share the spotlight with her sassy younger sister.

Not only did Aunt Rosie gallivant around the world when the mood struck, but she'd made a tidy little nest egg with investments throughout the years, and she wrote one of the hottest advice columns in the country—*Dear Aunt Truth.* Justine had been wanting to share that golden nugget with Xavier, since he and her aunt advised people for a living. But her aunt had a strict policy to never share her information with anyone.

What would Aunt Truth say about my feelings for Xavier? Feelings she'd only come to recognize as deeper than mere affection. Huh. Maybe she should reach out and ask. But not over the phone. Anonymously, of course. Heck, she still didn't know exactly what she felt for the guy she'd only known a month. Yet it felt like they'd known each other forever.

He reached for her hand under the table and held it, smiling into her eyes while the bride and groom said a few words to the crowd. Justine heard none of it, only the beat of her heart as she looked into her lover's warm gaze.

Everyone clapped, breaking the mood, and she did her best to relax and live in the moment, enjoying Xavier's presence while trying not to make too much of it.

Dinner went well, everyone mannerly as they talked to Xavier, asking questions and subtly digging to see when and if Justine might next be getting married.

Xavier parried every inquiry with aplomb, and she noted her father's amusement and admiration for her wedding date.

Later, after several people at the table, including Xavier, got up to stretch their legs and use the restroom, her father sat next to her. "Xavier's pretty damn good at deflecting, isn't he?"

"He's a master, all right."

Lyle laughed. "I like him, Justine. He balances you."

She didn't know what to say to that. Her father rarely got super personal with her. Mostly, he badgered her about her poor career choices, and of course her terrible decision to leave Mitch, a steady companion with an upward-moving career as well as a true financial partner.

They both paused while her sister and Ted walked around, talking to people. They did make a lovely couple, she had to admit. Mallory glowed with happiness.

"Mallory looks so pretty," she said. "And Ted looks handsome."

"She could have done better," he admitted in a lower voice. "At least Ted I can handle."

"Dad."

He chuckled. "You know what I mean."

"Sadly, I do." Her dad had only to dangle a promotion at work to keep Ted in line.

"But Xavier, I don't see pushing him around. He seems to have no interest in joining the firm or in my financial expertise. I asked him when he came for dinner. But no, he's strictly into being a therapist and can handle his own portfolio—a bunch of Earth-friendly companies who give back." Lyle snorted. "He seems a bit too altruistic for my taste, but I like him for you."

She blinked. "Are you drunk?" He had tolerated Mitch but hadn't liked him nearly as much as her mother and sisters had. Come to think of it, her dad hadn't liked any of her prior boyfriends all that much.

Lyle chuckled. "Not yet. I'm just feeling sentimental, is all. Two of my three girls are married. Now there's just you." He shocked her anew by kissing her cheek. "I know I don't say it often, but I do love you. Even if you're a bit too stubborn like me. You have to make your own way, and I respect that." He glanced up to see Jeanine waving at him from across the room. "I'd better get going before your mother drags me away by my ear."

"I'd like to see that happen."

He grunted. "Save me a dance."

"Yes, Dad."

He left her bewildered to realize that a real heart beat beneath the financial machine that was her father.

Needing a short break herself, she left the table and headed for the ladies' room. The Kimberly Whitestead Hotel downtown on the water was the perfect place for her sister to get married. The fancy hotel had cost a pretty penny, according to Mallory, but their parents didn't care. Classy, richly appointed, and full of old-world charm, the hotel catered to a wealthy clientele, as evidenced by the expensive rooms. Justine would have gone home right after the wedding if her parents hadn't paid for her hotel stay.

She had her priorities, after all, like paying her bills for the month. Frankly, if she ever got married, she'd favor a small, intimate gathering with less crystal and champagne and more rum in the punch bowl. Still, though, the hotel added to the fairytale wedding her sister had been clamoring for and rightly deserved.

Nearly reaching the restroom, she noticed Mikayla up ahead talking to Mallory and Angela. Ugh. She could do without talking to Mitch's new girlfriend. Before any of them could spot her, Justine noted what looked like a small library through a door slightly ajar, saw it was unoccupied, and darted inside. The classy sitting room, surrounded by books, had a private balcony overlooking the water.

Despite the chill temperature, the balcony doors were open, the filmy curtains hiding the glass panels and framing the deepening sunlight and indigo skies outside. The scent of saltwater and lilac filled the room, fresh flowers on the side tables adding to the rich appointments inside.

She studied the paintings on the walls as well as book titles, wasting time before she felt it would be safe to venture outside again.

"I told you, I can't."

That was Ted's voice.

She moved quietly toward the balcony, keeping behind the curtains. But as she peeked, she saw Ted standing next to the long hem of a pink dress.

"Come on," came a throaty whisper. "I won't tell."

Justine swore she heard the sound of kissing and froze, shocked.

"Sasha, no," Ted said, his voice gentle. "Honey, it's over."

"That's not what you said to me two months ago on that trip to Vancouver."

"That was a mistake. I told you that. I'm married now."

"Oh please. That means nothing."

"It means something to me." A pause filled the space between them. "I need to go find my wife."

Praying no one would see her, Justine hid behind the left balcony door and watched Ted leave the room. Then the woman who'd been trying to seduce her sister's new husband followed, muttering under her breath.

Justine just stood there, not sure what to do about what she'd seen. On the one hand, Ted had turned down an affair. Shot Sasha down flat. Yet it sounded as if they'd been seeing each other while he'd been engaged to her sister.

Should she tell Mallory? On her sister's wedding day?

Bemused, she left the room and ran into her sister on her way to the powder room.

"Hey, Justine. Isn't this great?" Mallory's eyes were shining, her smile wide and joyful.

Justine feigned enthusiasm and took her sister's hands in hers. "Seriously. This wedding has got to be the hit of the year. You look gorgeous. I couldn't be happier for you."

Mallory squealed and hugged Justine, twirling them around. "I want to stay and talk to you but I'm supposed to get back for toasts."

"Go. I'll be back soon. And Mallory, I'm so happy for you and

Ted." She could only hope Ted would be the husband her sister deserved.

After hearing the emcee urge everyone to return to their seats, she hurried into the powder room to take care of business. Unfortunately, when she moved to leave, she found Mikayla sitting with a friend in the outer powder room, laughing. Then the friend departed with a wave, leaving Mikayla and Justine alone.

Can I please just catch a break? "Hi, Mikayla," Justine said as she headed for the door. "They're getting ready with all the toasts."

Before Justine could pass, Mikayla stopped her. "Can we talk?"

"I really need to get back."

Mikayla stood. "I just wanted to let you know that Mitch has moved on from you."

Crap. We're going to do this right now. "I know. You guys look like a terrific couple."

Mikayla blinked. "Well, thanks. It's sad, but the relationship between you didn't work."

"Um, I know. That's why I broke it off."

"You did?" Her eyes narrowed. "Mitch said *he* ended things."

"Does it matter? You're with Mitch. I'm with Xavier and couldn't be happier." If only it were real. "I hope you've had fun tonight. I know I have. The wedding has been terrific. I wish you and Mitch the best. Bye." She hightailed it out before Mikayla tried to continue the needless conversation.

On her way down the hall, she ran into Xavier.

"I was just coming to find you." He tucked a stray strand of her hair behind her ears. She'd left it down and long, and it looked great cascading over her shoulders of the strapless navy-blue dress. "I was ordered by your mother to get your ass back in your seat. Her exact words. I think she's stressing."

"Mikayla cornered me in the bathroom," Justine whispered,

glanced over her shoulder and saw the woman bearing down on them. "Quick, kiss me."

"Wha—"

She meshed her mouth against his, but any notion of pretending went out the window as desire flared between them. The taste of him, of something sweet mixed with Xavier, went straight to her head. He felt so strong and solid against her, and she leaned into him, needing that connection.

"Justine," he whispered as he pulled back, staring into her eyes as if he really saw her. And with Xavier, she thought maybe he did. "I think I lo—"

Mikayla's eyes widened as she passed them, breaking the moment.

Relieved, Justine turned back to Xavier, only to frown in concern. He looked poleaxed.

"Xavier?"

"There you are." Jeanine speed-walked to them and hooked her arm in Justine's, dragging her away. "We're starting the toasts! Get back to the table."

Xavier followed after, a wry grin on his mouth. "Sorry, Jeanine."

"Don't you worry, sweetie. I'm sure my gorgeous daughter distracted you." She winked at Justine. "I saw that kiss. Oh my. Might we have another wedding on our hands soon? It's best if you're married before the baby arrives. I'm just saying."

"*Mom.*" Mortified, Justine glanced at Xavier, only to see him amused and shaking his head.

But was it just her imagination, or did she see a flicker of fear in his beautiful brown eyes?

CHAPTER 31

Xavier didn't know what had come over him. He'd nearly confessed to being *in love* with Justine.

The toasts went well. Then all the dancing. First, the newlyweds. Then the father and daughter, mother and son, and everyone started pairing up on the dance floor. But he kept wondering how he had managed to lose control of his feelings with Justine, and if she'd seen him acting like a lovesick moron.

"Our turn." Justine dragged him onto the dance floor for a slow song.

Xavier could hold his own when it came to dancing. He knew he was skilled because if he'd been anything but just okay, Auggie would have brutalized him with the truth. But he'd been to his share of Marine Corps Balls and fancy work dinners, enough to know how to handle himself.

A slow dance with Justine, however, stole his ability to do anything but move with her in slow steps. The feel of her swaying with him, moving in time together, was like making love but with their clothes on. Nothing they did could be construed as inappropriate, but he felt as if they danced under a shower of love. Especially when she smiled up at him and met his short kiss.

Short but overpowering.

He was dazed for the rest of the night, saying all the right things and laughing at the right jokes. But as they entered their room upstairs, he was glad to see he hadn't been the only one affected.

Justine eyed him like a hungry wolf. "Clothes off. *Now.*" She slipped out of her dress with real speed. He had just dropped the last of his clothes and reached for her at the same time she flew at him.

They kissed and groped, caressed and stumbled to the bed, where they sank into pure decadence.

She moaned as his lips found her breasts, and when he tried to trail his mouth down her belly between her legs, she wouldn't let him. "Next time," she said on a hitched breath. "I want you in me."

He couldn't reason, need pressing him to sink inside her. His desire to be a part of her fogged his mind, and he slid home, Justine already wet and hot for him.

"God, you feel good," he managed and lost himself to her taste and touch. The sex was both frantic and fantastic. No barrier between them, an unspoken consent so that when she cried out and seized around him, he felt no urge to pull back. Instead, he fucked her harder and came on a roar, jetting into the woman he loved with nothing but pleasure.

She tightened around him and stroked his shoulders, and he groaned as he continued to spend.

"Man, you're sexy." She kissed him, leading him back to her lips as he came down from his orgasm.

"Holy fuck."

She laughed. "What a compliment."

"I'm sorry. I think you broke me." He swiveled his hips then had to stop, the sensitivity overbearing. "I came so hard. All in you." Just saying that turned him on, and he shuddered when his dick twitched.

"I love it." Justine gave him a naughty wink and kissed him gently, her touch more than welcoming. "I can't believe what you do to me. And in that suit. I was dying for you all night."

"Yeah? Because you in that dress made it difficult not to show everyone how hard I was for you all night. Justine, you're beautiful. So damn gorgeous."

She flushed with pleasure. So he had to kiss her some more, so gone for this woman it wasn't funny. No, it was scary, but fear had no place in bed with them tonight. Not when he hadn't gotten his fill of her yet.

"Let's soak in the tub. Can you believe this room?" Justine rubbed his chest, toying with his nipples, and he hissed.

"Keep it up and you'll find yourself fucked again before we hit the water."

"Promise?" Her naughty grin shouldn't have surprised him, but every time he thought he knew the woman, she seemed to shift his impression of her. So much for the sex-kitten-girl-next-door vibe. Now she looked like a hungry seductress out to eat him alive.

He rolled them over and sat her over him. "Ride me so I can watch your tits."

Her eyes narrowed, and the flush that stoked her cheeks returned. Justine liked the dirty talk, and he liked arousing her. She started moving on him, willing his dick back to life. Already wet, the feel of being inside her had him stiff and aching in no time. As she moved, he sat up and drove deeper inside her while he latched onto her nipple, teasing her to a fevered pitch.

She writhed and moaned on top of him, dragging her body up and down.

The sound of her passion excited him, and he pumped up as fast and hard as he could while she took her pleasure. He slid his hand between them, grazing her clit, which made her bounce harder. The thought that they could have made a child before, and perhaps again, if she weren't on birth control pushed him to get as close to her as he physically could.

"I'm coming, Xavier. So hard," she moaned just as he shoved up one more time and spilled into her.

They remained locked together, their bodies in sync as they shared in the joy of belonging.

She hugged him, smothering him with kisses while she caught her breath.

It was some time before they relaxed and eased back, watching each other with hazy surprise.

Justine blew out a breath. "I just...*wow*."

He nodded. "I agree."

"And now we need to make it to the bathroom without making a mess." She nibbled on his lower lip and kissed the tiny sting away. "You came a lot inside me." She shifted slightly, and they both groaned. "So sexy."

"Justine, it's like you want me to come inside you again." But he needed a much longer break this time.

"I do. All night long." She smiled. "But first, the bath. Because you're my love slave for the night, I expect a lot of pampering."

"As long as that includes me buried inside you somehow, I'm in."

They paused, stared at each other, and said, "Literally," before laughing.

Later in the bath, as she lay on top of him, cradled in his arms, Xavier knew he'd never had a more perfect night. Too tired now to be afraid of what came next, he stroked her breasts and belly and let the hot water, and the even hotter woman, soothe him.

"What do you think I should do about Ted?" she asked after having confided what she'd witnessed earlier.

"Well, I'm no expert."

She snorted.

He grinned into her hair and kissed the top of her head. "But if it were me, I think I'd say nothing. Not because what Ted did with that woman wasn't wrong, but because it's over. You heard him end it. Besides, it's your sister's wedding day. You don't want to ruin it for her. And you don't want to be remembered as the one who ruined it either."

"Yeah." She sighed. "That's what I thought, but I wondered what you would say."

"Well, I can say I'd never cheat on you like that. I've never cheated on anyone. I don't believe in infidelity. I mean, hey, everyone makes mistakes, and I'm no one to judge. But trust is a big sticking point with me."

She turned in his arms and kissed his chin, stroking his beard. "Me too."

"Ted and your sister need to communicate in their marriage. And I'm not even going there with their sex life. Because none of this is my business."

"Mine either." She made a face. "On the one hand, I was really impressed Ted turned Sasha down. But now I'm wondering how he knows her. If they work together. What happens the next time they take a trip to Vancouver together?"

"*If* they take one."

"If, yeah. But still. I worry for my sister."

"Which is sweet." Xavier hugged her tighter and had to kiss her. "But it's her life. Trust me. I know all about butting in when I'm not invited. I've lost a few friends that way, and it's taken me some time to learn. Not everyone wants good advice. Sometimes they need to live in the muck they make of their lives before they can clean up after themselves."

"You mean, clean up like we are right now?"

He grinned. "Yeah. Where did I drop that soap?"

It took him a while to find it, but by then, they'd both forgotten why they wanted to be clean in the first place.

JUSTINE GROANED THE NEXT MORNING. It turned out Xavier was a cheerful morning person. Not necessarily a deal breaker, but it came close.

Her lovely man didn't try to wake her though. At—she turned a bleary eye toward the clock by the bed—seven am, he kissed her on the forehead and left the room. Once again ensconced in silence, she went back to sleep.

An hour and a half later, he nudged her. "I'd let you sleep, but you have to show up for family breakfast. Remember?"

She groaned. "My freaking parents. It's not like Ted and Mallory will be there."

"Aw. Poor Justine."

She found herself grinning as she cussed at him. Her shower felt good, and awake, she had no problem sharing the hot water with her sweaty guy. "So you used the hotel gym? Was it nice?"

He lathered up, oblivious to her intent gaze. "It was great. They have updated equipment even my sister would approve of."

"Nice. How is Auggie by the way?"

"Great, I'm sure. She's got a new mystery guy she's trying to hide. But breakfast the other day was more or less the same." He sighed when Justine kissed her way up his clean abdomen and nibbled on his upper chest. He cupped her cheek and stopped her cold when he said, "Auggie wants to spend more time with you, I think."

She froze. "What? Why?"

"No, no. Keep going."

She smiled around his nipple but got distracted while he showed her what "getting wet" really meant in the shower with Xavier. Goodness, but she had a tough time keeping her hands off him.

Once dressed and ready to leave the room, she asked again, "What's this about Auggie?"

"Auggie thinks she likes you—which never happens—so she wants to get to know you."

Justine fiddled with the belt of her cute sundress. "Your twin wants to get to know me? Your fake girlfriend? Hanging out with the guy's family is something a real girlfriend would do, right? But we're not?" ended in a question.

Could he read the hope on her face, that want for something more?

"Hell. I'm sorry. I'm pushy when you want to keep things normal." He ran a hand through his hair. "I always do this. I—"

"I want more," she blurted.

"What?"

"This, us. It's amazing, and maybe it's all because we know it's fake so we're not stressed about a relationship. Or it's just that we're amazing in bed together. Or that you made Katie laugh and I entertained your sister. My folks like you. Your mom likes me. It's like everything is pushing us together but us. And I feel guilty because I'm really into you and you were only doing me a favor to begin with, so how can I have the audacity to rope you into more Justine-shenanigans?" She had to pause to catch her breath.

Xavier just stared. "I don't think I've ever heard you say so much at once." His smile was blinding. "Justine, I really like you too. I think we need to end this fake relationship and start a new, real one." His smile grew even wider, but to Justine, it looked wrong. Brittle.

"I'm sorry, Xavier." Now she felt terrible when after her shower she'd felt on top of the world.

"For what? For wanting to be with me?" He pulled her in for a warm hug. "Honey, I'm so into you it's not funny. I guess I'm just scared I'll screw us up, like I screw up all my relationships."

"I understand. Trust me." She pulled back to see him looking at her as if he truly cared about her. As more than a friend. Perhaps she hadn't been wrong to blurt out what she felt. Or maybe she had her hormones to blame. Xavier had *destroyed her* last night and this morning, in total control of her body and mind. "I just don't want to stress you with what *I* want. It has to be something we both want."

"So much," he agreed. "So much want for you, I have." He paused. "And I have no idea why that came out that way. I sound like a bad Yoda."

"Love for you, I have, young Skywalker," she teased, then realized what she'd said and felt lightheaded with embarrassment. "Oh man. You know what I mean. Not love. I mean, like. I like you a ton. A lot. So much. Yes." *Could I babble any more?*

In a bad Yoda imitation, he said, "Understand you, I do." Then he started humming "Here Comes the Bride," which had her blushing harder while laughing.

They found her family in the dining room, the pair of them still laughing and walking arm in arm.

Finally, a real couple. A woman in love, a man in like and in lust.

And for now, Justine could deal with that.

DEAR AUNT TRUTH

Dear Aunt Truth: I think I love him, but I don't know what he feels for me. What should I do? I don't want to ruin our friendship.

Dear Frady Cat: If you love him, tell him. Love doesn't ruin friendships; it defines them. As the Doctor would say, "What's the point in two hearts if you can't be forgiving now and then?"

CHAPTER 32

"So let me recap your weekend," Katie said over lunch Monday afternoon. "Mikayla tried to bitch up and protect her man, but you wouldn't let her act all high and mighty by being super nice. Then she caught you sucking face with Xavier, which nailed how much you *don't* want Mitch back."

"Yeah." Best moment ever. And Justine had Xavier to thank for it.

"Your father told you he loves you at the wedding. That right there is miraculous."

"I know. But my mom and Angela weren't overly sentimental, so they made up for my dad's weirdness."

"Right." Katie grinned, a dimple showing. "But the end-all to this miracle event, beside you catching the groom doing the right thing by his new bride, is that you finally came clean with Xavier about dating for real. This after marathon nookie in a dream hotel room." Katie sighed. "It's like a Disney movie married a porn flick and gave you a weekend you'll never forget."

"Not exactly how I would have put it. You have a unique view of the world, don't you?"

"You have no idea." Katie munched on her salad. "So now that the wedding is taken care of and your studly neighbor is servicing you, what's left?"

"Katie."

"Of course. Frank. How's work going?"

"And...you had to bring up work."

"Sorry. But we had to catch up on your daily misery at some point."

Justine groaned. "I'm spending so much time trying to get up to speed on Laura's job—I'm sorry, I mean *my* new job—that I'm behind on the one I had. Have." Justine frowned. "I actually swallowed my pride and asked Frank for a helper, at least to get me caught up with her projects. He said no. So now I'm behind on the new tasks, the old tasks, and I have a ton of emails and phone calls to return. By the time I get home, I'm so exhausted I eat then go to bed. Or I just go to bed. Alone," she said before Katie could say something about Xavier...which she did anyway.

"That sucks. No more happy fun time with Xavier."

"I know." Justine sighed. "Work sucks. But Katie, he and I— I can't describe it. We're so great together. Being with him is so natural. I don't have to work hard and he still likes me."

"Another miracle."

"Ass."

Katie snickered. "I'm kidding. I'm happy for you. He's a great guy. And he survived the wedding with you. That's something. But if you can't have an argument with him and stay together, you're doomed for failure. No one's happy all the time."

"You make a good point."

Katie studied Justine. "What about Ted? What did you decide to do about him?"

"Nothing. I overheard something I wasn't meant to hear, but he was ending things. I want to let my sister have a clean slate with her husband. Now, if I catch him cheating, I'll definitely narc him out. But I can't see what telling her now will do but make her upset. She deserves to have a honeymoon period."

"I agree. Besides, she knows Ted better than you do. For all you know, he and she had a cheating pass. You know, that bucket list nookie. Maybe Mallory had her own affair."

"I can't see it."

"Well, neither can I. I was just trying to spin something positive. It's what I do for a living, you know."

"Ha ha." Justine poked at her noodle salad. "Speaking of your living, how's your job going?"

Katie shrugged. "It's much better with my new boss. But I'm like you, unsatisfied and feeling overwhelmed. I actually took some contract work from Kenzie this past weekend."

"Oh? I haven't gotten a chance to contact the person for the job she offered me. I plan to do that after lunch."

"For shame! On company time?" Katie smirked.

"You bet. I'm so done killing myself with overtime. Today I'm going home at a regular time. And I'm giving myself an extra ten minutes for lunch. Considering I've been working hours I won't be paid for, I figure they owe me that much."

"You go, rebel girl."

But that night, Justine stayed an extra hour trying to slog through the emails she hadn't gone through from last week.

She felt guilty all night and into Tuesday, only texts with Xavier during her lunches made her smile. Wednesday proved just as busy with no time for anything but her job.

Justine worked her butt off, stayed late—alone—and went unappreciated and underpaid.

But after she got home, she marched down to Xavier's. He'd texted that he was free all night, so she decided to take him up on some fun.

Unfortunately, she spent the evening complaining about work. He listened and agreed with everything she said. Such a great guy. They got in a few kisses before he had to take a phone call. By the time he'd come back to her, he'd found her asleep on his couch.

She woke when he kissed her goodbye and tucked her into her own bed.

"Come see me tomorrow. And don't stay one minute over your normal quitting time."

She mumbled something back, she was sure.

Thursday at four-thirty, Justine decided enough was enough. She shut down her computer, grabbed her bag, and headed home.

Frank peeked out of his office at her as she passed. "Oh, Justine. Did you get that report for Nash done yet? He needs it like yesterday."

Her stomach fluttered with nerves. It went against everything she'd been taught to go against management, but she stood her ground and gave Frank a wide, nonthreatening smile. "Nope. I'll have to get to it tomorrow."

"But you can't."

"See you bright and early tomorrow, Frank." She added a wave and left feeling lightheaded. She also quickened her step, not giving him the ability to confront her face to face.

Practically running to her car, she laughed with wild abandon. *I did it. I left on time.*

Back at home, she allowed herself to decompress then answered a few questions from Kenzie's—no, *Justine's*—new client. But this time, she didn't dread working on a project. She *wanted* to create a new social media platform for the elderly-friendly company Kenzie had handed over.

Feeling enthused about her work for the first time in ages, she even changed into running gear and enjoyed a slow jog, getting her blood moving.

She returned to the building in a good sweat and nearly ran over Auggie.

"Oh, I'm sorry, Auggie. Been visiting your brother?" Duh. Obviously.

Auggie fiddled with her ponytail, the deep red like a flame that burned with Auggie's energy. "Yeah. But he got busy. He's going back to work soon, you know."

"He had mentioned he was returning but I didn't know when." That bothered her. Had she been talking so much about herself that Xavier hadn't been able to share about his own life? Or did he deliberately not tell Justine because they weren't as close as she thought they were?

"Yeah. He acts like he's made of money, but he actually has to work for a living. And doodling isn't gonna cut it."

"Doodling?"

Auggie blinked. "I meant him taking time off. Goofing off. Doodling his time away. You know, being a doofus doodling." She chattered like a chipmunk high on caffeine. "So what are you up to?"

Before she knew it, Justine was confiding in Auggie about how much she hated her job but loved her new contract work, how much she loved spending time with Xavier, and how happy she'd been to finally open up about them being a real couple. "Your mom was so sweet at dinner. My parents could take lessons from her."

Auggie grinned. "Yeah, my mom's a keeper for sure. She's a little too nice though."

"Oh? She had no problem putting Xavier in his place."

"Well, she's good like that. But I meant with guys. Her last boyfriend was a total tool. But it's been a while. I think she's lonely. I wish she'd let us set her up on more dates. It takes a while before you find a good man."

"Ha. I know."

Auggie snorted. "Preach."

"Are *you* still searching for a good man?"

Auggie was beautiful, built, and seemed full of positive energy. If she couldn't find a significant other, Justine had little hope for Katie and her other single friends. But not herself—because she had Xavier.

"Maybe. I'm not sure yet." Auggie looked thoughtful for a moment before her trademark snark reappeared. "I'm not sure any men really deserve me." She shook her head, and her ponytail fluttered behind her. "Ah, sorry, Justine. I have to go. Got to get more training under my belt if I want to win this upcoming fitness competition. We should do coffee some time."

"Sure. Just let me know and I'll make it happen."

Auggie raised a brow. "Yeah, sure. Just as soon as you dump your crappy boss and find a job that lets you live a little." A one-two punch that hit home.

"Good point."

"Later." Auggie left in a rush just as Benji entered the courtyard.

He spotted Justine and froze.

"Hi, Benji. Don't mind me. I'm just heading upstairs. The fountain's all yours." She noted him holding a nylon bag.

"Uh, yeah. Okay." He glanced around then left.

Odd.

She didn't run into Sam or his family as the group had gone on their Hawaii trip. She only knew because Sam had left a note by the door Monday morning. Her third floor neighbor, Kai, remained gone, along with Aunt Rosie. So only Justine, Xavier, Benji, and Top remained in the building. She found she missed Sam, who brought youth and fun into the place.

Even Top with his grunts and stern expressions enriched the TCA, because didn't every building need at least one grumpy guy?

Back upstairs, she decided to pop over to Xavier's without showering and changing first. He wouldn't mind.

She knocked, and the door immediately opened.

"Who are you?" asked a drop-dead gorgeous woman. She had

rich brown hair, blue eyes, and an hourglass figure. She looked Justine up and down. "What do you want?"

"Christine, stop it," Xavier said from inside the apartment. He spotted Justine and looked instantly relieved, not the expression one would think to find on man guilty of cheating on her.

Such an odd thought to have, but Justine was so gone on Xavier that she kept waiting for something bad to happen.

Xavier crossed to her and pulled her inside the apartment. "Hi, Justine. Christine, this is my girlfriend. Justine, this is my ex...who was just leaving."

"Are you serious?" Christine eyes turned shiny. "You're dating already?"

Justine wanted to feel bad for her, but from all Xavier had said, the woman refused to leave him alone. She held tightly to his hand, standing close. His presence felt so good, something she'd needed for the past few days.

He put an arm around her shoulders. "Christine, I wasn't lying. Your brother wasn't lying. Neither was my boss or our receptionist," he growled. "*Please* don't come to my workplace again. Get some help. This obsession isn't healthy for you."

"Fine. I'm done with you!" She glared at Justine before leaving, slamming the door in her wake.

"Wow. And I thought my exes were bad."

Xavier sighed. "I'm sorry. She showed up at my clinic ranting about me. They called me, so I came to get her. The only way to make her leave was to agree to swing back to my place to talk. We started downstairs in the lobby, but she followed me up here because she had to use the bathroom." He looked abashed. "I thought she was just using that as an excuse to come inside my place, but I couldn't tell. And I didn't want to be rude."

She hugged him, seeing his anxiety. "I'm sorry. That had to be tough."

"It was. I just don't understand. I'm great, but am I *that* great?" he asked with a half-laugh.

Yes.

Poor Christine had likely waded back into the dating pool, where finding a gem like Xavier was as rare as finding the back of an earring after dropping it in a mass of shag carpet.

She'd been there. Dating men who didn't listen or weren't thoughtful. Dates where the men acted like Mitch or Frank, where a woman was expected to cater to them. And then if she did find a great guy, he only wanted a hookup or had no job and still lived with his parents, who did everything for him.

She studied Xavier, the opposite of so many men she'd dealt with.

"I think you're pretty great." She beamed at him. "You listen to me. You even hugged me after I got sweaty on a run."

"I didn't want to say anything, but you stink." He made a face.

"Jerk."

His big smile turned him from handsome to extraordinary.

She tried to cover how she felt about him by joking. "It's good that I'm calling you a jerk, you know."

"Is that right?"

"According to Katie, if we can't argue and still be friendly, we're not meant to be."

"Katie makes a valid point. Couples who can't agree to disagree on minor things often have issues with the larger obstacles in a relationship."

"Is that you with your therapist hat on?" she teased. "And speaking of therapists, I saw Auggie downstairs. Were you going to mention you're going back to work soon? Do you have a date in mind?"

"Wait. Auggie?"

"Yeah, you know. Your sister?"

"I haven't seen her." He scowled. "My sister was here, downstairs?"

"Um, yes."

"Huh." He shook his head. "Well, anyway, I did want to talk to you about my work. I planned to tell you tonight, actually."

"Should I be happy for you?"

He kissed her. "Yes. Because of you, and because I took time off, I'm in a much better frame of mind to help others." He gave her a long look. "In fact, I was planning to make us dinner."

"Oh?"

"But I think I could help you better by taking off those tight shorts of yours and giving you one heck of a glutes massage."

"Is that right?" She'd been missing this. Missing *him.* The teasing, the fun. Xavier brought the joy in life she'd been lacking for so long.

"Yep, massages for Justine. It's on my to-do list."

She took his face between her hands and kissed him. "You make me happy, Xavier. I like everything about you."

He flushed. "Even when I'm bossy and try telling you what to do?"

"Even then."

"Then you're in for a treat. Take off those bottoms, Ms. Ferrera. I have some therapy you're definitely in need of…"

CHAPTER 33

Xavier didn't mean to, but it had been a few days. And after their marathon sex-capades at the wedding, he felt bereft, not having Justine in his arms whenever he wanted.

He tried to go slowly, but she wasn't having it. Justine stripped naked and bent over the back of his couch, taunting him with that fine ass.

"Come on, sexy. In me."

He took the time to drop his shorts and underwear and that was it. Stepping between her spread ankles, he positioned himself at her sex and slid inside her in one big push.

She moaned and reached between her legs, turning him on even more because she was so wet and ready for him. Nothing better than having his girlfriend want him so badly she dropped her clothes and bent over without him having to ask.

His *girlfriend.*

The notion made him wild, knowing she belonged to him. His. Possessive and raw, he took her with a ferocity she encouraged. Her hand moved between her legs, and as she touched herself, he surged deeper.

She cried out as she came, and her body tightened around him.

Gripping her hips and never wanting to let go, he thrust once more and lost it, jetting so hard he saw black, the ecstasy overpowering.

It took him a few moments to stop coming, his orgasm savage yet so much sweeter with Justine in his arms. Or in this case, bent over the couch. He'd never been so compatible with anyone. Sexually, mentally, emotionally. She was perfect for him.

"Damn, Xavier. You always feel so good in me."

He leaned over her to kiss her shoulder and continued his kisses up to her ear. "Yeah, so good inside you." He swiveled his hips, felt one final jolt as he spurted once more, then eased. "I feel like a walking hard-on around you. And yes, that's a compliment."

She laughed. "Such a way with words."

Usually, but around her he started to feel tongue-tied, afraid of saying or doing the wrong thing. He always screwed up his relationships, found fault with one thing or another. But this time, he could find no fault with Justine, and that freaked him the hell out.

He winced as he withdrew. "Come on. Let's get cleaned up."

After some quality time between Justine's legs in the shower, they managed to get clean. He leant her a shirt and pair of his shorts, which she had to cinch with a drawstring. The shirt lovingly cupped her breasts, teasing the points of her nipples when she shifted.

"I love you in my clothes." *Hell, I love you out of them too.*

She gave him a shy grin, and he was overwhelmed with feeling for her. "I like wearing them. They're so soft." She smirked at his crotch. "Unlike you."

"Ha ha." He was thickening, though he should have been too tired to go again. Wanting to look like a man capable of thinking past his dick, he sat her down with him on the couch and turned to watch her. "I'm going back to work next week."

"So you said." She toyed with her hair.

He loved the dark color, so rich that when the sun hit it, her hair shone like umber silk. "My time will be a little more constrained, but I hope nothing changes between us."

"Changes how?" She frowned.

"I still want to see you when you have time. But I won't be available for a daytime quickie." He gave a mock sigh. "Not that you've taken advantage of any nooners."

She flushed. "I would if I could, but I'm stuck at work."

He had been waiting forever to comment, but he had to say something. "Are you sure you want to keep working there?"

"No. I don't. But I have to have a job to earn money. See, I have this pesky thing called rent."

"Very funny." He pulled her hair from her fingers and played with the satiny strands.

"I did finally take a call from my friend's client. I told you she recommended me for some outside contract work. I really liked it, feeling as if I'm making my own hours."

"Nice. Yeah, I don't exactly miss needing to be in the office to see people. Though I like it much better than online meetings. You can't get a great feel from them. I can't explain it."

"No, I understand. Much of what I do is online or through phone calls. But I'm not delving into mental health. I'm all about ads and PR and marketability."

"Which actually does tie into mental health. You want people to buy into what your client is selling, so you tap into their wants and needs."

"Huh. I guess you're right." She gave him a bright grin. "What are your wants and needs, Xavier?"

He tugged her hair and let the strands fall from his fingers. "I'm pretty sure we already took care of those."

She laughed.

"Just being with you makes me happy," he admitted, her blush enchanting him. "You're so pretty."

"Xavier." She turned even pinker. "So, um, can I ask about Christine's visit?"

He sighed. "If you must. But you're ruining the moment." He was glad to see that she didn't blame him for the woman being here. She didn't seem jealous either. Hmm. That kind of bothered him.

"Is she dangerous?"

He blinked. "Ah, no. At least, I don't think so. She's just trying to hold onto someone who's moved on."

"She was really pretty. Gorgeous, actually."

"Yes, and she's very aware of that fact. Look, Christine is a good person, but we didn't mesh. She got too needy, which made me pull away even more." Something he'd already told her.

After a pause, Justine asked, "Am I too needy?"

"Hell, no." He hurried to reassure her. "You have a terrific sense of self-worth. Although…"

"Go ahead. Say it."

"Although you don't always act like it. Stand up for yourself with your boss. Demand they pay you what you're worth or leave."

She frowned. "I left on time today."

"That's great. Keep doing that while demanding to be compensated for your work."

"I will. But baby steps work better for me than just ripping into my boss."

"I didn't say rip into him. I just worry they'll keep taking advantage of you if you let them."

She looked annoyed. "You sound like my father."

"Ouch."

She sighed. "I'm sorry. You're right."

"You asked." He shrugged, a little hurt she didn't seem to be listening to him. "This is why I have trouble with relationships. Sometimes I should just listen, but you did ask."

"I know." She leaned forward to kiss him. "I'm just frazzled because I made a big leap forward. Leaving on time when my boss wanted me to stay. It might not seem like a lot, but I hate confrontation."

"Most people do." He stroked her hair and kissed her. "You're so smart and talented."

"You've never seen my work." She smiled.

"But I know who you are, and your intelligence shines through."

"That's one of the nicest things anyone's said to me."

"It shouldn't be, though I can see men commenting on your looks before your smarts, only because you're gorgeous."

"Keep it up and my head will swell."

"You mean, more than it already is? You're pretty and all, but yeah, what a big head."

She laughed and knocked him back. "Take it back."

"Make me."

Their wrestling match turned into a tickle fight. Except he got the better of her.

"Stop tickling me, you monster," she said between giggles.

"Nope. I want to hear the words."

"Your beard makes you look like a red panda?"

"My—what?"

She laughed harder. "My aunt's dog used to tilt its head like that when you called its name. I'm gonna start calling you Sparky."

He tickled her some more. "Not the right words."

"Okay! Okay!" She writhed under him until he gave her a reprieve by kissing her.

Their kisses turned passionate, and he lost himself in her until a glimmer of self reared its head. Too much feeling, too soon. It scared him, the depth of his need. He pulled back and studied her. What was it about her that called to him?

"Xavier?"

"The words," he said, his voice deep.

"I love you."

OH MY GOD. Justine hadn't meant to admit that. Not yet, when she wasn't sure of it herself. What was love, really? Because she thought she'd been in love before. But the feeling had never been so all-consuming.

Staring up into his fathomless eyes, she couldn't help herself.

He didn't respond at all, which started to feel awkward. But then he kissed her, and she felt so much unsaid in that kiss that she released any sense of tension and indulged in the passion between them.

He kissed her until they were left breathless. And then their clothes were gone, and Xavier stared into her eyes as he made love to her. The intensity of their joining stole any need to keep herself apart from him, and she gave all of herself, letting Xavier have everything.

That love pushed her orgasm into a different realm, the pleasure so intense, made even more so when he stiffened and released, their bodies joined as one.

The ecstasy seemed to last forever, but when he finally pulled back, he stared at her with love in his eyes. "Justine…"

"You don't have to say it, Xavier." But she wanted him to. "I know it's soon, but it just popped out." And she'd allow herself this moment to revel in feeling so much for someone again.

"I feel the same way," he admitted in a rush.

She wanted to cry out with joy but saw his hesitation and waited.

He blew out a breath. "You scare the crap out of me."

"Me?" She'd never made anyone afraid. "Why?"

"Because you matter so much. Look, when I eventually get stupid, just remember I'm a guy and I overthink everything. Promise you'll give me a little leeway when I upset you."

She laughed. "You're overthinking things right now. You're buried inside me, we both love each other, and you're warning me of your downsides. Relax, baby. And feel what you do to me."

She distracted him with her body, her heart so full she couldn't handle much more. But after they spent the evening playing, she went back to her apartment with promises to talk the next day.

She needed a little space after all that sharing, and she could tell he did to.

Because when she said she would be heading back to her place for the night, he didn't try to stop her.

CHAPTER 34

Justine sat by Xavier on the ride to his mother's house for a July 4th cookout. The last few days had been magical, filled with an eager need to see each other while also maintaining some healthy space.

Xavier had explained it all the following day. "I need you to trust me. I've seen so many couples rush into things. I want you all the time. But I don't want to overwhelm you. I suggest we keep things the way they are. You set the rules for us, and if I have a problem, I'll tell you."

Again, the man wanted her to set boundaries, giving her a sense of control over their relationship that took all the pressure off her trying to meet *his* demands. Yet... He seemed to want space between them but wouldn't admit it. And that told her to keep a bit of distance. How strange for Xavier to act skittish after admitting he loved her. He hadn't exactly said the words, but he kind of had. Hadn't he?

She didn't know much, only that she walked on clouds, in love with a man who gave her orgasms, made her laugh, and made the world a little brighter just by being with him. She could almost put her work worries behind her, though after the 4th, she'd have to get back to the grind.

"You're quiet." He squeezed her knee.

"Just thinking that being with you is amazing…and totally unexpected."

"Oh?"

She petted his beard. "I'm dating a furry man."

"This is an amazing beard, woman. You're lucky to be touching it."

"Lucky? You want to get lucky later, maybe rethink your words."

He grinned. "Now that you're warming up, you sure you're okay?" He paused. "With us?"

"I am if you are." She scrutinized him. "I feel like you're at an advantage because you deal with people and their emotions for a living. Like, you could manipulate me pretty easily if you wanted."

"'With great power comes great responsibility.'"

"Sure thing, Spiderman." She rolled her eyes.

"I'm kidding. I would never deliberately try to manipulate you." He frowned at the road. "That's dishonest. I'm all about honesty."

"So if my butt looks huge in my dress, you'll tell me?"

"I'm not stupid."

"That's what I thought."

He shrugged. "There's honesty and then there's not wanting to hurt your girlfriend's feelings." He winked. "But that dress you're wearing shows off your amazing legs and butt, so don't look to me for criticism."

It warmed her how readily he kept labeling her his girlfriend. He hadn't mentioned any feelings though. Neither of them had brought up the big L word since she'd said it four days ago.

Nothing like disturbing your boyfriend by being too close to smother the flames of love.

"You went quiet again. I'm serious. You look amazing in that dress."

She toyed with the thin strap. "It's a sundress. And I wore sneakers with it."

"Cute and approachable, yet strikingly sexy. I like your vibe."

She laughed, tucking away her caution. "You're a goof."

"I'm your goof." He brought her hand to his lips and kissed her. "Now remember, Auggie will be there today. And Mom will be all over you once she finds out we're dating."

"She already thinks we're dating."

"Yeah, but she'll know it's real." He sighed. "She kind of knew it was real before. I'm not good at hiding my feelings from my mom."

"Aw, you had a big crush on me, didn't you?"

"Oh stop." His cheeks turned red.

She hooted. "You're blushing! So cute."

He grumbled as they pulled into the driveway.

"A lot of cars out here," she noticed, counting a few in front of the large home.

"It's the 4th. Time for picnics and barbecues."

She brought the potato salad she and Xavier had fixed—well, Xavier had made it while she'd watched. Auggie opened the door before Justine could knock and tugged them both inside.

She put a finger to her lips and snuck them into the side office, which had been turned into a craft room. Justine liked the light colored furniture and big desk upon which a sewing machine and basket of yarn had been set.

"What's up?" Xavier asked.

"Shh. Do you not see me sneaking you inside?" Auggie poked her head out then closed the office door. "Quick notes: Top's here as Mom's 'date.' I invited Benji because he looked sad when I saw him wandering the street outside the condo."

"Wandering the streets?" Xavier's brow went up. "Really? He barely leaves to go to work."

"And the gym," Justine added. "What? I saw him with a gym bag the other day."

Auggie cleared her throat. "I was swinging by to pick you up. I hadn't realized you'd already cozied up to the upstairs chick." Auggie nodded at Justine, her gaze on her brother. "Thanks for telling me."

He snorted. "Like you didn't already know. You forced it out of me at Roxie's." He turned to Justine. "We also share a twin brain."

"Ah." Twin brain?

"I did know," Auggie admitted. "But it would have been nice for you to tell me, like, officially. Without me prying the truth from your stubborn mouth. I had to hear it from Judy at the bagel shop. She saw you two smooching in public. Disgusting."

Justine blushed. "PDAs aren't really my thing, but your brother is impossible to resist."

He turned to her. "I am, aren't I?"

Auggie's lips twitched. "Super disgusting."

"Right. So why did you pull us in here, exactly?" he asked her.

"So you don't act like a jackass when you see Top and Mom making eyes at each other. And be nice to Benji."

"I'm always nice to Benji." Xavier frowned. "What do you mean making eyes at each other?"

"See?" Auggie turned to Justine. "He won't admit it, because my brother thinks he's above such things, but he gets jealous when Mom finds a guy she really likes."

"What? That's not true."

Justine watched the twins go back and forth, amused at how alike they were, despite Xavier's claims that Auggie was super dramatic.

Auggie sounded smug. "It's totally true. Mom didn't date all that much while we were around. Dad died our senior year of high school. We were already in the Marine Corps when she'd opened up to seeing anyone. But when we'd visit, Xavier would bristle if she seemed to like a guy."

"Now you're just lying."

"Oh? Seems to me you only tolerate the idiots she's gone out with. But if there was someone decent, you picked him apart."

"I never did that." Xavier sounded angry.

Auggie turned to Justine and shrugged. "See? Her last boyfriend was a real jerk, but we tried to be nice to him for Mom's sake. My brother can do fake-nice really well. But when Mom was into Jared eight years ago, you weren't so fake nice, were you?"

He looked even angrier, and Justine had the notion Auggie might be right about him. "Your point is we should act normal about Top and Benji being here," she said before Xavier could argue with his sister.

"Yeah." The woman glared at Xavier. "Be. Nice." She turned and left.

Xavier rubbed his beard and glared at the doorway. "I do *not* have a problem with my mother being happy. I love her."

"Maybe you love her so much you don't think any man is good enough for her," she suggested, something her aunt had once advised in her *Aunt Truth* column.

He opened and closed his mouth. "I don't know. Maybe."

She hugged him. "Xavier. You love your mom. That's nothing to be upset about. So you're protective. You're a good son."

"Am I if I don't want her to be happy?" He looked miserable, so she kissed him.

Top happened to catch them in the act, standing in the doorway. "Ah-ha. Auggie was right. When you're done locking lips, your mom wants you in the kitchen." He smirked and left.

Justine grabbed the potato salad, embarrassed, and hurried to the kitchen. Xavier followed.

She hoped she hadn't made a mistake sticking her nose where it didn't belong, but when she had a moment's pause between peeling carrots and carving watermelon balls, Xavier leaned close to kiss her and whispered, "Thanks, Justine. For being there for me."

She turned and caught his smile, glad she hadn't ruined anything between them.

XAVIER HATED that he now saw himself through a distorted lens. Had he been a good son? Was he being a good boyfriend? A good brother?

He hadn't thought himself capable of being so selfish, wanting all his mother's attention. Heck, he and Auggie shared everything and always had. When his father had died, they'd all been lost. The man hadn't been a saint, but he'd been as perfect a father and husband as a man could get.

So naturally, the first man his mother had dated, two years after his father passed, hadn't measured up. But then, none of them had. Damn. Maybe Auggie had it right after all.

"Um, pass the potatoes?" Benji asked.

Top grunted and pushed the bowl closer to Benji, who looked as if he'd jump if Top breathed too hard.

Auggie frowned. "Easy, Marine."

Top gave her a look that she gave right back, the pair of them glaring so hard it was a wonder their brows didn't get stuck together. He wasn't the only one who noticed either. Justine looked as if she was trying to hold back laughter. His mother too.

"Oh my God. Would you two relax?" he said on an exasperated sigh. "You've spent the whole meal trying to see who's is bigger."

"Mine, clearly," Auggie sniffed.

Top stared at her before laughing. "Damn, girl, you might just be right."

Cynthia shook her head, her eyes filled with mirth. "Stubborn jarheads."

Was it his imagination, or did Benji hide a smile as well?

"Well, Max," Cynthia said. "We might as well tell them."

"Tell us what?" Xavier asked.

Top—Max—cleared his throat. "We wanted to let you know that we're getting married."

Auggie and he stared. "*What?*" they said as one.

"I'm soon going to be giving you a baby sister," Cynthia added with a smile. "Can you believe that?"

"Hell, no." Xavier wondered if he might be hearing things. Then he noticed Justine and Benji trying to hide their laughter. Auggie had believed the lie, though, so he didn't feel so bad. She looked pale.

"Ha. Told you." Top guffawed. "The look on your faces. Relax, you two. Your mom and I are well past the age of having babies. But we are dating, so if you got a problem, now's the time to spit it out."

"I think it's wonderful," Justine said.

"Yeah, cool. Old people dating. It's nice." Benji turned bright red after saying that and focused on his plate again.

Cynthia rolled her eyes. "Old people. Thanks, Benji."

Auggie smacked him on the shoulder. "Nice going, doofus."

Benji shrugged but seemed to relax.

The look and feeling he sensed from his sister made Xavier reexamine the pair. That Auggie refused to meet his gaze told him he'd clearly missed the match-up going on in front of him.

"Is everyone at this table dating someone else at this table?"

Top stared at Auggie and Benji and grinned. "Seems to be."

"Benji and Auggie?" Justine goggled then gave a slow nod. "Huh. Now I see it."

"What? I don't." Xavier didn't know how he could have missed all the feelings floating over the table. But he didn't know that he liked it, and he felt like an ass for feeling that way. So he put on his best smile. "Well then, a toast." He held up his root beer, waited for everyone else to do the same, then said, "To the lonely

Hanovers, lonely no more. May your hearts be full and your bellies stuffed with potato salad and watermelon."

"That was just lovely, Son," Cynthia said, dryly. "You all had better eat! I don't want any leftovers."

Top shot her a smile. "I think I can handle that."

"Me too." Benji dug into his food then paused. "Wait. I'm not dating Auggie."

"Shh. We'll talk about it later, okay?" Auggie patted his hand on the table then ignored him.

Benji looked confused but continued to eat.

Everyone kept talking and smiling, and Justine's laughter made him warm all over. But Xavier knew something inside him had shifted.

He just didn't know what.

CHAPTER 35

Friday, July 8th

Justine didn't know why she sensed a change between her and Xavier, as she couldn't fault him for his attentiveness. But something seemed off with her boyfriend.

Her *boyfriend.*

Whenever she thought of him as her significant other, she felt warm and fuzzy inside.

"Justine, where are the specs on Anweiss Tech?" one of the project managers asked over the wall of her cubicle.

"What?"

He frowned. "The social media presentation for Anweiss Tech? We have a meeting on Monday to discuss our projections." At her silence, he added, "Laura's files should have had them listed as a priority."

"Well, Nash," she said with her super-friendly voice, "I still haven't gotten through all of Laura's files. I just finally got caught up on my own projects. Next, I have some emails and calls to return. Then I can get to Laura's stuff."

"That won't work." He shook his head. "We need to talk to Frank about this."

"Yes, let's." She'd had her fill of her boss. Every day he grew more obnoxious, asking her to stay later and later. She'd gone back on her promise to herself to stop being weak and had stayed late Monday, Tuesday, and Wednesday. Yesterday she'd worked through lunch but had gone home on time. Not early, on time.

But today, in addition to his earlier email about putting in time this weekend to help him finish an overview presentation for one of his new clients, with Nash's attitude and Frank's idiot thinking that Justine would be everyone's assistant on everything, she'd hit her breaking point.

Xavier had been subtly mentioning every day for her to own her strengths and acknowledge she deserved better. And Kenzie's business had offered her another client if she so desired.

Justine had a glimpse of what her future might hold. But she needed to reach out and grab it.

Or kick it squarely between its legs, for once.

She followed Nash down the hall to Frank's office, where he sat getting chummy with his boss and two of his project managers. How the hell did any of them have time to drink coffee and trade jokes when she had to stay late to get her work done?

Nash knocked on the doorframe. "Hey, Frank. We need to talk to you about the Anweiss Tech meeting coming up."

Frank's companions joked as they left the office. "Oh, Frank. You're in trouble now."

He laughed them off and stood, looking handsome and smarmy as usual. The guy practically oozed incompetence.

Justine looked around his big office, seeing all he'd earned on other people's backs. Hers especially.

"Frank, Justine hasn't gotten me the files I need to get ready for Monday's meeting with Anweiss. And I can't figure out…"

She tuned him out while he continued to complain.

Is this what I want? To always be catering to someone else who will take all the credit? To continually stress out because I'm not putting myself first? Why the hell do I need Frank's validation? Or anyone's?

Her more practical side chimed in. *Well, you do need the money. Your savings will only take you so far.*

Yeah, but I'm my father's daughter, my aunt's niece. And I've been saving up forever. It's not a lot, but it's enough to give me breathing room. Especially if I do a great job on Elder Care 4-U, the new client she'd picked up from Kenzie.

Justine's heart raced. Could she do it? Should she? Aunt Rosie would have told her boss to screw off months ago, even before Justine's "promotion." Her father would tell her to ride it out but make provisions to secure a better work environment while her mother would tell her to just get along and not make waves.

Xavier... He'd be practical yet supportive, as he'd been from day one. And then he'd tell her to take responsibility for herself because no one but her could make the decision for her future.

"Justine, are you even listening?" Frank sighed. "This has become a real problem, you know. You—"

"I quit."

Frank and Nash stared.

"I've been underpaid for the past year. I work harder than anyone in your department." The dam had burst and she couldn't stop. "You use me all the time to help you on *your* work while taking away time to finish mine. So I work long days and nights and never get paid for it or comped time."

"But—"

"I'm talking now," she said over Frank. Nash just stared, his mouth open, and she continued on a full head of steam. "You told me I'd be getting a raise, one I deserved. Instead you gave me another job for no pay. Yeah. No. Pay. And that's...bullshit." Her heart threatened to explode from her chest. "I'm done. No more doing your work for you. No more doing work I'm not even getting paid to do. Not even a thank you for everything I've done to help 'the team.'" She scowled. "So take my job and Laura's job and your own and shove them up your ass."

She turned on her heel and flew back to her cubicle, where she dialed Katie. "I did it. I quit and told Frank to shove it up his ass."

"Holy shit! I'll be right down."

Justine hastily packed up her things, using an empty cardboard box from the supply room. She didn't have much. A plant, a few sketch pads, some watercolors she'd brought from home.

"Justine, I don't think you've thought this through," Frank said as he came to her cubicle, walking gingerly, as if expecting a bomb to detonate.

She ignored him.

Katie arrived with a huge grin. "Finally!" She turned to Frank. "You've used my buddy for the last time, bucko."

Breaking into hysterical laughter would make her look doofy, so Justine kept her mouth shut and continued to pack. A small glance at Frank showed him looking ill.

"Justine, I think you're just under a great deal of stress."

"Ya think?" Katie snarled. "You shoved Laura's work on Justine instead of hiring a new employee. And you stiffed her on the raise you said you were giving her." Katie's voice continued to rise, and a small crowd gathered around them.

"That's not true," Frank huffed. "We're downsizing, and I—"

"Got a new admin assistant," Justine had to say. She turned to glare at him. "You have a big office with plenty of time to sit around and chitchat while I stay until seven or eight just trying to get through my day. You have used and abused this employee. I'm reporting all this to HR too. I don't give a damn if they don't care. I do, and I'm tired of not being appreciated for all I do for this company." She said over him, "And to all of you who I've helped for months on end, you're fucking welcome!"

She grabbed her box and her purse. Katie grabbed her plant. She headed straight for the door, glad Frank had moved and the crowd had parted because she would have walked right through them out of the building.

Once at her car, after stowing her things, she turned to Katie, still not believing she'd done it. "I quit. I cursed. I'm done here."

Katie pumped her fists in the air. "Fuck, yeah." She glanced at a beep on her phone. "Shoot. I have to get back for a meeting and tie things up. Then I'm quitting too!"

"No, you like your job." *I quit. Oh my God. I quit.*

"Not really. I just like it a lot more—but still less—with my new boss. But the work isn't challenging, and I'm tired of having to fit myself into the corporate mentality. Did you know Kenzie wears jeans to work? Sometimes shorts? And Rachel and Lila take turns getting energy smoothies and donuts whenever they want and start their days whenever they want."

"Huh?"

"You remember, Kenzie and her coworkers, who work out of Kenzie's basement? That's such a terrific office! So what are we going to name our company?"

"Huh?"

"You said that already." Katie snickered. "I can't wait to go back in there and see how Frank handles his job without you to keep him going. Talk to you later. Drive safe." Katie hugged her then darted back inside the building.

The entire way home, Justine kept flashing back to telling Frank off, and it was the absolute best feeling. Up there even with sex with Xavier. She felt euphoric, excited, and nauseated all at once.

As she parked her car, she got a phone call.

"Aunt Rosie?"

"Hey there, my favorite niece. I hear there might be wedding bells in your future."

"Not exactly, but I did just tell my boss to kiss my ass."

"Oh, ho! Then we do have something to really celebrate. Take me through it, play by play. This sounds juicy."

"It was. It *soooo* was."

CHAPTER 36

When Justine came bouncing into his apartment later in the evening, Xavier felt as if spring had returned, the scent of flowers and joy bundled tightly with her.

"What's the occasion?" he asked as he saw her wide smile.

"I quit today, Xavier. And it was glorious!"

He caught her as she jumped into his arms and twirled her around, captivated by her laughter and her newfound sense of freedom.

"I have never been so happy as I was leaving that awful place behind."

"Tell me all about it."

But as she went through her day, he thought about his. Counseling three couples on the verge of divorce and a teen with anxiety hinting at family problems at home.

Ever since hearing his sister's take on how he didn't like his mother's boyfriend, Xavier had been reexamining himself. Looking deeper inside and not liking what he saw.

"Hey, are you okay?" Justine tugged his arm.

They sat at his kitchen table, and he got up to fetch them two lemonades. "Sorry. I'm thirsty."

"And distracted."

"Ignore me." He forced a smile. "I'm being a bad listener, and I hate that. So you really told Frank to shove all those jobs up his ass?"

Her proud smile had his heart racing. Even though they'd committed to dating, he still felt nervous, his heart fluttering when he saw her. Mooning over a girl. How high school.

Yet she got to him the way no one ever had. A love so deep he feared dipping even a toe into its water.

He swallowed down his panic. "What are you going to do now?"

She shrugged. "Finish the new client's project and call the other one Kenzie gave me. Hunt down more future clients." She paused. "Maybe start my own business. Katie mentioned us working together. I'm not sure, but… I don't know. I kind of like the idea of taking charge of my future."

He felt so proud of her but didn't want to come across as condescending. "Yeah, that's how I felt when I joined MYM. I work with other doctors and therapists, but I take my own clients and run my own schedule. Well, mostly. None of us work nights."

"Heck, I was working day and night for a long time, and it got me nowhere." She huffed. "What a great team player I was."

"But you stood up for yourself. I am so happy for you."

"How happy?"

Despite needing to figure out why he'd been having such a tough time mentally committing to Justine, emotionally, he loved her. And physically… He couldn't get enough of her.

She stripped him down and had her mouth on him in seconds.

He moaned, lost in lust and love and tired of stressing over it.

Pumping harder, he cupped her head, unsure how he'd lost all control around the woman. She licked and sucked, nibbling under the head of his crown, and he came hard, moaning her name.

What is she doing to me?

He was breathing hard when she stood, stripped, and led him back to his bedroom. He couldn't be anywhere in his apartment without thinking of her. She'd ingrained herself in his brain, in his bed, in his heart.

Yet a part of him remained distant, unsure why when the pleasure between them was so damn good.

He followed her down to the bed and immediately sought the wet heat between her legs. Feasting on her sex, he pumped a finger, then two inside her, loving how she trembled and sighed his name. He wanted to celebrate with her, to show her how much he cared while the words failed to pass his lips.

He would bring her close but not close enough, edging her several times before he crawled up her body and thrust fast and deep inside her. She keened his name as she came, squeezing him, so that he thrust twice more then came again.

She continued to kiss and hug him, shivering as she experienced that rush of pleasure. A combined meeting of mouths and bodies.

He kissed her back until they lay spent, together.

And he stopped thinking so hard about what everything meant and why he couldn't make that last step to give Justine what she needed. What she deserved.

JUSTINE HAD NO IDEA WHY, but she felt Xavier retreating into himself. It had only been a few days since they'd confessed their feelings, but she felt like she knew him so much better now. And something had been bothering him for a while.

Now dressed and sitting on his couch, they felt like a couple, and also like a couple about to break up. It was so odd.

"Xavier, what's going on with you? Did I do something?"

He blinked. "What?"

"You seem, I don't know, like you're not really here with me."

He sighed. "Being back at work is taking some getting used to. I need to remember to distance myself from it or I can get kind of depressed."

"I'm so sorry."

They held hands, and he squeezed hers before pulling away. But the separation felt more than physical.

"I am too. I think…" He stood and started pacing. In all the time they'd been together, she'd never seen him so frazzled.

"What's wrong?"

"I don't know." He sounded genuinely confused. "I love being with you. Spending time with you. You make me laugh and feel good. But lately, I don't feel… I can't describe it."

Her stomach dropped. She'd just lost her job—her choice, but still. Was she about to lose him too? What had she done to jinx her life?

"This isn't you, it's me." He gave a sharp laugh. "I know that sounds so trite. But it's true. Ever since the barbecue at Mom's, I've been processing what Auggie said."

Justine studied him. "Auggie?" So his distance had nothing to do with her? Why then didn't she feel any better?

"I feel like maybe I haven't liked any of my mom's boyfriends because I'm selfish. Like, maybe I need her attention or her love all to myself. But then, I don't think that's quite it." He kept pacing, and she watched, amused, confused, and angry, because why couldn't at least one point in her life work in her favor?

He continued, almost talking to himself, "I mean, I love her. I love Auggie. So why do I have a problem with the people I love finding love themselves?" He looked at her. "I think Auggie and Benji might seriously have a relationship going. And it bothers me."

"The way I bother you?"

"You don't bother me," he replied so quickly, with so much honesty, that she believed him.

And she settled, feeling a spark of compassion for this man who tried to help others all the time, and maybe at the cost of himself.

"I don't bother you, but maybe how you feel about me bothers you."

"I, no. Well, maybe."

Yet how did he feel? He'd never actually said he loved her, had he?

Quitting work and putting herself first had freed Justine. Perhaps tomorrow she'd feel differently, but today she knew just what to say, how to feel. And she didn't regret loving Xavier. Not one bit.

She gave him a sincere smile. "I know I love you. I feel it deep inside." She patted her chest. "You've let me be in charge of our relationship from the beginning. Treated me like an equal and like a person who knows her own worth. And I thank you for that."

He looked upset. "Are you breaking up with me? This sounds like a breakup speech."

She laughed, simultaneously sad yet strangely happy. "No. But I'm going to do you a favor. I want *you* to take charge of this relationship. You tell me what you want when you know what that is. I love you. I'm not afraid to say it or feel it."

She just looked at him.

Shame crossed his face. "But I am."

"I think so. I just don't know why. You're the most grounded, emotionally mature man I know. You're not afraid to say what you think or communicate. So why has our relationship changed?"

"It hasn't."

"It has." She knew the truth, could see it in his eyes. But love made no sense. She knew that. She gave a sad grin. "WWXD?

What would Xavier do? That's how I've decided on some of the choices I've made, because you're such a well-adjusted person. Probably the most balanced guy I've ever dated." She stood and kissed him on the cheek. "Figure out what you want, Xavier. You know how I feel. You should also know I'm taking back control of my life. And I'm worth someone who can admit how they feel without regret."

"I know." He didn't look sad as much as baffled, and that gave her hope.

But Justine had things to do. A job to find. A life to figure out. For herself.

Xavier would have to muddle his way to his own truths. She could only hope they'd bring him back to her.

CHAPTER 37

Xavier didn't know what had happened. Three days later, he remained baffled at how he'd had the nicest not-breakup breakup ever.

"All right brother of mine." Auggie sighed and played with the straw in her juice glass. Hermione had already been by twice to challenge Auggie into a few rounds of "Your Mother" jokes and a glare fest. "What the hell did you do?"

"What?"

"You've been glum, chum." She chuckled, amused with herself. "What's up? Did you lose your girlfriend? Because I'm sensing you've joined the lovelorn."

"I don't know."

"How can you not know?"

He sipped his coffee, his appetite absent though he'd ordered food to keep Auggie off his back. "That's what's so baffling. We had the best time at her sister's wedding. We only argue about TV shows that she's clearly wrong about."

"You and your Daleks."

He ignored that. "We have the most amazing connection. And,

I mean, in bed…" He cleared his throat. "Let's just say it's off-the-charts hot."

"Good for you, studly. So what's the problem? Is she not emotional enough for you? Too 'dramatic,' as I've often been accused of being?"

"No. She, uh, she told me she loves me."

Auggie stared, her smile slow but wide. "No kidding. Way to go, slugger! You have them dropping hearts for you left and right, don't you? Any more signs of Christine?"

"No." He absently rubbed the back of his head. "What's wrong with me? I've got the most beautiful, perfect woman in love with me. She's sexy and giving. I don't want to be with anyone else but her. So how did we break up?"

"That's a mystery, for sure. Who broke it off?"

"No one. Well, maybe her. I don't know." Mystified, he had no idea how he'd sabotaged this relationship.

"I bet she did." Auggie leaned in, her gaze piercing. "I bet she got sick of your distance bullshit and called you on it."

"What?"

Auggie shook her head. "Bro, you know I love you. But you live too much in that fat head of yours."

"Up yours."

"See? It's that attitude I'm talking about. You call me dramatic."

"You are."

"So what if I am? I try my best to find love and laughter in this big ball of worry we call life."

"What are you talking about?"

"I'm trying to converse on your level, professor." She lifted her nose in the air.

He had to laugh at that. "You are so annoying."

"Yeah? Well so are you when you don't like what you're hearing."

"What does that mean?"

They both paused as Hermione returned with their breakfast orders.

"Try not to choke on it, demon spawn," she said to Auggie, then with a bright smile, to Xavier, added, "Eat up, honey. You look like you need it. Still handsome though. Always." Hermione winked, gave Auggie the finger, then left.

He watched their server flirt all the way to the counter. "I don't understand your relationship with Hermione."

"Meh, few do. But that's her way of telling me not to be late to tonight's roller derby match. We bet serious money on it." Auggie tucked into her food and said, "You have issues."

"With my sister's table manners, yes I do."

She chewed with her mouth open and swallowed loudly. "Yet another issue. Your intolerance for all things fun."

"Fun? I saw you masticating eggs." He felt pretty proud for working "masticating"—his word of the day—into common conversation.

Auggie gave him a thumbs up. "Nice job."

"Thanks."

"But let's get back to why you and Justine broke up."

"I'm not sure we did." Were they maybe on a break?

"Well, dumbass, have you talked to her?"

"Um, no." He scowled. "And how about you lighten up on all the insults?"

Auggie laughed. "Yeah, right. Look, you're acting like a teenager too afraid to talk to his crush and avoid a simple misunderstanding. You told me that Justine told you to figure things out. So what are you figuring out?"

"I... Hell. It's your fault," he snapped.

"Me?"

"Yeah. You made me think about how I acted with Mom's boyfriends."

"It's not like she's had a million of them. Six, no, seven, right? And of those, only three were long-term. That's not counting her coffee dates. I'm mean real dating, like, a relationship that last more than a month."

"How do you keep track?"

Auggie snorted. "I love how you pretend you don't know about Mom's social life."

Sadly, she was right. He did know. He just didn't like to think about it. "I'm uncomfortable with Mom dating. And you're right. I didn't like Jared, and I'm not keen on her with Top. And I actually like Top."

"You didn't like Noel, but you accepted him because he was a dick. You knew Mom would never stick with him. I know you because I'm the same way. I just realize and accept my shortcomings. You try to pretend they're not there." She softened her voice. "Xavier, you've dated a bunch of women over the years. But you always find a flaw with them. Why do you think that is?"

"Because I'm looking for Ms. Right." It wasn't wrong not to want to settle.

"Who you'll never find. She will never exist for you because you're afraid if you do find her, something will happen and she'll leave. Then you'll be as sad and freaked out as Mom was when Dad died." She shrugged. "You should already know this."

"What? That's not true."

She quirked a brow, just like he often did, and he stared at her, as if trying to see the truth in the mirror of his twin. "Look, I went to a lot of therapy while you were going to school to be a shrink."

"Therapist."

"Whatever. I know my issues. I love excitement and have a flair for—sure, fine, I'll admit it—drama. But I *know* when I'm picking a trainwreck of a guy. I'm not ready to settle down yet, so I go for flashy and fun. Or at least, I used to."

He stared. "What? So what's the deal with your new boyfriend? Is it really Benji?"

She blushed. "Shut up."

"Ha! I knew it. You're into the yeti."

"Don't call him that."

"Hell. I never called him that. You did!"

"Well, it's not like we're actually dating or anything. Not really."

"Is that who you were visiting the other day when you stopped by the complex but never stopped in to see me?"

"What?"

He gave her the eye. "Justine saw you. You talked to her, dumbass."

"Hey, you said no more name calling."

"As applied to me. Not you."

"Say what you want, loser. But at least I'm giving the yeti a chance. You want to cut Justine off before she can be someone special. Because you stupidly think if you lose her now, you won't be as hurt when you lose her later."

He just stared at his sister, startled she sounded so intelligent about processing emotions.

"Hey, I keep telling you I'm more than a pretty face."

"Huh."

Hermione walked by, overheard, and laughed and laughed.

"I need to talk to someone about this," he muttered.

"Damn skippy." She lowered her voice. "For someone moonlighting as Aunt Truth, you sure are adverse to hearing it. We should call you Aunt Moron."

"Oh, that's mature."

"Yeah? You want mature? I'll give you a few more names. Imagine me giving up true love because I'm scared. *Oooh.* How scary. Love is *terrriffyyinnng.*" She made fun of him for the next few minutes, during which Xavier wondered how his overly dramatic sister had learned to be so smart.

And how he'd become so vacuous.

And double points for me for using another word of the day.

CHAPTER 38

Tuesday evening, Justine stared at her phone in shock and asked her aunt, "What's that?"

It had been four days since her super sweet breakup from Xavier. He'd texted her once, just to say he missed her. But other than that, nothing.

She should have felt worse. But she'd gone from quiet acceptance to grief to anger to a kind of numbness, broken only by her deep dive into contract work and Katie's inane phone calls, doing her best to cheer Justine up. And even then, Katie still liked Xavier, feeling sorry for him rather than angry.

"He's messed up, J." Katie had said. "Just give it time. I've seen the way he looks at you. He's a goner. He's just acting stupid on account of having a penis." Such wise words from her best friend.

Her aunt's voice on the phone sharpened. "I said I'm coming back in a month. Kai's coming too. But don't worry. You can stay on the couch. It'll be like a big old sleepover!" Aunt Rosie chatted a bit more about Italian men and fine wines. Or fine men and Italian wines. Justine wasn't sure because her aunt rambled without taking a breath for quite a while.

"Are you still there?" her aunt asked. "It's should only be five-thirty. I think. It's after eight here."

"In the morning? Why are you awake?"

"I haven't gotten to sleep yet." Aunt Rosie laughed and said something to someone in the background.

Justine frowned. "Um, what was that?"

"I said, your mother called to tell me how much she likes your new *boyfriend*."

Justine groaned.

"I knew you and Xavier would be perfect for each other."

"Too bad, because Xavier didn't get the memo."

"Oh? Dish, girlie. Tell Aunt Rosie all about it."

So Justine did, praying *Aunt Truth* would have some sage advice for her.

"Well."

"Well what?" Justine asked. "Is it over between us? Are we on a break? What do his problems mean?"

"I doubt either one of you knows. Why the hell haven't you talked since Friday? It's almost been a week."

Five days, three hours, and twenty-four minutes, to be exact. "I don't know. I wanted to give him space. I'm still not sure where we are. I mean, I know where I am. Soon to be homeless with a few contract jobs that might pay for groceries for the month. Oh, and my cell phone bill."

"There you go. Great job, honey." Her aunt tittered. "I'm sorry for not joining your pity party of one."

"Aunt Rosie," Justine growled.

"Oh stuff it, Justine. You finally got the gumption to leave that awful job and told off your boss. I'm super proud of you!"

"Will you be proud of me when I'm living with you three years later, stuffing hot dogs, PBJs, and Ramen down my throat?"

"Ah, the meals of champions. I love a good PBJ."

She groaned.

"Lighten up, honey. Xavier's a thinker. He needs to go through all the reasons why he can't handle a long-term girlfriend, see that he's being ridiculous and fear-based, then declare his undying love for you."

"He never even said it," she mumbled. "I did. Put myself out there only for him to say he 'felt the same way.' What the heck is that?" She liked the anger stealing through her numbness.

"That's a young man who can't get over past trauma," Aunt Rosie said with authority. "Now stop wallowing and enjoy life. Just think, in another month, Kai and I will be back with a bunch of stories. And maybe even a step-uncle in your future!"

"Really?"

"Well, maybe. He hasn't shown me his estate yet, so we'll see."

"Estate?"

"He's a count. Honey, I don't settle for just anyone. And you shouldn't either. Your life will work itself out. If Xavier can't see how wonderful you are, then he's not the man I think he is. And that's one from Aunt Truth. You can take that to the bank."

Justine disconnected and wound her way down to the fountain in the courtyard. She sat glumly, staring up at the clear night sky while the fountain bubbled and the flowers scented the air.

"Hey, whatcha doing?" Sam came to sit next to her looking tanned and happy.

"Welcome back, Sam." She gave him a hug, amused that he clung to her like a limpet she had to pry away. "We missed you."

"Aw. I missed you too." He grinned, adorable with his bright Hawaiian shirt and a plastic lei. He took the necklace off and put it over her head. "For you."

"That's so sweet."

"Yeah, it is. So when are we going out?"

She laughed and shocked herself by starting to cry.

Sam's eyes grew wide. "Oh my gosh. Are you okay?" He paused. "Is it...that time of the month?"

"What? No." She hiccupped on a laugh. "And don't ask women that."

"Sorry. I won't. My bad."

The goofball made her feel better. "Sorry for breaking down. It's been a rough couple of days."

He sat closer. "What happened?"

"I quit my job for my fathead boss. Aunt Rosie's coming back so I need to find a new place to live." Because she loved her aunt, but that apartment was *way* too small for her aunt's personality and anyone else. "And Xavier and I are…taking a break."

"Oh." He paused and his face lit up. "*Oh.*"

"Sam. I'm too old for you to date. But not too old to be a friend." She held out a hand.

He sighed and shook it. "Rylan said the lei wouldn't work, but I tried."

"Tell me about your trip."

He expounded on the virtues of scuba diving with a trained guide, told her about swimming with his uncle and messing up Adam's chances with a lifeguard, and showed her a handful of shells he'd bought at a gift store.

They talked for quite a while, the young boy and nearly thirty-year-old woman with little in common, and laughed and enjoyed themselves before Sam had to turn in.

Justine stared at the night sky, not so sad anymore, and hoped that Xavier soon came to his senses. Or she might just be tempted to wait until Sam turned twenty-five and take him out for real.

CHAPTER 39

Wednesday evening, Xavier stared in shock at Adam's youngest nephew. Cute Sam with his crush on Justine didn't hold a candle to the angry kid reading him the riot act for making Justine cry.

"Yeah, and now she's moving away."

"Wait. Seriously?" How had his not-breakup turned breakup become a real thing? "She can't leave."

"Well, she is. Rosie's coming back, and Justine has no job and no boyfriend." Sam shot daggers at him. "What's wrong with you?"

Xavier groaned. "I don't know, Sam."

Sam watched him then sighed. "I'm glad I'm not an adult. You people are stupid." He then regaled Xavier with tales about dolphins he'd seen before leaving.

Xavier waited for the boy to depart the fountain area before admitting to himself he'd made a huge mistake. A lot of introspection, a short discussion with Rosie last night on the phone, and time spent talking to Ava at the office and getting a gentle, therapeutic rebuke had put him on the path to owning up to his mistakes.

That was if it wasn't too late.

He hurried upstairs and saw his sister rushing into Benji's place and slamming the door behind her. *That* he'd discuss with her later.

He banged on Justine's door and jumped back when it was yanked open.

"What?" Justine growled, looking haphazard in shorts and a ragged Tee. "Oh, Xavier. Hi."

He freaked out at thoughts of her leaving. "Oh fuck. I love you. Now we need to talk."

She stared at him wide-eyed, and he had to move her back to enter, shutting the door behind him. "I'm sorry. I heard you cried over me."

Her eyes narrowed. "That little punk. I did not. Well, maybe. It was everything hitting me at once." She poked him in the chest. "And I know I said you didn't have to say it back, but it hurt when you didn't."

"I know." He groaned and reached for her, and like the giving, loving woman she was, she hugged him back just as tightly. "I'm sorry, Justine. I realized I have a huge issue involving relationships and love and trust. It's past trauma from my dad dying and leaving my mom and us kids a mess." He groaned and sniffed her hair, relaxing into her arms. "What's even worse is Auggie understood me more than I understood myself. I'm never going to live that down."

She laughed, and he had hope he hadn't ruined everything.

He put her back so he could look into her eyes. "I'm nice and smart and responsible. And I rock this facial hair."

"You do." She grinned.

"But I'm not good at relationships that last. Eventually my partner does something that triggers me, I guess. Either they're too neat or too sloppy. Too demanding or not demanding enough. But with you, I fell hard. Fast. In love. And you scared me, because with you, I knew it was so much more than lust at first sight. I've never had a friend like you. And I've missed you like crazy."

"Me too."

He leaned close to kiss her. "I can't even explain how I went from happy to needing space so quickly. It just hit me so hard, how much I love you. How much I'd be broken if you left me."

"We can't predict the future, Xavier." Justine shook her head. "No matter how much I wish we could. But I've never felt for anyone the way I feel for you."

"Not even Dr. Douche?"

She grinned. "Not even him. My mom and sisters have been asking about you, you know. My mom called asking you to dinner again. I had to tell her I'd get back to her."

"Dinner with Jeanine? Count me in."

"And my father."

"Lyle? Sure. No problem."

She sighed. "I really do love you, and I'm not sure how it happened. But you're my best friend, Xavier." She whispered, "Don't tell Katie."

"I won't," he whispered back. "And I apologize wholeheartedly for being an ass and not talking to you. I had no idea what to say, to be honest, because I couldn't tell you what I was feeling. Panic, fear, but most of all, love for a woman who fits me." He blinked. "Ah, there's one other thing you should know."

"That you help my aunt write *Aunt Truth?*" She smirked. "I saw one of your doodles when I was in your apartment. And lately, Aunt Truth uses Dr. Who references in her advice column."

He swallowed. "I wanted to tell you, but I didn't think I could since it didn't seem like Rosie had confided the truth."

"She did a long time ago. She's great, but Xavier, I can't live with her here. She'll drive me bonkers."

He laughed. "She's a… well, a lot to take, I grant you."

"I have to move."

"Move in with me."

"I did that with Mitch, and it didn't work."

"But he's just a doctor. He's not an animator or LMFT like me."

"Well, that's true, but I want to think about it."

"That's fair." Though he had every notion to convince her why living together would be ideal.

She wound her arms around his neck and let him pull her in for a breath stealing kiss. "He might be a doctor, but you know all about *The* Doctor—as in, Who."

"That's true. My fascination with that show is real."

"I know. And I don't mind it. But if I had to admit to being obsessed over something, the one thing I can't get enough of with you, it's making love."

"Love, yes."

"I'm talking about having sex, bumping uglies, grinding hard."

"Fucking like bunnies?" he offered.

"Exactly." She laughed and kissed him again, rubbing her cheek against his beard. "I love you, Xavier. Now let's get naked and celebrate."

"Yes, definitely. Oh, and remind me to tell you about Auggie and Benji when I'm done. And my mom and Top. They're dating just about every night. If this keeps up, we can move into Top's place when he moves in with my mom."

"You're joking!"

"I sure hope I am." He frowned as he tugged her to her feet and led her back to her room. "If that man expects me to call him Daddy, he's got another think coming."

"Another think? You mean another *thing*."

"No, no. That's the expression. 'Another think.'"

As they argued about the English language, and Xavier somehow inserted a Dr. Who reference into the conversation, he realized he had nothing but joy ahead of him with his best friend by his side. "Hey, about that best friend thing," he murmured as he undressed her and she undressed him.

"What about it?" She latched onto his nipple and had him hard and aching in an instant.

"Huh?" How did she do that with her tongue?

"The friend thing?" She gripped his dick, and he nearly lost it.

"We never tell Auggie you're my best friend. I don't think she could handle it."

"Gotcha. Now shut up and kiss me, Dr. Who."

"The Matt Smith one, right?"

She raised a brow and quoted the Doctor. "'Do what I do. Hold tight and pretend it's a plan!'"

"Have I told you how much I love you?"

"Tell me again. Better yet, show me."

♡

A NOTE FROM MARIE: *You can stop right here. This is a happily-ever-after ending. Everyone's in love. Justine and Xavier are doing just swell together, and Justine and Katie will start a new business. Cynthia and Max are falling for each other, and Auggie and Benji are making magic together. But Katie, well, she's been on one heck of an adventure.*

If you want a hint, check out the Epilogue, and don't miss the follow-on link for an Auggie/Benji short story.

EPILOGUE

Saturday, July 16th
Sea-Tac Airport

Justine waited by the baggage claim at the airport for Katie while Xavier spent the evening with Auggie and Top in some weird Marine thing at his sister's gym.

Katie's Single and Ready to Mingle celebration with their now single friend, Jon, had gone down in Vegas the past weekend while Justine and Xavier had spent their time mostly naked with a variety of succulent fruits, melted chocolate, and whipped cream.

She smiled to herself, so in love it wasn't funny. And love seemed to be in the air, because dinner last night at Cynthia's house had been a night for couples. Cynthia and Top were adorable, with Top blushing and trying not to show his softer side. Then there was Auggie calling him "Daddy" at every turn, which had both Xavier and Benji—now sporting a shave and haircut showing off a very attractive man—laughing. Apparently, Benji and Auggie had become a couple, and all of them, including Benji, had no idea how she'd wormed her way past his door.

Not to be left out, apparently Adam had found a special someone he hadn't yet shared with Sam. But Sam didn't mind, because he'd scored a date with a fellow ninth grader he planned to take to the movies. Poor Rylan, unfortunately, hadn't passed his driver's test and would have to take it again.

Justine couldn't wait to get Katie all up to speed on her life, planning to lead with the fact that they'd gotten four more clients thanks to Kenzie shuffling more people their way. And in even better news, Kenzie was looking to expand her business and offered them both positions, if they wanted them.

So much to think over!

Right after she moved into Xavier's apartment. Was it a bad move to live together so quickly? Only time would tell. But they both wanted more togetherness and less distance, and he promised to do better sharing what he felt. She actually liked that he wasn't so perfect. It put them on an even playing field, so to speak.

Where was her bestie—*other* bestie? Katie was late.

She finally found her frazzled friend looking less than her best, her pink skirt stained, her blouse wrinkled, as she hustled toward Justine with her bag and Jon in tow.

Jon kept looking at her and laughing, his smile way too wide compared to Katie's pinched expression. Odd, because Jon and Katie were like peas in a wacky pod.

Justine hurried over to them. "What's wrong?"

Jon broke down in hysterical laughter.

"It's not funny," Katie seethed and tried to push back her flyaway hair.

"You smell drunk."

"I think I *am* drunk." She moaned and ripped at the tangle on the side of her head.

And that's when Justine spotted a ring on her finger.

A *wedding band.*

"What the hell?"

"Celebrating being single, and my best friend gets married." Jon continued to chortle. Yes, actual evil chortling.

"Married to who?"

"To me," said the tall, good-looking guy trailing them. He was tall, with a military short haircut and straight posture, wearing jeans, an olive green tee-shirt, and black boots. And whoa, momma, but those biceps were *huge.*

Sergeant Hot Stuff held out a large hand. "Hi. You must be Justine. I'm Theo." He gave a wide smile, showing bright white teeth and a dimple as he gently took her hand in his. "Katie's husband."

Thank you for reading Justine and Xavier's story! Sign up for my newsletter to read a bonus **Auggie and Benji** short story! And look for Katie and her *new husband!!!!* coming soon.

ACKNOWLEDGMENTS

Huge thanks to author Kai Strand, who gave me the title and makes a cameo in the book. You rocked it with *Love in 3D*!

And to my beta readers; Angi, Sarah, Tracy, Jen, and Jean for helping with consistency and typos, I truly appreciate it!

ALSO BY MARIE
(SEE PARENTHESES FOR CONNECTIONS!)

CONTEMPORARY

THE MCCAULEY BROTHERS
The Troublemaker Next Door
How to Handle a Heartbreaker
Ruining Mr. Perfect
What to Do with a Bad Boy

BODY SHOP BAD BOYS
Test Drive
Roadside Assistance
Zero to Sixty *(Pets Fur Life Charity)*
Collision Course

THE DONNIGANS *(Theo Donnigan)*
A Sure Thing *(Ava's love story)*
Just the Thing *(Gavin's love story)*
The Only Thing

ALL I WANT FOR HALLOWEEN

THE KISSING GAME

THE WORKS
Bodywork
Working Out *(Jameson's Gym)*
Wetwork

VETERANS MOVERS

The Whole Package

Smooth Moves

Handle with Care *(Kenzie's love story)*

Delivered with a Kiss

TURN UP THE HEAT

Make Me Burn

Burning Desire

Hot for You

Turn Up the Heat

WICKED WARRENS

Enjoying the Show

Closing the Deal

Raising the Bar

Making the Grade

Bending the Rules

GOOD TO GO

A Major Attraction

A Major Seduction

A Major Distraction

A Major Connection

BEST REVENGE

Served Cold

Served Hot

Served Sweet

ROMANTIC SUSPENSE

POWERUP!

The Lost Locket

RetroCog

Whispered Words

Fortune's Favor

Flight of Fancy

Silver Tongue

Entranced

Killer Thoughts

WESTLAKE ENTERPRISES

To Hunt a Sainte

Storming His Heart

Love in Electric Blue

TRIGGERMAN INC.

Contract Signed

Secrets Unsealed

Satisfaction Delivered

PARANORMAL

BETWEEN THE SHADOWS

Between Bloode and Stone

Between Bloode and Craft

Between Bloode and Water

Between Bloode and Wolf

Between Bloode and Death

Between Bloode and Gods

CROSS STEP

Namesake

Kate Complete

COUGAR FALLS

Rachel's Totem

In Plain Sight

Foxy Lady

Outfoxed

A Matter of Pride

Right Wolf, Right Time

By the Tail

Prey & Prejudice

ETHEREAL FOES

Dragons' Demon: A Dragon's Dream

Duncan's Descent: A Demon's Desire

Havoc & Hell: A Dragon's Prize

Dragon King: Not So Ordinary

CIRCE'S RECRUITS

Roane

Zack & Ace

Derrick

Hale

DAWN ENDEAVOR

Fallon's Flame

Hayashi's Hero

Julian's Jeopardy

Gunnar's Game

Grayson's Gamble

CIRCE'S RECRUITS 2.0

Gideon

Alex

Elijah

Carter

SCIFI

THE INSTINCT

A Civilized Mating

A Barbarian Bonding

A Warrior's Claiming

TALSON TEMPTATIONS

Talon's Wait

Talson's Test

Talson's Net

Talson's Match

LIFE IN THE VRAIL

Lurin's Surrender

Thief of Mardu

Engaging Gren

Seriana Found

CREATIONS

The Perfect Creation

Creation's Control

Creating Chemistry

Caging the Beast

AND MORE (believe it or not)!

ABOUT THE AUTHOR

Caffeine addict, boy referee, and romance aficionado, *New York Times* and *USA Today* bestselling author Marie Harte has over 100 books published with more constantly on the way. She's a confessed bibliophile and devotee of action movies. Whether hiking in Central Oregon, biking around town, or hanging at the local tea shop, she's constantly plotting to give everyone a happily ever after. Visit https://marieharte.com and fall in love.

facebook.com/marieharteauthorpage
twitter.com/MHarte_Author
goodreads.com/Marie_Harte
bookbub.com/authors/marie-harte
instagram.com/authormarieharte
tiktok.com/authormarieharte

Manufactured by Amazon.ca
Bolton, ON